I0819950

DEVA LEELA

SHUNYO MAHOM

Swami Shunyo Mahom Publishing

© 2022 Shunyo Mahom

All USA and international copyrights reserved.

"Deva Leela" Second Edition – ISBN 978-0-578-33145-4

www.shunyo.org

Books by Swami Shunyo Mahom Publishing:

"Being Human" by Osho

"Zen Pearls" by Osho and Shunyo Mahom

"Mama Llama's Pajamas" by Shunyo Mahom,

Children's Book Illustrated by Carene Villejas

“This is the dawning of the Age of Hilarious.”

Dilai Dalai 630 A.D.

Invocation

My shadow is kind to these wrinkles.

I see my whiskers are long.

Circles of years embrace me,

soothe me like a song.

Laughter is the song of my being,

its melody the soul of my art.

The song I sing is Osho love

flowing from my heart.

DEVA LEELA

CHAPTER 1

The Dream has no beginning.

But sometime after that, on May 27, 1848, Bunny, a lovely young blonde angel in a shapely white satin gown, sat on a fluffy white cloud sipping champagne.

Next to her sat her elegant clean-shaven devil boyfriend, Lloyd, looking relaxed and suave in his red silk smoking jacket, matching trousers and socks, and brown leather sandals.

Bunny set her champagne glass on the cloud and saw God parking his huge white motorcycle on the cloud to her right.

"Well look who it is!" she shouted. "What are you doing in these parts?"

God squinted through his thick sunglasses. He stroked his long white beard, bent down, and wiped his black leather boots with the bottom of his long white robe.

"Taking the census," he said finally, "and I suspect..."

Suddenly the Almighty paused and stared at Lloyd in disbelief.

He whisked over to Bunny and Lloyd's cloud and asked, "Who is *THIS?"*

"Lloyd," Lloyd said. "You must be..."

"GOD!" God cried. Then he turned to Bunny and asked, "What's a devil doing up here?"

"No problem," Bunny replied, "he's with me."

"I see that!" God blurted. "But, but...

Bunny seductively fluttered her eyelashes and slowly bent over, revealing her peachy bosom.

The nearsighted Holy of Holies was awe-struck and speechless at the sight.

"You know how I looooove company," Bunny purred.

God's eyes widened. "Yes, I, I, I..."

"You and I have always had an open relationship, right?"

"Y-yes, b-but..." God stuttered.

"Then be a darling and let me have some fun. Lloyd is helping me with Leela and Mark. You don't want me to do it alone, do you?"

God looked down and saw Deva Leela, a young French Indian mystic, sitting on a yak-skin rug in Bodhi Cave in Northwest India.

"No, I, ah... where's Mark Trimble?" God asked.

"Don't worry, he's fine," Bunny said, "in San Francisco now. Anyway, just let us be, okay? I'll be responsible for Lloyd."

God shrugged his shoulders. "Okay," God said, "a temporary arrangement. But just until Mark and Leela no longer need any guidance from you... ah, two."

"I know," Bunny said, "Now I bet you have lots of angels to count. I don't want to take up any more of your precious time."

"Yes, yes," God said, "I'd better be going." He flew to his motorcycle, revved it up and sped off to Cloud Nine.

"Whew, that was close!" Lloyd said.

Bunny nodded. "A little *décolleté*, a little cleavage, helps even out the playing field with God.... Now about Deva Leela down there..."

Bunny sipped champagne then glanced far below at the tiny figure of 23-year-old Deva Leela meditating in Bodhi Cave.

"Leela looks radiant," Lloyd observed.

"Beauty that shines from within," Bunny agreed.

Then Bunny and Lloyd bent over to watch Leela below...

The sun silently set in the west as Deva Leela sat in Bodhi Cave and gazed in awe at a lone eagle soaring high above the fertile Dilai Valley below the cave. The valley stretched east-west for fifty miles before merging with the larger Swat Valley region of Northwest India.

The cave had been Leela's home for two years and was an aesthetic marvel. Like sparkling diamonds in a night sky, hundreds of clear quartz crystals glimmered within the black granite walls of the cavern. One felt as if on holy ground: thirteen centuries of mystics meditating there had transformed the earth into a living being, radiating subtle vibrations of love and silence.

Now as the last rays of sunlight disappeared behind the snowcapped mountains to the west, Leela was filled with gratitude for the miracle of Existence.

Ah, this...

The night slowly descended, and the deep emptiness of the black velvet sky brought up mixed feelings of joy and sadness in Leela. Tears rolled over her high cheekbones and fell from her chin onto her beige cashmere robe. Another day was disappearing into the infinite void, and she felt a longing for something long ago and far away.

Minutes later, Leela stood, walked past the brightly burning campfire and gazed at a pile of 21 black rolled up cured yak skin scrolls in the middle of the cave. Upon the scrolls were 99 sutras written by the Chinese mystic, Hueng Tsiang, affectionately known as "Dilai Dalai" to seventh century Swat Valley residents in 630 AD."

By 1848 a worldwide religion, Dilai Dalai Jai, had evolved with the sutras as their sacred scriptures. Thousands of devotees around the world worshiped Dilai Dalai as "the Patron Saint of Fun".

Leela picked up a scroll, untied the leather string, rolled out the yak skin, and read the ancient Chinese calligraphy in gold characters by the fire's light. She knew the sutras by heart. The English translation of the four sutras on this scroll read:

If, according to physicists and mystics, all matter in the universe can be reduced to the size of a matchbox, why diet?

Love is a rose with thorns,
consciousness the fragrance.

How can energy and matter exist if not for space to exist in?
The mystic $0 = e = mc^2 =$ loving

Temporary Insanity: A woman shopping, saying,
"I can't afford it."

Leela smiled, rolled up the scroll, tied the leather string, and laid the scroll down. She turned around, walked back to the mouth of the cave, felt a knot in her throat, and took a deep breath.

An inner voice whispered, *A longing for...*

She didn't know for what. She was only aware of a strong energy inside her navel center. She shook her head and her long silky black hair fell over her shoulders and down the middle of her back. She closed her almond eyes, pursed her full lips, took a deep breath, and let her awareness settle inside her navel center.

An hour passed...

Leela opened her eyes and saw the full moon rising above the mountains on the horizon. She smiled, closed her eyes and watched her breathing circle in and out, in and out...

Soon her silent inner sky reflected the vast night sky, and she felt flowers of sublime emptiness showering upon her.

Suddenly a bolt of energy rushed up Leela's spine to her throat! Her eyes opened wide, and her body vibrated with ecstasy. She jumped up and roared with laughter! She danced, danced, danced in wild ecstasy, until finally, exhausted, she stood and bowed to the luminous silver moon above.

Laying her hands over her heart, she thought, *Enough for today...*

Leela walked inside the cave and lay on a pile of yak skins. She pulled one of the skins over her body, closed her eyes, and watched her breathing...

A long-forgotten scene passed before her mind's eye...

It was monsoon in the ancient city of Srinagar in North India. Raindrops trickled through the thatched roof in a corner of her father's pottery studio. Leela was five years old, singing a lullaby as she sat on a cushion next to her twenty-four-year-old mother, Taichia:

"What's one more raindrop?
Soon the tears will surely stop.
What's one more raindrop to an open heart?"

Leela's father, Satchitta, was a potter. He sat across from Leela and Taichia, spinning a wet clay pot on a wheel. His long black hair and beard framed his balding head, handsome face and fathomless eyes, and covered the broad shoulders of his stocky forty-year-old frame.

Taichia had been raised in England, her parents were French. Her tanned olive skin, blue eyes and sensual Mediterranean features resembled other exotic women in southern France. She kissed Leela on her cheek, stood, smiled, nodded to Satchitta, and gracefully walked out of the studio.

Leela's orange robe was a rainbow of red, yellow and blue dabs of paint. Her little hands, nose and cheeks were speckled with blue and white.

She picked up a paint brush, giggled, stood, and walked to Satchitta and watched as he turned the pot. Then she made a few playful blue strokes on Satchitta's nose.

Satchitta smiled and continued to spin the wheel.

"Satchi, I'm bored," Leela said.

Satchitta glanced at the pot Leela had just painted. "No problem. Beautiful."

"Yeah," Leela said, returning to her cushion and sitting, "but I'm bored."

Just then Leela's chubby little friend, Prema, peeked through the window. "Leela," she whispered, "let's play."

Leela jumped up and ran to the window. "But it's raining. Play with Satchi and me inside."

Prema walked around to the front door and shyly peeked in.

"Come in," Leela said, picking up a pot. "Let's paint."

Prema shuffled inside the studio and hung her head. "No, I told you: I can't paint."

Leela handed her a brush. "Yes, you can!"

Prema set the brush on the floor. "I'll mess it up again."

Leela looked to Satchitta for inspiration.

Satchitta smiled as he continued spinning the pot.

Leela turned to Prema and said, "There are no mistakes, only learning. Come on, it's fun!"

A smile crept over Prema's face. She shrugged her shoulders and sat down. They took turns painting a pot, until to Prema's surprise, an exquisite pattern of vibrant colors graced the pot.

Prema's face beamed. "I didn't know I…"

Suddenly, a thunderous voice shattered the playful mood in the studio! Northern India's most powerful citizen, Rakan Kailin, screamed, "SATCHITTA!" and bolted through the front door, dragging his terrified five-year-old son, Asanga, by an arm behind him.

Rakan was short and mean. He had an enormous belly and a permanent scowl on his face. His twisted nose and beady eyes were flush with red as he stormed into the studio like a raging bull. He stopped and glared at Leela.

Then he rushed to Satchitta and shouted, "It was her again! Asanga confessed! You'll have to pay for the damages this time!"

Satchitta stopped spinning the wheel. He calmly wiped off the wet paint on his nose and the clay on his hands with a cloth.

"Who did what?" he asked.

Rakan's body shook with rage, and his bloodshot eyes glared menacingly at Leela. "This, this demon here!" he said vehemently. "She stole crystals from the chandeliers in our temple again! I know it was her because she conned Asanga here to help her. How many times have I told you that I don't want her playing with him? I took care of him but--"

"Asanga?" Leela interrupted. "You hit him *again?"*

Little Asanga shook as he stood slouched over in his torn cotton robe. He cowered behind his father and nodded. He had bruises on his tear-stained face and arms.

"That's none of your business!" Rakan retorted.

"Wait, Rakan!" Satchitta said. He turned to Leela and asked, "Leela, how many?"

"Oh, maybe ten," Leela said. "The crystals are so pretty. Asanga and Prema and I were climbing on the--"

"You *see!"* Rakan screamed.

"Do you still have the crystals?" Satchitta asked.

Leela lowered her eyes. "Some."

"I still have three," Prema said. "We were going to give them back, like last time."

Satchitta smiled. "There, you see, Rakan? No problem. They were going to return your crystals. What do you say to Rakan, Leela?"

Leela's face lit up. She turned to Rakan and innocently asked, "Do you want to paint with us?"

Rakan threw his hands up in frustration! "There, see?" he shouted. "No discipline! Two peas from the same pod!"

Then he glanced at Prema and added, "Three peas! You're corrupting the morality of your daughter *and* the other youth in this city, including my son! I'll put an end to it, you'll see! But for now, I want those crystals! *NOW!*"

"In good time, Rakan," Satchitta said calmly. "Leela, Prema, can you get the crystals and bring them to Rakan?"

Leela and Prema nodded.

"I'll get mine," Prema said, and rushed outside. Leela stood and looked at her father.

"So Rakan," Satchitta said, "you'll have your crystals today. I'll talk about the situation with Leela and Prema. *Namaste*."

Rakan shook his fist. "Next time I'll call the police!"

"Please," Satchitta said, "no more games. The whole police department sits during your sermons in your temple every week listening to your false rumors about how I am corrupting people and how I should be stopped. But don't involve police in matters regarding children. You and I can--"

"How do you know about my sermons?" Rakan interrupted. Then he glanced at Leela and pointed a threatening finger. "Ah-ha! *YOU!* You are not to sneak into my temple again, do you hear?"

Satchitta turned to Leela and said, "He's right. We talked about this before. It will only mean more trouble. Do you understand?"

Leela nodded sadly.

Satchitta continued, "As for me, Rakan, I claim no authority. No one is being corrupted here. My friends and I are living here consciously, creatively, nothing else. It's our choice if we want to live communally or not. Our ashram has grown organically, like our farm. It's our right to live in peace without being threatened or harassed by your false rumors of orgies and beatings here."

Satchitta turned and looked at Asanga's bruises. "And speaking of beatings," he continued, "why do you have to--"

Rakan's face turned beet-red. He interrupted Satchitta, declaring, "It's Rufus's will - God's will - that I handle my son accordingly! That's none of your business! I've had enough of Asanga sneaking out and playing with this, this little demon here! Tomorrow I'm taking him to Military School in Delhi. Then he won't be corrupted by, by.... I'm putting an end to this nonsense! And I want those crystals back today! You know where to find me." Then he stormed out of the hut, dragging Asanga behind him.

Satchitta turned to Leela. "Did you see his anger?"

"He's always angry," Leela said.

"True. His God, 'Rufus', is pure imagination. He is a fanatical moralist and wants himself and everyone else to be as perfect as the God in his imagination, and no human is perfect. He's angry with himself really."

"Why?"

"Because he falls short of the perfect saint he tries to be in his imagination."

"What is imag...in...ation?"

"In a minute," Satchitta said. "The point is, Rakan will call the police if there *is* a next time. Do you want that to happen?"

"No."

"Then what are you going to do?"

Leela pursed her lips. "Well, give him back his dumb crystals and stay away from him, I guess."

"You guess?"

Leela took a deep breath and huffed, "He's no fun anyway! A big grouch!"

"All the more reason to stay away from him. The only reason he didn't call the police this time was because Asanga was involved. He didn't want his son to get into trouble again."

Leela winced. "He beat Asanga again!"

Satchitta nodded. “There’s nothing that I or the police can do about that. He owns the police. Can you agree to tell me or your mother when you are going to play outside the ashram again, and agree not to play inside Rakan’s temple again?”

“Yes.”

Satchitta picked up a clay image of a smiling green frog. “Is this frog real, alive, natural?”

“No.”

“But sometimes I see you talking to this frog and to your dolls as if they are real. Yes?”

“Yes.”

“It’s your imagination that lets you do that.”

Leela’s eyes fluttered as she tried to understand. “You mean when I pretend something is real that isn’t real? That’s imag...ination?”

“Yes, and when you behave as if something that isn’t real is real, that’s imagination. That’s what Rakan does.”

Leela nodded, then knitted her eyebrows. “And... God?”

“God to me is being conscious of inner and outer Nature.”

“Real frogs?”

“Real frogs.”

Leela’s dream in Bodhi Cave suddenly ended. She opened her eyes and glanced at the stars above. Then she closed her eyes and sleep swept over her like a gentle cloud of forgetfulness. The last words she heard before she fell into a deep unconscious sleep were, *A longing for...?*

In the middle of the night Leela’s eyes suddenly opened as a soft inner voice whispered, *“...a longing for the source of love inside.”*

CHAPTER 2

Bunny gazed at Leela sleeping in Bodhi Cave and sighed, "Leela's doing fine. Let's see about Mark."

"Okay," Lloyd said.

Bunny and Lloyd projected the image of being on a cloud above 23-year-old Mark Trimble through their third eye centers. And *Whoosh!* - they were transported to a pink cloud high above Mark as he strolled on a San Francisco Bay beach.

They sat and watched Mark for a few minutes, then Lloyd gazed at Bunny sipping champagne. "What are you thinking about?" he asked.

"What's real and what isn't," Bunny said.

Lloyd adjusted his forked tail. "So, what's real?"

"I don't know," Bunny said. "It's strange being an angel. I once felt something when I drank champagne. I miss having a physical body. What's in this?"

Lloyd shrugged his shoulders. "Champagne? Don't know. I like the bubbles."

"Me, too," Bunny agreed. "About Mark down there..."

Bunny and Lloyd peeked over the edge of their cloud.

"You know," Bunny said, "Mark's kind of cute."

"Ruggedly handsome," Lloyd agreed.

Three gulls - a white adult and a brown adult - and a small light-brown gull - alighted from the cloud next to Bunny and Lloyd. The gulls flew below and landed in front of Mark Trimble as he walked along the sandy beach in the late morning sun.

Mark stopped and gazed at the gulls. He had been lost in a daydream about his brother Floyd's suicide in Missouri. The gulls awoke him to the present moment.

He sat on a weathered redwood stump, took off his muddy boots, and rubbed his feet. He took a few deep breaths of salty air and gazed through his clear blue eyes at the vast expanse of the bay before him.

Amazing...

He stretched his solid six-foot frame, scratched his full red-brown beard, and began to write the first entry in his new leather-bound journal:

•

San Francisco Bay, May 27, 1848.

The mystery and majesty of the sea: alive, dynamic, changing, yet somehow always the same.

Alive...

Like the sea, I'm alive, and in the moment grateful to be so. But Floyd's suicide woke me to the fact that this, too, will pass. Like Floyd, I'll die someday, disappear like a wave into the ocean. Then what? Don't know. How could I?

Like Merschel once said, "The point is to risk everything to discover the truth of your nature before death, to live the mystery of life to the fullest - no compromise! Then death is no longer the villain we're led to believe, but a friend, a gilded frame giving context to the sacred work of art life can be.

"Mark," Merschel continued, "you and I aren't on some hero's journey. Heroes are spiritually asleep, villains are asleep. We're here to spiritually wake up, that's all. So, if you're looking for security, consolations, for solutions to life's mystery, forget it! I've been with a live Master, Gopal, in India, looked into the fathomless eyes of a Master, and I can tell you that a Master will take away all solutions from you and will make you aware of mysteries which are going to remain mysteries forever."

Mark laid down his pen, considered Merschel's statement.

True so far...

Then he continued to write:

Can't say I really understood you, Merschel. But a Master.... I wonder if one exists: someone who has transcended life and death? Truth is, I don't know, haven't met an enlightened Master yet. Don't know if I ever will.

Merschel's Master, Gopal, said, "Truth is already the case. Inside our navel center is a direct spiritual connection to a cosmic energy that pulses and activates each breath, keeps us alive even when we are asleep.

"We are dreaming we are disconnected from the source of life. But we are connected, naturally, like waves in an ocean of Existence. So, relax and enjoy! Go In! There's no one to become. You are already who you need to be inside. Go In."

But mostly those are just words to me. Me, an enlightened being? All I know is, Merschel, thank you! Something in the depth of your eyes told me that beings like Gopal do exist and I aim to meet one and see for myself.

India now or bust!

The only way to know if death is an enemy, a friend, both, or neither, is to meet someone who does know from their own experience and go from there.

Sitting here on the beach now... the salty scent of the seaweed and ocean air, waves crashing, sea lions, pelicans, and those three gulls playing yonder...

Been in San Francisco for two weeks now. Interesting town. Interesting people: arrogant, roughneck Americans; runaway black slaves; poor Chinese, Mexicans and Chileans; Europeans of every sort; Australian criminals; housewives; prostitutes of every nationality. Quite a group, all in some way or other infected by the get-rich-quick disease which has swept through this area like a plague. There are one or two luxury hotels, but mostly there is a wreck of temporary buildings, shacks, canvas tents and houses, mud and broken bottles all around. By the looks of it, this town should have been named, "Havoc"!

There are hundreds of temporary buildings of wood, canvas, straw, cardboard and tin rising from the muddy streets and standing in stark contrast to several of the well-constructed office buildings along the main streets.

The noise from the new construction can be deafening at times, and the racket seems to amplify the frenzied greed and impatience which drives most of this hodgepodge of bewildered humanity.

Because of the language barrier among folks of different tongues, fights are frequent, and theft is common, especially in business. Shots ring out often and there are times I feel I'd be safer back near Sutter's Mill panning gold, or back home in Missouri. But my ship, *The Emerald Queen,* is leaving for India in a week or so, and soon all this frenzy will pass.

Funny... browsing in the White Cloud Emporium yesterday, this thick leather-bound journal fell from a shelf. I was pulling out the book next to it when *plop!* - there it was in my hands.

I thought, *Why not? You've got time before your ship leaves. Writing might be fun.*

So, I walked to this beach to write about what has happened since Floyd's suicide, but something else happened...

Since the gold fever has hit California, San Francisco has been flooded by all kinds of eccentric characters coming to ride the wave of greedy excitement here. I was sitting on this beach yesterday starting to write in this journal when I saw a gaudily clad, bearded Union military officer in the distance holding court to ten sea lions. And the sea lions were listening! Attentively!

I looked around and saw no one else on the beach to whom this strange officer could have been talking. It was the sea lions.

The officer had his back to me, so I put my boots on, and slowly, quietly, walked to within ten feet behind him to listen as he bellowed, "...and no one shall take away these rights! Give me liberty or smell my breath! I now ordain you Right Honorable Dukes and Duchesses of Seaweed, Esquires."

The strange officer picked up a clump of dry seaweed and ceremoniously draped it over his shoulders.

"Repeat after me," he continued, "I do solemnly swear..."

The officer paused and the sea lions honked in response:

"Honk! Honk! Honk!"

"...that I will uphold the duties entrusted in me by the Lord Emperor George Bull Goose Beatty..."

"Honk! Honk! Honk!"

"...hitherto, that no creature shall swim these waters without a license..."

Honking...

"...and that the fine for transgressing this order..."

Honking...

"...shall not be more than five dollars..."

Honking...

"...or less than imaginable."

Honking...

The Lord Emperor pulled a sandwich out of the old, weathered leather mail bag hanging from his shoulders, sat down, and began to eat the sandwich.

The sea lions came closer and closer...

...and closer...

Bull Goose Beatty saw this, and smiling, threw the sandwich into the throng of honking mammals. They all made a mad dive for the sandwich.

The Emperor quickly turned around and saw me watching. He stood and walked to within a few feet of me as the Dukes and

Duchesses of Seaweed fought over the sandwich. The stench from the Emperor's body almost knocked me over.

"You!" he said in a snappy tone. "Do you have any mustard?"

His directness scared me. I jumped back, stuttered, "N-no."

"Then what do you have for me?"

I took a deep breath, reached in my pocket, and pulled out a beautiful pink and white conch I had picked up on the beach.

"Put it to your ear," I suggested, and handed him the conch.

The Lord Emperor George Bull Goose Beatty inspected the conch then put it to his right ear. As he did so I looked into the depths of his sparkling brown eyes.

A lot like Merschel's eyes, I thought. *Mystic's eyes*.

The other-worldly beauty of his eyes was in stark contrast with the rest of him. He smelled like moldy Limburger cheese; his long brown hair hung in braids to his shoulders; and his bare toes were sticking through his tattered leather boots.

Two of the ten or so handmade medals pinned on the front of his military jacket were inscribed, "Eat well," and "Obey your mother."

With the conch to his ear, the Emperor finally declared, "Ah, yes, it is God speaking to me. Yes," he continued, obviously in a dialog with somebody, "I will write my mother.... Yes, the cards are on the table.... No, I wasn't cheating.... A banana?"

Bull Goose Beatty looked at me sheepishly and asked, "Do you have a banana?"

"No," I replied.

"Neither of us has a banana," he said into the conch. "Yes, I will ask him." He lowered the conch, peered at me intensely, and asked, "Do you love yourself?"

"Don't know what love is," I said.

The Emperor smiled approvingly, and asked with a glint in his eyes, "Then do you accept yourself?"

I felt uncomfortable, squirmed, then blurted, "Who's going to do the accepting, the part of the mind that rejects me?"

"Um, okay," the Emperor nodded, "we'll leave it at that."

Then the Emperor studied me closely. "Mmmm... I have a feeling about you... please... sit."

I sat on the sand.

The Emperor paused, then said in measured tones, "When Gautama the Buddha was asked about God and such, he often told this story...

"There are four kinds of horses," he would say. "The first is one who, when you whip him, will not budge. The second, when you whip him, will begin to move. The third, you only need to show him the whip and he will move. The fourth, he only needs to see the shadow of the whip and he moves."

The Emperor paused and asked, "Which kind of horse are you?"

I shook my head. "Depends, I guess."

"On what?" the Emperor asked.

"Sometimes I'm the first kind, sometimes the second, sometimes one of the other two."

The Emperor smiled. He pointed to my journal and asked, "What's that for?"

By this time, I felt in tune with the bizarre nature of the circus that the Emperor created around himself, so I said, "To chronicle your reign."

"So be it!" he pompously declared and waived his hand across the sky. "Let us inspect my domain!"

The Lord Emperor George Bull Goose Beatty slid his right arm through my left my arm and led me into town. Most folks recognized the Emperor and waved as we walked by. A few children taunted him, and one boy threw a rotten apple at him. George deftly caught the apple, took a bite and handed it back to the child.

"Thank you," George said to the boy with a gracious nod. "Generosity is its own reward."

An old woman walking a raggedy black poodle stopped the Emperor and asked him to heal the mutt. "She's been acting strange," the woman said. "I think she has worms. Can you help?"

Bull Goose knelt and tenderly kissed the poodle's feet. The poodle rolled onto its back. The Lord Emperor rubbed the poodle's belly gently for a minute, then said softly, "She'll be fine. She's pregnant."

On this went, like a parade of sorts as we walked down the muddy streets of San Francisco.

People waved, we waved back.

People jeered, we waved back.

My impression of the Emperor began to change as I watched him do his magic. *He's got something,* I thought. *A bit cuckoo, but definitely the real deal.*

At one point George stopped and turned to me. Our eyes connected. There was silence for a moment. Then George chuckled, waved his arms across the sky, and dramatically proclaimed:

"Laugh when the mind cries, so foolish,
and closes the heart to the seed
of wisdom which grows with awareness
of each moment the soul breathes."

Dumbfounded, I stared at the Emperor, who continued,

"Words are a salad of lollipop dreams,
bluebirds mumbling, pastures green,
Lucy and Lucky rolling in cream,
symbols empty of feeling."

Bull Goose smiled innocently and handed me a copper penny. "Keep the change," he said, then sat on the muddy street and closed his eyes.

I, too, sat and closed my eyes.

After a while I sensed movement and opened my eyes.

George stood towering above me. I saw that he had taken off his left boot and balanced it on his head. I stood up and together we silently walked to the Farmers Market. There we were fed a free lunch by different vendors, each of whom first saluted George, then handed us produce, nuts and fruit as we passed by their crude rickety stalls.

After lunch I followed George as he walked down the street dropping breadcrumbs behind him, leading a procession of quacking Mallard ducks into the police station where Chief O'Reilly and ten amused officers lined up for the Emperor's inspection.

During the inspection, the Emperor stopped in front of one of the uniformed officers, frowned, then asked the ducks, "What do you think of this one? A bit sloppy, eh?"

The ducks quacked their agreement.

The officer looked down at his dirty shoes. He lifted one foot at a time and shined the top of each shoe on the back of the trousers of his other leg.

The ducks quacked their approval.

George smiled, dismissed the officers and the ducks, and he and I walked out of the police station.

Later in the evening, we ate an elegant dinner at *La Premiere Restaurant* adjacent a theater. The meal was scrumptious, and the waiter accepted the Emperor's personal currency as payment.

I did most of the talking during dinner, mostly about why I was going to India: about Floyd's suicide; about the books on mysticism that I had read in Colonel Holgate's library in Missouri; and about how a mystic, Merschel Whistle, had taught me meditation and inspired me to want to be in the presence of his own Master, Gopal, in North India.

For the most part, the Emperor listened silently and enjoyed his vegetarian meal without commenting.

Outside the restaurant, I asked George if I could have a closer look at his currency notes. He handed me a three-by-six-inch green paper twenty-dollar note with white lettering.

On the front side under an engraving of the Emperor's noble profile, were the words, "No nation, no religion, just some guy getting along."

On the back side was an etching of an ostrich with its head in the sand. Beneath the image were the words, "In the Mystery we doubt."

I recognized this statement as part of one of the ancient sutras I had read in a book in Colonel Holgate's library a few years back - "The Dilai Dalai Sutras".

I pointed to the statement. "What's this?"

"Ah, just some rubbish I pinched from Dilai Dalai's sutras," he replied. "The whole sutra goes something like, 'In God we trust? It's more like, In the Mystery we doubt.'"

"You've heard of the sutras? Read them?"

"Just by word of mouth. Can't help hearing about them now, can I? Amazing how so many idiots have made a Dilai Dalai Jai religion out of those ancient scriptures. No one has even seen the original scrolls!"

"I met someone who's seen them," I said. "My friend, Merschel Whistle, saw them near the Swat Valley in Northwest India."

The Emperor frowned. "Maybe so, but now there are thousands of Dilai Dalai Jai priests and nuns around the world! I heard that on April first worshipers gathered by the thousands back East to praise Dilai Dalai on his supposed birthday. How does their devotional song go?

"Praise to thee, O Blessed One,
ears bigger than the sun,
giving joy to everyone
on this, your birthday.

"Praise to thee, O Blessed Dilai,
knowing that indeed it's silly
to worship you willy nilly
on this, your birthday.
Or is it tomorrow?"

"I heard about that, too," I said.

The Emperor sniffed. "Never mind, we've got better things to do tonight."

"Like what?"

Bull Goose Beatty smiled. "Come on."

He led me next door to the Grand Theater, where we sat in the Emperor's reserved box seats and enjoyed a marvelous production of Shakespeare's "Midsummer Night's Dream".

After the performance we walked outside the theater and the Emperor looked up and howled at the rich plethora of diamond stars and full moon above. Then he and I bowed to each other.

He turned and shouted, "Rickshaw!"

A ragged young bowlegged Oriental man ran up with a dilapidated rickshaw in tow and George climbed aboard. The Emperor silently nodded to me; then with a sudden jerk, the spindly-legged runner hauled Bull Goose's fading apparition into the clear starry night.

I took a deep breath and slowly walked back to the wharf and onto my ship, *The Emerald Queen*, home for the last two weeks.

I walked below the deck to the sailors' quarters and grabbed a few wool blankets from my hammock, then went back on deck to the stern and wrapped the blankets around my body. I lay down with this journal as a pillow and gazed at the infinite tapestry of stars and planets twinkling above.

Soon I felt a deep silent connection with something bigger than myself and surrendered to the familiar feeling. I had had glimpses of this feeling during lovemaking with Shelly back home and recently with Wo Lin here in San Francisco: a feeling of disappearing into love. But lying on deck last night this feeling slowly changed, and I felt a silent longing in my heart for the ultimate love affair, a longing to be at the foot of Merschel's live Master, Gopal, in India.

Finally, I took a deep breath, closed my eyes and fell asleep. All-in-all, it was a day filled with cheers and tears dear to my heart.

•

CHAPTER 3

Leela lay with closed eyes between two yak rugs in Bodhi Cave, visualizing when she had felt closest to the source of love: making love with Asanga on her seventeenth birthday.

Asanga...

She dreamed of the fun she had had with Asanga as five-year-old children in Srinagar: jumping off high cliffs into the raging Jhelum River; playing with Bengal tiger cubs while their mother hunted nearby; sleeping overnight in dark depths of the wild forest.

Leela and Asanga were often punished by Rakan for their mischief, but the punishment bonded them as much as the fun they had. Leela was heartbroken when Rakan sent Asanga off to Military School in Delhi soon after Leela, Asanga and Prema were reprimanded by Rakan for stealing crystals in Rakan's temple.

Leela had been born in Gazabha, the commune in the Dilai Valley that her father, Satchitta, his younger sister Shanti, and their father Gopal, had lived in. Gopal had become enlightened the year before Leela was born. Little Leela loved Gopal dearly. Together they painted, danced, and played whatever games Leela wanted to play.

When Leela was almost four years old, one of Gopal's disciples, his dearest childhood friend, Amritam, inherited 35 acres of riverfront property, 720 kilometers away in Srinagar.

Amritam gave the land to his guru, Gopal.

Gopal knew it was time for his son, Satchitta, to be on his own, so he and Satchitta talked and agreed that Amritam's gift was "a chance to spread the love".

Three months after Gopal inherited the land in Srinagar, Satchitta, Taichia, Leela, Amritam, and 20 adults and 9 children moved from Gazabha to Srinagar to develop the lush fertile farmland along the Jhelum River. Shanti remained in the Gazabha commune with Gopal.

Leaving Gopal was hard for little Leela. She felt the searing pain of loving someone and having to part. But Gopal made the transition as easy as possible by reminding her again and again, "Always remember, beloved, you are loved."

Leela kept the Master's words close to her heart...

Srinagar was a challenge for Satchitta and his friends from the beginning. Language was one challenge. They had spoken Pukhto in Gazabha but had to learn Kashmiri in Srinagar. Also, at Satchitta's request, Taichia taught everyone English, one of the main languages used in commerce throughout India.

The main challenge, however, was the constant harassment by Rakan and his father, Bezuhl, who together ruled over a commercial and religious empire which extended far beyond Srinagar into most of Kashmir. The two despots believed that Satchitta's ashram was a threat to their commercial empire and did everything in their power to subvert the construction and settlement of the new ashram.

Despite this harassment, within eleven years, Satchitta's ashram blossomed into a vital creative international community of 191 adults and children. Leela blossomed into a playful rebellious teenager.

Late in the evening of Leela's seventeenth birthday, as she was walking in the moonlight through the Srinagar ashram, she was awestruck by the sight of a handsome young gypsy stranger walking towards her.

The gypsy had dark copper skin, chiseled masculine face, penetrating brown eyes and a black goatee. He was wearing a peach-colored turban and shawl, patchwork rainbow quilt shirt, maroon balloon pants, sandals, and carried an *aektara*, a small one-stringed instrument, and a *duggi*, a small kettledrum.

It had been twelve years since Leela had last seen Asanga, but she intuitively knew the gypsy was him!

She slowly walked up, looked the gypsy in the eyes, and sheepishly asked, "Asanga?"

Asanga was ecstatic when he saw how beautiful his beloved Leela had become! He beat out a rhythm on his *aektara* and *duggi* and began to dance wildly!

A minute later, he suddenly stopped and yelled, "Leela!"

Leela shrieked, leaped, and hugged Asanga! They spun around and around like two whirling tops in ecstasy.

A crowd gathered to watch, until finally Leela and Asanga laughed hysterically and collapsed in each other's arms on the grass by the pond.

Leela raised her eyebrows and asked, "Is this how you dress in Military School?"

Asanga laughed, and replied, "No. I escaped three years ago, when I was fourteen. Went to Bengal, lived with Baul mystics."

"Oh, right!" Leela said. "I've seen a few Bauls. Wonderfully mad mystics! Why Bengal?"

"My mom was a Baul, used to live there."

"Kijna?"

"Yes. Without Rakan knowing it, mom told me stories about the Bauls when I was a kid, how their religion is singing, dancing, celebrating, loving. I knew Rakan would try to track me down after I escaped from school and had heard mom talk about how the Bauls lived in the hills away from the villages. I found a beautiful group of Bauls living in a remote village and felt I would be safe there. I loved those folks!"

Leela looked puzzled. "Then why... did you leave?"

Asanga looked directly into Leela's eyes and said, "You."

Leela's eyes fluttered. She blushed and stroked Asanga's heart. "I missed you, too," she said tenderly. "But are you safe *here*? Rakan has spies all around."

Asanga nodded. "I know. I think one saw me come through the front gate, but I don't think he recognized me. Anyway, what about you?"

Leela smiled. "Mostly it's been great here. My folks and the other adults gave me freedom to do whatever I wanted as long as I didn't hurt myself or others. If my folks saw that I was causing a problem, they would ask me questions to provoke me to explore some situation or behavior. I'd muse over their questions then share my understanding. We've always had an open dialog, more like friends than father or mother and daughter. They trusted me enough to let me make mistakes and learn from them. And I made plenty!"

Asanga laughed. "Me, too!"

Leela took a deep breath. "A lot changed though when I moved into the ghotul."

"The what?"

"The ghotul. Come on, I'll show you."

Leela took Asanga by the hand and together they walked to the ghotul at the south end of the ashram.

On the way Leela said, "The present ghotul structure hadn't been set up here when you and I were kids, but a ghotul has existed for 2,000 years in Gazabha. Satchitta lived in the ghotul as a teenager. The Gazabha ghotul was like the one here now: a large circular bamboo and thatched leaf structure. All sexually mature boys and girls in the ashram - each 'Sane' - lives in the ghotul until they are 21."

"Teenagers?" Asanga asked.

"Yes. Eight parents monitor the forty Sanes who live in the ghotul. We Sanes are responsible for maintenance, cooking and cleaning, and parents take an active part in our schooling. We have conscious sex with all the other kids of the opposite sex."

Asanga's eyes widened. "Really? Great!"

Leela laughed. "There are 5 small 'womb rooms' where we explore our sexuality in private. One of the rules is that no one can remain more than three days with the same person until each Sane has known all the others of the opposite sex.

"Each Sane is then given an opportunity to choose, by mutual agreement, which of the other partners they would like to be with for a longer trial period. This process continues until a Sane leaves the ghotul at 21, usually with a partner with whom they want to raise children. We have no formal marriage ceremonies, but it's rare that any couple separates after leaving the ghotul.

"Really? Most stay together their whole lives?"

"The ghotul allows the natural hunting and conquering instincts of the male mind to be satisfied before committing to raising children. A natural trust usually develops among Sanes, and after someone leaves the ghotul, the trust is strengthened each day through seven Zahn meditations."

"Zahn?"

"We had the same tradition in Gazabha," Leela explained. "A large brass gong is rung at two-hour intervals for a total of seven times each day; then the entire community sits silently in meditation with closed eyes for ten minutes. Children under seven play in the communal daycare during Zahn."

As Leela and Asanga approached the ghotul, Asanga asked, "What do you mean a lot changed when you moved into the ghotul?"

Leela's eyes became misty. "Um… that's hard to answer. Come in. Let me show you the place first, okay?"

"Sure."

Leela took Asanga by the hand and gave him a brief tour of the ghotul: 10 bedrooms, 5 womb rooms, a creative arts room, a communal bathroom and kitchen. She made hot chai tea in the kitchen then led Asanga into one of the womb rooms where they sat on cushions and sipped chai while Leela shared her story:

"I was 14 when I moved into the ghotul from my folk's bungalow. A few months later, I was sitting next to Satchi at the weekly commune meeting, when Satchi said, "Enlightenment has happened."

Asanga sat back and gasped, *"Wow!"*

"Yes, that's what everyone said... except me."

"Except you?"

"Well, I had heard Satchi and others talk about enlightenment, and it seemed like something I might look into later, but I was too busy having fun to be impressed. For four years before Satchi's announcement I could tell that Satchi had really changed, had begun to spend a lot of time in his bedroom and had become very silent. But at that meeting, I thought, *What's the fuss about? Sure, Satchi has changed. So what?*

"At the meeting Satchi said, 'A new phase of the ashram will begin. We will open our doors to the world.'

"And immediately things changed! I had no idea what enlightenment was, and didn't understand at first when, at that same meeting, Satchi's old friend, Amritam, threw himself at Satchi's feet and asked, 'Master, please accept me as your disciple.'"

"Wow!" Asanga said.

Leela nodded. "Yeah. Satchi gently touched Amritam's head, smiled, and joked, 'You'll be the next one to pop, Amritam!' We all laughed, then celebrated!"

Asanga rolled his eyes. "Amazing! Amritam became Satchitta's sannyasin, his disciple, open to exploring inner mysteries."

"Yes. Taichia and I also became Satchi's disciples that night. The rest of the commune became sannyasins at the next community meeting. Personally, I felt like I was playing another game with my dad, but it was no game after that."

"How so?"

"Well, remember Prema?"

Asanga mulled over the question. "Prema... Prema... your little roly-poly friend in Gazabha?"

"Yes, I had known her since Gazabha. Anyway, soon after that meeting, Prema began to tease me, calling me 'The Master's Daughter', and somehow an icon was born.

"Icon? Wasn't she just kidding?"

"It was more than kidding. She was and still is, chubby, overweight. She doesn't accept her body and isn't as popular as I am with boys in the ghotul. She has always felt, well, jealous of me."

"Oh..."

"Her name-calling was more like ridicule, and it spread to some of my other old friends. I remember one time, about a year after Satchi's announcement, I was about to enter the kitchen here when I overheard Prema and two other girls gossiping.

"Prema said, 'Leela always gets what she wants, the cutest boyfriends, most fun work to do!'

"Kilia said, 'She thinks she's perfect, the Master's daughter! Everyone thinks her paintings are the most beautiful.'

"Lonu said, 'No wonder she's Satchitta's favorite!'

Asanga shook his head. "Ooh, mean stuff!"

Leela nodded. "I was shocked! I wondered, *Who are they talking about? Me? I am the Master's daughter, so what?*

"Anyway, I shrank away from the kitchen and crept into a womb room and cried for hours."

Asanga saw that Leela was on the verge of tears and hugged her for a minute.

Finally, Leela looked up and stroked Asanga's head. "Thanks," she said. "Anyway, that was the beginning of two years of growing pains for me and everyone else in the ashram. The ashram grew like wildfire. Westerners came to be with Satchi. Many became disciples. Now there are 191 resident disciples here.

"Since I've lived in the ghotul, life has been enriching and challenging. Enriching because I've had lots of lovers and have had the opportunity to consciously mature in many ways. But it's been challenging because to some new disciples from other countries, I've become an icon - 'the Master's Daughter'. A few new disciples have treated me like I'm special, have tried to do favors for me to get close to Satchi. Sometimes when I see through their phoniness, I consciously try to piss them off to change their idealistic image of me."

Asanga smiled. "You're a fireball! You and I used to fight sometimes, too."

Leela shrugged her shoulders. "True. Anyway, sometimes Prema, Kilia and Lonu still gossip negatively behind my back. And to top it off, during these last six months, Rakan has intensified his attempts to destroy the ashram."

Asanga lowered his head and shook it as he considered his tyrannical father. "Really?"

"Really. Sannyasins have been beaten in the marketplace and on the road. Two nearly died. Recently I've felt like I'm somewhere between heaven and hell. The love here is heaven; the threats from Rakan, the jealousy and phoniness of some of my old friends and new disciples, hell. Everyone's pretty tense lately."

"Don't these Zahn sessions help?"

"They do. But remember, we surrender to a Master *because* we're unconscious flawed humans with egos! Me included! Yeah, Zahn helps. I'd be nuts without Zahn and the other meditations we do. And Satchi has addressed these ego issues during his discourses. But dropping the ego has been a challenge for all of us. The mind is so tricky! Now though, I want to forget all about it and have fun. It's my birthday!"

Asanga whooped. "It is? Let's celebrate!"

Leela smiled shyly. "I've been celebrating all day!"

Then she stood, walked over to a window, and silently gazed at the full moon. Slowly she turned around and said, "Right now I just want to be with you... you know, *be* with you!"

Asanga's eyes widened. He nodded then stood and walked over to Leela. He looked in her eyes as the moon poured its radiant nectar onto Leela's face. Leela closed her eyes and placed her hands on her chest. Then she and Asanga each took a deep breath.

Leela opened her eyes, reached out and held Asanga's hands. Their hearts pounded.

In the warm Spring moonlight, Leela slipped off her fuchsia wool robe, undressed Asanga, and gently draped her arms around his waist.

They stood naked and began to synchronize their breathing.

Soon they were breathing one rhythm.

The moon smiled.

Two cuckoos sang in harmony.

Asanga's legs and feet felt like cypress roots deep in the earth. He put his fingertips on Leela's nipples, and his *lingam* hardened.

Leela began to breathe faster and fuller. She put one hand on Asanga's chest and wrapped the other hand gently around his *lingam*. The energy in Asanga's sex center smoldered. His breathing deepened.

Within a minute Asanga's breathing changed to a shallower rhythm. The energy rose to his heart. He trembled.

Leela trembled.

Asanga took Leela's left hand and walked her to a bed. They lay on the bed and tenderly played with each other's body for thirty minutes.

During that time, they could hear loud voices arguing outside the open window, and the commotion outside continued until Leela rolled over, stood up, walked to the window and closed it.

Asanga stood, walked to Leela and hugged her. Leela put her right foot outside Asanga's left foot, wrapped her left leg around his hips, and slid his *lingam* into her warm, wet *yoni*.

Immediately Asanga's energy went back down to his sex center. His breathing changed to slow, deep breaths. He breathed into his heart, gave space to the energy, allowed it to just be there - a witness of the energy, detached yet present with the energy.

Asanga widened his stance and leaned back. Leela leaned with him and slowly moved up and down his *lingam* inside her.

Leela took a deep breath and groaned. Asanga gently kissed Leela's breasts and touched her chest with his right hand.

Suddenly Asanga's sex energy shot to his heart! He groaned and shook like an earthquake! Leela wrapped her arms and legs around Asanga and slid her tongue deep into his mouth. They lowered themselves onto the bed and melted into a rhythmic symphony of orgasmic ecstasy.

Leela and Asanga went through a dozen conscious cycles of orgasmic energy. Asanga would relax and allow his energy to build, and then when he felt ready to ejaculate, he slowed down his breathing and pumping until the energy cooled down. He did this again and again: pumping, relaxing, pumping, relaxing, and building his energy to higher, subtler levels, over and over. Leela simply remained open, receptive, and surrendered to the energy building up inside her.

Finally, the two lovers reached full-body orgasms and disappeared into some space unknowable - gone, gone, beyond the beyond, into the source of love inside...

The next thing Leela knew she was gazing into Asanga's eyes, into two dark fathomless oceans reflecting the moon.

Suddenly, the couple heard a fierce shout from outside the womb room: "HE'S IN THERE!

Leela and Asanga sat up in bed with a start! The shout had come from one of the spies Rakan had hired from Asanga's Military School. The spy had recognized Asanga entering the ashram.

Rakan burst into the womb room with four armed Hassas, his elite storm-trooper priests dressed in black uniforms. Rakan ordered three Hassas to drag Asanga out of the room naked. Leela rushed to help Asanga but was thrown to the ground and pinned down by the fourth storm-trooper. She screamed for help, but no one came.

Finally, the trooper got off Leela and left the room.

Leela ran naked outside the ghotul and discovered that the whole ashram had been under siege by Rakan and fifty Hassas.

Everyone was screaming!

Worst of all, Satchitta had been dragged from his bed and carried away by four Hassas! The Master was imprisoned in the dungeon below Rakan's Temple for 12 days.

Satchitta was the spiritual magnet of the ashram, and Leela, Taichia, and the other disciples were in utter chaos during his imprisonment. Satchitta's body had become super-sensitive after his enlightenment, and everyone feared for his life.

Finally, after 12 torturous days, Satchitta's disciples had gathered enough signatures to petition Srinagar's government to free Satchitta.

At a price...

Soon after Satchitta's release it became clear that the Master had been poisoned during his imprisonment. His health quickly deteriorated, his back was in incredible pain, he could not walk, his gums and teeth hurt, his eyesight failed him and other senses, too.

Finally, after a month of intensive care, Satchitta's health stabilized, and against Taichia's insistence that he remain in bed, he began to walk and give alternating Kashmiri and English discourses again each morning.

The month after the Master's release was hell for Leela. Her agony intensified daily because she felt responsible, guilty and heartbroken over what had happened. Satchitta was chronically ill. Asanga was prisoner in Rakan's temple, and she didn't know if she would ever see him again. And Prema's malicious gossiping was fraying Leela's nerves. She was miserable, her heart clouded with pain.

Lloyd looked down from his cloud and saw Leela dreaming with tears in her eyes as she lay between two yak rugs in Bodhi Cave. He flipped his forked tail around and tapped Bunny on the shoulder.

"What?" Bunny asked.

"It was natural for Leela to feel responsible for what happened to Satchitta and Asanga," Lloyd said.

"I guess so," Bunny agreed, "Her tears are honest. But I don't know... I need a break from the drama. Leela's only dreaming."

Lloyd chuckled. "A break? Okay." He snuffed out his cigar on the sole of his sandal and said, "Jacob Bloom meets a sexy young redhead at a bar, and they begin to discuss human nature.

"'Would you have sex with a stranger for a million dollars?' Jacob asks.

"'Yes, I would,' replies the woman.

"'Okay,' says Jacob. 'Would you have sex with me for 25 dollars?'

"The redhead huffed, 'What kind of woman do you think I am?'

"'We've already established that,' Jacob replies. 'Now we're just haggling about the price.'"

Bunny chuckled. "Um... the price we pay for love. The price Leela has paid for love, for the source of love inside."

Leela continued to dream…

In the dream she'd agonized over seeing her father in chronic pain after his poisoning, and everyone in the ashram terrified waiting for Rakan's next attack.

During the month after the siege, 12 adults and 6 children left the ashram in fear. Work had begun on a large secret underground escape tunnel out of the ashram in case there was another attack. A tall bamboo fence was quickly constructed around the Master's house. Full-time guards patrolled the fence. The stifling atmosphere of fear intensified until late one evening, the volcano exploded...

One full moon after Satchitta's release, Leela was about to step into the ghotul's kitchen, when she heard Prema and five other girls gossiping. Leela stopped and peeked around the corner to listen.

Prema said, "It looks like Satchitta is going to die. Who will be his successor?"

Kilia said, "Someone enlightened."

Lanu asked, "Is anyone in the Inner Circle enlightened?"

Prema said, "I don't think so."

"How about Leela?" Lanu asked in ridicule.

Everyone roared in laughter.

"Leela's too attached to Satchitta," Prema said. "She'll never be enlightened."

Leela was shocked! *Too attached to Satchitta? Never be enlightened?*

Leela had reached her boiling point! After years of living with "the Master's Daughter" stigma and tolerating her old friends' negative gossip, Leela had had enough! Her nerves were frayed, her heart was suffering, and her mind was calling for revenge. Prema's words felt like a knife to Leela's ego. Leela's eyes flashed red as she burst into the kitchen and slapped Prema hard on the face!

"Idiot!" Leela shouted. "He's not going to die! Not now. Successor? Who do you think you are? I'm sick and tired of your stupid lies and gossip!"

Leela turned to the rest of the Sanes and said, "I'm sick of all you cowards! Sick of you!" Then she stormed out of the ghotul and straight to Satchitta's bungalow.

Leela was livid. "I need to see Satchi!" she demanded to the guard at the gate to the bungalow.

"Wait here," the guard said, then closed the gate behind him.

Leela waited at the gate for ten seconds then pushed the gate open and ran to the front door of the bungalow just as the guard was about to enter.

The guard turned around and shouted, "WAIT! Stay here! I'll see what I can do."

Leela nodded, then the guard went inside and locked the door.

Within a minute the guard opened the door and said, "Taichia said Satchitta is in pain. His back. Come back in the morning."

Leela began to shout, "Satchi! Satchi! I'm dying! I'm dying!" She continued shouting as the guard stared at her in horror.

Within seconds Taichia appeared at the front door. "What is it, love?" Taichia asked.

Leela pushed her mother aside and rushed to Satchitta's room. She pulled open the door and ran to the Master's bed. Satchitta was half-lying, propped up with pillows.

Taichia ran to Leela and scolded her: "You can't be here! He's in pain!

"It's okay," Satchitta said weakly. "Let us be."

With that, Taichia scowled, then nodded hesitantly and turned around. She walked out the door and closed it behind her.

"Those idiots again! Prema! Kilia! Lanu!" Leela shouted. "I've had it with all this jealousy and Asanga locked up, and you, so sick! You're not going to die, are you?"

Satchitta was silent for a moment, then said, "The body is going to die someday but not now. What is the real problem?"

"Real problem?" Leela said loudly. "The real problem is, is... Prema! Rakan! EVERYBODY is the problem!"

Satchitta said, "Forget Rakan. Prema and the others are jealous of you, but that's their problem, not yours. They are mirroring some unconscious jealousy in you. Who are you jealous of?"

Leela was dumbfounded and remained silent.

Satchitta continued, "You can let the others affect you or not. You have the right to remain undisturbed."

Leela wasn't really listening. She was recalling Prema saying that she was too attached to Satchitta and that she would not get enlightened. She vaguely heard Satchitta's final words, then snapped: "The right to remain undisturbed?! What are you talking about? Do something about those idiots!"

Satchitta was silent for several moments. Finally, he said, "I know it's hard. Surrender is hard. Seeing things as they are is hard. The ego doesn't want to give up its dream. You dream that Rakan, Prema, and the others should change. But that hasn't worked. Now you're suffering. But you have a choice. You can be more aware, surrender your dream, let others be as they are, or continue to demand that they change and be miserable. You have the right to remain undisturbed."

Leela's volcano erupted a second time!

She screamed, "The right to...!" She stopped, threw her hands up in disgust, shrieked, ran out the door and back to the ghotul, threw clothes into a backpack, took a knife from the kitchen for protection, and left home!

For where, she didn't know...

With *"the source of love inside"* a shattered dream, Leela wandered aimlessly around the Srinagar countryside for an hour. Then she remembered Gopal's last words to her before she moved from Gazabha when she was almost four years old:

"Always remember, beloved, you are loved."

Immediately Leela began to walk towards Gazabha and her grandfather, in search of an oasis in what she perceived to be an unbearable desert of futility, heartache and despair.

Leela's intense dream ended as she awoke inside Bodhi Cave. She opened her eyes, turned her head, and looked outside. The morning sun shone brightly on her face as she lay beneath the yak rugs. The intense dream from her past had stirred feelings deep within her heart. She took a deep breath, tossed off the yak rugs, stood, picked up an empty pitcher, and walked to the freshwater spring deep in the recesses of the cave.

CHAPTER 4

The morning after Mark's wild jaunt with the Emperor around San Francisco, Mark lay huddled in a blanket on the deck of *The Emerald Queen* in the dim predawn light.

The Emerald Queen was a glorious monarch of the high seas. The clipper's three main masts were over 100 feet high and supported a large expanse of square hemp sails controlled by a complicated web of rigging which rose above a pointed bow and sleek narrow white hull.

Suddenly, Mark was awakened by a soft voice and a gentle hand shaking his right shoulder: "Mark? Mark?"

Mark had been dreaming about his younger brother, Floyd. In the dream Mark saved Floyd from certain death by shouting to him, "Stop! Don't do it!" just before Floyd was about to jump off a cliff.

"Mark? Mark?"

Mark opened his eyes and saw a concerned look on the sweet face of Wo Lin, who had been his young Chinese lover for the past week.

Wo Lin lay on the deck facing Mark and wrapped her left arm around him. "You no come last night," she said sadly.

Mark yawned. "Um... sorry."

Wo Lin's face turned sour. "You with... other girl?"

Mark chuckled. "No. I met a strange old goat on the beach yesterday, spent all day with him."

Wo Lin sat up with a jerk. Her long black silken hair fell over her shoulders. "Goat? You with *goat?*"

"No goat. Look, I, ah... let's take a walk. I'll tell you all about it, okay?"

Wo Lin took a deep breath. Her deep brown eyes softened.

"Walk? Um... no goat?"

Mark chuckled. "No."

"Don't understand."

"That's okay, neither do I."

Mark tucked his journal under his brown leather jacket, then he and Wo Lin stood up. The fog was thick, the air chilly and damp, so Mark wrapped his blanket around Wo Lin and himself, and with their arms around each other's waists, they slowly walked to the beach.

Mark had had back pain from panning gold the previous few months, and a week earlier had had an acupuncture treatment in the sterile white office of the venerable Dr. Li Chang. It was then that Mark met Wo Lin, Dr. Chang's intern. After Mark's initial session with Dr. Chang, the doctor invited him to join Wo Lin and himself for lunch and tea.

Dr. Chang and Wo Lin spoke only broken English, but during lunch it was clear to Mark that Wo Lin was engaged to Dr. Chang's son, Wei Ding, who was due back any day from a business trip to China. Regardless, Mark could see by Wo Lin's glances that she was attracted to him.

Mark was also attracted to her. Love happens, and Wo Lin's smiling almond eyes, rosy complexion, silent grace, and petite figure drew him like a moth to a flame.

After lunch Dr. Chang told Mark how to boil Chinese herbs, strain the liquid from the solution, and drink it to ease his back pain. Mark paid for the session and Dr. Chang instructed him to follow Wo Lin to her shack behind the office where the fresh herbs were kept.

Wo Lin's hut was Zen sparse and clean. She weighed the herbs, and as she handed them to Mark, she stood for a full minute silently gazing into Mark's friendly eyes. They agreed to meet for a walk on the beach that evening and had secretly been lovers ever since.

During Mark and Wo Lin's walk from T*he Emerald Queen* to the beach, Mark shared the story of his adventures with the Emperor - the "old goat" - and Wo Lin calmed down.

Once at the beach, they sat on a large redwood stump.

After a period of silence, Wo Lin finally said, "You rarely talk about why you came to California."

Mark hesitated before he responded. "Not much to say. I lived on a farm in Missouri..."

"Miss-ouli?"

"Close enough. Missouri. Far away. Lived on a farm with a big family."

Mark's dream that morning about his brother's suicide still lingered in his mind. Sadness swept over him. His voiced cracked and tears welled up in his eyes. "Maybe you're not going to understand this," he said, "but you see, my brother..."

Mark began to cry. Wo Lin hugged him and laid her head on his shoulder. Mark wept silently for a while, then said, "Sorry, I need to be alone. Just for a little while, okay? We'll go to the pub tonight."

Wo Lin's face brightened. "O'Doul's?"

"Yeah, we'll have fun, I promise. But now, please, I need to be alone."

Wo Lin wiped the tears from Mark's face, then kissed him on the cheek and stood up. "You… okay?"

Mark nodded.

"You play music tonight?" Wo Lin asked.

Mark managed a weak smile. "Sure."

"We dance?"

"Dance."

"Make love?"

"Make love."

Wo Lin solemnly stood up and walked towards the wharf, consoled that she and Mark would spend another fun evening together.

Little did either of them know that tumultuous events during the next couple of days would utterly change their relationship.

"This is where it gets juicy," Bunny said, putting her strip poker hand down on a fluffy cloud.

Naked from the waist up, Lloyd put two of his five cards on top of the cloud. "Why juicy? Two please."

Bunny dealt Lloyd two cards from the deck. "Well, you know The Men's Code: Be strong. Try hard. Please others. Hurry up. Be perfect. Do anything, but don't *feel!*"

Bunny discarded one card and dealt herself the top card from the deck. "Our boy Mark there is boiling with feelings, with grief about Floyd's suicide. *Juicy* feelings! There's hope for men after all."

"He'll work it out," Lloyd said. "What do you have?"

Bunny laid her cards down. "Full house, queens high. Off with your pants, *man!*"

Mark watched Wo Lin walk onto the wharf. He stood, trudged to a sand dune, sat down, wrapped the blanket tighter around his shoulders, took slow deep breaths into his heart, and began to write the second entry into his new leather-bound journal…

•

May 28, 1848.

The salty fragrance of the ocean... no sign of the Emperor...

Are those the same three gulls from yesterday - the white, the brown, and the light-brown one?

You guys following me around?

Okay, echoes of time speak to me...

My strange odyssey began back home on our Missouri farm, two months after my seventeenth birthday. It was a cold, humid, blustery November afternoon and started out normal. I can still see our rickety old two-story wooden farmhouse and red barn, hear the livestock, smell the manure, and see two of my four sisters helping mom hang laundry out to dry...

My buddies, Wayne and Jeff, and I were running through our cornfield towards Six Boy's Woods to check our rabbit traps. Wayne was my closest friend, a tall lanky blond, ever the comedian. Jeff was a stocky curly redhead with a flair for the dramatic.

It hadn't rained in a month and the drought had taken its toll. Corn stalks stood hunched over like sullen soldiers in the weather-beaten field.

Then just as we left the cornfield and were about to disappear into the woods, from out of nowhere my ten-year-old brother, Floyd, jumped in front of us. "Hey, where are you going?"

"To check our traps," I said.

"Think you caught any rabbits?"

"Don't know."

"Can I come?" Floyd asked excitedly.

"No!" Jeff said. "You're just a runt!"

"Yeah!" Wayne chimed.

Jeff and Wayne trotted off into the woods.

I shrugged my shoulders. "Look, Floyd, we gotta go, okay?"

Floyd's eyes saddened as I turned to run away with my buddies. Feeling an uneasy knot in my belly, I thought to turn around and shout, "Some other time, Floyd, I promise!" But my need to be accepted by my friends was stronger than my gut feeling, so I ignored the thought and ran straight into the woods.

Deep in the woods we checked the traps we had set a few days before.

No luck.

We spent a few hours in the woods then went to church for altar boy practice. On the wall outside the church was the sign I had painted the night before: "Our Lady of the Nice Legs Church".

After practice I got drenched from the steady rain that had begun to fall and arrived home late for dinner. Mom was serving dinner to my two younger brothers and four sisters. My stepdad, Hank, was absent. My natural dad used to call mom a "Wild Irish Rose", and she usually was. Usually mom's ready laugh, cherubic face and caring ways endeared her to all who knew her. But that night she was all business as she dished out corn, dumplings and string beans to her squabbling children at the table.

"Where were you?" Mom huffed.

"We checked our traps. Nothing. Then altar boy practice," I said.

"Hmm, avoiding chores most likely. But you know the rule about being late: in the living room till we're all finished. Lucky your dad's in town or he'd let you have it for being late again."

Dad? I thought. *Hank's a stepdad.*

But I said nothing, just went to a corner of the living room and collapsed in a chair. I closed my eyes and daydreamed about my natural dad who had died in a cave-in at Palmer's Coal Mine when I was five years old.

Suddenly, something woke me from my reverie - shouting and commotion from the dining room. I vaguely remember hearing Floyd call our eight-year-old brother, Eddie, "a fairy".

I looked up and saw Mom grab Floyd's plate. "I told you to never use that language!" she scolded. "That's a *sin!* Now go to your room! No more supper for you, young man!"

Floyd stormed dejectedly past me towards the stairs to his bedroom on the second floor. I felt a familiar knot in my belly, thought to say, "It's okay, Floyd," and follow him upstairs to console him. But I said nothing, just waited until everyone had eaten before I fed myself on cold beans, corn and dumplings. Then I went to my own little cubbyhole of a room upstairs to do homework.

A half-hour later, while dodging my history book and looking out my bedroom window at the merciful torrent of rain falling outside, I heard Eddie cry from the boys' bedroom, "FLOYD'S DEAD! FLOYD'S DEAD!"

Mom flew upstairs and right by me as we both rushed into Floyd and Eddie's bedroom. She quickly lowered Floyd's limp body down from the top edge of the door where he was hanging by a leather belt around his neck. On the floor was a wicker chair lying on its side, apparently the chair that Floyd had used to stand on so that he could reach the top of the door. Floyd's skin was milk white as was the foam at the corners of his open mouth.

Mom tried mouth-to-mouth resuscitation on Floyd for a minute, but Floyd remained eerily unresponsive and still.

In a surreal slow-motion chain of events, I followed Mom as she picked up Floyd and carried his body down the stairs past a pack of screaming kids and out the front door to our horse-drawn carriage.

Mr. Scott, one of our temporary farmhands, had been working late and must have heard the screams. From out of nowhere he jumped up on the driver's seat and drove us to Doc Moore's house in town as the rain poured down buckets.

Mom and I held Floyd's body on our laps and Mom kept crying and blowing air into his mouth. "God, no!" she gasped. "No! Not now!"

I was too much in shock to do anything but stare at Floyd's ghostly face and feel his limp legs on my lap. The bumpy 20-minute ride over the rutted muddy road was eternity.

Once at Doc Moore's house, Mom and Doc disappeared into the office with Floyd. Mrs. Moore held my head against her chest as we stood in the hallway. Mr. Scott stood silently inside the front door.

"What's wrong with Floyd?" asked Mary, the Moore's youngest daughter.

"Hush, child," Mrs. Moore said, hugging Mary. "Just pray. Just pray."

Everything was ghostly silent for a minute. I was still in shock and agonized over the thought that twice that day I had ignored my instincts to support Floyd.

Then suddenly, Moper, the Moore's old bloodhound, let out a loud howl from outside the office window, just as mom's heart-piercing wail came from inside the office.

Moper kept howling, but soon the wail from inside the office trailed off into a agonized whimper. About ten minutes later the office door opened slowly. Doc Moore walked out and closed the door behind him. He put an arm around my shoulder and said, "I'm so sorry, Mark."

"No! No!" I shouted and shoved Doc aside. "He's not!" I ran towards the door, but Mrs. Moore grabbed me. She wrapped her arms around me and said, "Mark, Mark..."

Just then my stepdad, Hank, burst through the front door, ran up to Doc Moore and shook him. I smelled booze on Hank's breath.

"Where's Floyd?" he demanded. "Bridget?"

Doc grabbed Hank's right arm and held it firmly. "Steady, Hank," Doc said. "Floyd's dead."

"No!" Hank shouted, and broke free from Doc Moore and yanked open the office door. I was standing at an angle where I could see the stunned look on Hank's face when he saw Mom bent down and crying over Floyd's body on the table. Hank rushed over to Mom and held her as she cried.

I stood frozen in Mrs. Moore's arms for a while, tears streaming down my face. Then suddenly I pushed her away, lashed out and punched the wall with my left fist. As I did, my hips shoved against the table next to the wall, and a vase with yellow, green and red wildflowers fell and crashed onto the floor.

"There, there, Mark," soothed Mrs. Moore, holding me in her arms, "everything will be fine. Floyd is in heaven now."

"HEAVEN?" I screamed. "HEAVEN? NO, HE'S NOT! HE'S DEAD!"

The next thing I knew, Mom was helping me up from the floor where I lay huddled in tears. I stood up, looked down, and saw that Doc Moore had wrapped a bandage around the bloody knuckles of my left hand.

I heard Doc Moore tell Mom and Hank that he would take care of the body and that it was best for everyone to go home and get a good night's sleep. Then my folks and Mr. Scott and I drove slowly home beneath the stark rainy sky.

What a heartbreaking day!

•

Mark closed his journal, took a few deep breaths, and stared at the soft grey mist above the San Francisco Bay. Then he stood, tucked the journal under his arm, and walked to O'Doul's Pub for breakfast. He passed by Dr. Chang's office on the way and waved at Wo Lin through the window. She smiled and waved back.

In that moment one of Dilai Dalai's sutras crossed Mark's mind: "Death is life's shy lover."

CHAPTER 5

Lloyd emptied his pipe's ashes into a pink seashell, and said, "The past is an anchor around Mark and Leela's necks."

Bunny nodded. "It's all about love."

Lloyd's eyes widened. "You taught me a thing or two about love. And sex!"

Bunny shrugged her shoulders. "Oh?"

"Yeah," Lloyd said. "I was a power-tripper with women before I met you. You straightened me out, like on our honeymoon during our first lifetime together."

"On Ios in Greece?"

"Right. I was a macho man and thought I would set things right the first night of our honeymoon. I took off my pants, handed them to you, and said, 'Here, try these on.'

"You put on the pants and said, 'These are too big. I can't wear them'"

Bunny laughed. "I remember. And you said, 'I'm the one who wears the pants in the family and don't you forget it!'"

Lloyd nodded and said, "Then you slipped off your panties, handed them to me and said, 'Here, you try mine on.'

"I tried your panties on and said, 'I can't get into your panties.'

"And you said, 'That's right! And if you don't change your smart-ass ways, you never will!'"

Bunny chuckled. "You were more understanding after that."

Then she peeked over the edge of the cloud, looked down at Leela sitting on a yak rug in Bodhi Cave. "Pathen just arrived at the cave," she said, "and Leela seems ready to crack."

Lloyd nodded. "Um, we'll see..."

It was mid-morning and Leela's teenage cousin, Shanti's son, Pathen, stood dripping with sweat in the hot May sun at the entrance to Bodhi Cave. Leela was nowhere in sight.

Pathen stretched his long slim body and slipped a heavy backpack of fruit, nuts, and vegetables from his shoulders. He laid the pack on top of a yak rug, took a deep breath, then gazed at the breathtaking panorama of Dilai Valley before him.

Below, Pathen saw a carpet of tall evergreens framing tiny Khidir Creek. The creek flowed due west for eight miles through Gazabha village, then another forty-two miles before entering the Swat Valley and merging with the Swat River. Above, high plateaus adorned with an ocean of vibrant flowers rose into a string of rugged mountain peaks in the distance.

Dilai Valley was a small part of the Swat Valley region of Northwest India in the nineteenth century. Before the beginning of the eleventh century, the vast Swat Valley was known as the Kingdom of Uddiyana, "The Royal Garden", with the city of Mingora as its capital. Men wore white turbans and dark blue and saffron yellow cashmere robes, and women were dressed in colorful saris. Forest chapels flourished where mystics meditated. Hundreds of Buddhist stupas stood, wherein lay the relics of Enlightened Beings. Merchants plied their trade, offering silks, rubies, emeralds and exotic spices from the Orient, as well as cashmere wool, copper utensils, and sandalwood carvings from India and beyond.

Uddiyana was a paradise on earth and was well described in the 630 AD journal of the Chinese mystic, Hueng Tsiang, during his travels in India.

The Kingdom of Uddiyana met its demise around 1000 AD when it was pillaged by Mahmud Gaznavi, who destroyed most of the temples and monasteries, burned the literature and art, killed all the Buddhist men, raped the women, and put children into slavery.

Perhaps because of its remote location, Gazabha's tiny population of 200 men, women and children was spared Mahmud's wrath.

Hueng Tsiang lived in the Gazabha commune for three months, then spent the next seven years in silent meditation in Bodhi Cave. After this Sadhana he continued his travels in India - now with Rajaba, a consort from Gazabha.

According to one biographer, "During Hueng Tsiang's stay in Gazabha, he taught Zen Calligraphy and Dhyana, the inner science of meditation, worked in the communal garden, and did a lot of nothing. His playfulness and bizarre sense of humor inspired the Gazabha villagers to dub him Dilai Dalai, 'Ocean of Delight'."

The name stuck, and although Dilai Dalai never claimed to be enlightened, the ninety-nine sutras he wrote on twenty-one yak-skin scrolls in Bodhi Cave had been revered and passed down through the ages through oral tradition, translated into over one hundred languages, and published in books. The sutras became the cornerstone for hundreds of Dilai Dalai Jai sects throughout the world by the mid-nineteenth century, even though the location of Gazabha, Bodhi Cave, and the original scrolls were known to few people outside Dilai Valley.

Pathen took deep breath then sat on a yak-skin at the mouth of Bodhi Cave. He had been the Premion for the two years that Leela had lived in the cave.

The Gazabha tradition of Premion - "Beloved Guardian" - and Prasad - "Beloved Gift" - began with Dilai Dalai's seven-year meditation retreat in Bodhi Cave. The tradition began during the first week that Dilai Dalai spent in the cave, when a fourteen-year-old boy from Gazabha carried a backpack of fruit and vegetables to Dilai Dalai. The boy returned to the cave with a bounty of food week after week during Dilai Dalai's seven-year Dharma, and the tradition then continued for thirteen centuries.

The Gazabha tradition of Premion and Prasad involved twenty-one elders of the Gazabha Community – ten men and eleven women, "the Inner Circle" - meeting every seven years and selecting a Prasad from among men and women in the community twenty-one and over.

A Prasad was to spend seven years in silent meditation in Bodhi Cave. Concurrently, a Premion was selected from among the young males in the ghotul to carry the heavy load of fruit and vegetables up the steep, rocky path to the cave once a week for the same seven years.

Over the centuries most Prasads, including Satchitta's sister, Shanti, returned to Gazabha after their Dharma was completed. Eleven Prasads left Bodhi Cave before their Dharma was up. All were welcomed back into the Gazabha commune, and another Prasad was elected to replace them for the remainder of those seven years. Nine Prasads had chosen not to return to Gazabha after completing their Dharma. Thirty-six Prasads eventually became enlightened, five within the first year in Bodhi Cave.

Leela's father, Satchitta, was born in Gazabha and learned as a young child that he had a natural creative urge to mold, bake, and paint pottery. Satchitta lived in the ghotul as a teenager for seven years, and although he had many lovers, he was deeply in love with a young woman, Archa. He and Archa were both both sixteen when Archa drowned in a freak accident in Khidr Creek.

Satchitta was devastated by Archa's death. He put his total energy into meditation and creativity for the remainder of the time he lived in the ghotul, becoming a Premion and later a Prasad. He never had a steady partner again until his thirty-fifth birthday.

It was on that day that an eighteen-year-old French-English nursing student, Nadine Fleur, stopped in Gazabha during her travels in India. Upon meeting Satchitta, Nadine felt as if her heart was drawn by the largest magnet in the world and she never returned to Europe. Leela was born nine months later. Nadine changed her name to Taichia, "Peaceful Energy", when Leela was two years old.

Pathen took another deep breath. He sat silently for several minutes, stood, gazed at the vast lush green beauty of the Dilai Valley, stretched, turned around, and looked inside the cave… at another world entirely.

It took a minute for Pathen's almond-colored brown eyes to adjust to the morning light within the magical cave. Then he looked around…

A large clay bowl partially filled with water sat in the middle of the space. Another small bowl with a few fruits and nuts sat beside it. Twenty-one rolled-up yak-skin scrolls were stacked upon each other. Finally, there was Leela's yak-skin-rug bedding, along with several wool robes, socks and shawls.

Suddenly, Leela cried from the back of the cave: "Pathen! Oh, am I happy to see you!"

Startled, Pathen jumped back towards the edge of the cave, thirty feet above the rocky trail below. He was shocked, didn't know what to say. Leela had just broken the two main rules for a Prasad: absolute silence and aloneness.

Pathen stared in disbelief.

Leela emerged from the dark shadows at the back of the cave carrying a pitcher of water from a freshwater spring. Smiling, she laid the pitcher down, ran to Pathen, and hugged him.

"Thank you for coming!" Leela said, then stepped back and studied Pathen: *Only sixteen, tallest Sane in Gazabha, most popular among the women in the ghotul. Beautiful young man, honest smile.*

Pathen was in shock. "You're, ah, welcome."

Leela laughed. "Oh, sorry, the silence thing. Look, Pathen, I'm sorry but I might have to leave here. Soon!"

"Leave? Why?"

"I'm not sure why. That's why I need to talk with you. I need to decide what to do. Don't say anything about us talking, okay?"

Pathen would do anything for his cousin, and she had a crucial decision to make. *To be a Prasad is a rare opportunity, a gift,* Pathen thought. *For Leela to leave now would mean...*

"Okay," he assured her, "I won't say anything."

Leela smiled. "You must be hungry. Mind if we snack on the goodies?"

Pathen wet his lips with his tongue. "Love to," he said.

Leela knelt on the yak rug next to Pathen's backpack and motioned for Pathen to join her, which he did. Leela took out a few dried apricots from the pack and handed them to Pathen. Then they sat in silence and nibbled on dried fruit.

The silence helped Pathen relax and consider the situation:

Leela was seven years older than he and had always been an enigma. It was a mystery how Leela had spent most of her life in the Srinagar commune and had then lived in Gazabha for a total of only seven of her twenty-one years before she was chosen from among twenty-two other teenagers to be a Prasad. It was also a mystery why Leela would consider dropping the gift of being a Prasad after only two of the seven years of her Dharma.

Pathen shook his head, *Mystery follows Leela like a luminous shadow.*

Finally, Leela spoke as if she had been reading Pathen's mind: "It's a mystery why I was chosen to be a Prasad after all the trouble I caused with Rakan in Srinagar."

"I heard about that," Pathen said. "But wasn't it Rakan who caused the trouble?"

"Yes and no. That's why I need to talk with you. I'm confused. I'm thinking about moving back to Srinagar to be with Satchi. But

I don't want to stir up any more trouble with Rakan and his gang. Satchi supported me in every way, even when Rakan and others criticized him for not punishing me for my mischief. But being a Master's daughter has been..."

Tears welled up and coursed down Leela's cheeks. She gently wiped them off then continued:

"There's so much love around Satchi. That's why I might go back. Meditating in this cave has often felt so dry! It was so juicy being around Satchi and Taichia and the others! Yeah, there were hard times there, too.

"And Gazabha? Um… folks here are beautiful too, but I miss... hmmm… Satchi's *juiciness*! I don't know, I caused so much trouble in Srinagar, drove everyone nuts because I lived wild and free."

Leela handed a dried apricot to Pathen.

Pathen glanced at Leela and thought, *a living paradox…*

He had heard stories about how Leela had provoked Rakan's rage and got away with it, fantastic stories of her legendary mischief and love life in Srinagar.

But the strange thing for Pathen was that Leela had not been at all like that in Gazabha. Something in her had changed. During the four years that Pathen had known Leela before she became a Prasad, she was the epitome of a meditator. She had lived in the ghotul and had many lovers, but whenever she had the chance, Leela sat alone in silent meditation. To Pathen, Leela seemed to have made an easy transition from the ghotul to Bodhi Cave. But now she seemed so confused, nerve-racked, doubtful, needy. Pathen had never seen her like this.

"I never wanted to hurt anyone," Leela continued. "But somehow I was a threat to Rakan, especially after Asanga and I were lovers."

Pathen squinted and asked, "Asanga? Who's that?"

"Rakan's son. We were seventeen."

"His s*on!?* Rakan attacked the ashram because you were lovers with his *son!?"*

Leela shrugged her shoulders. "Rakan probably had planned to attack the ashram long before Asanga and I became lovers. I had a long history with Asanga; we were childhood friends.

"All I know is, Rakan's attack almost killed Satchi. And me! I was heartbroken! Rakan locked Asanga up after our tryst. According to rumors, Asanga is still a prisoner in Rufus Temple, and I don't want anything like that to happen again. Maybe it's best if I stay away from there."

Pathen leaned forward. "I heard things have settled down there now."

"I hope so, for everyone's sake."

"Except for..."

Leela saw a concerned look on Pathen's face and asked, "Except for what?"

"Well, recently we got word from friends in Srinagar that Satchitta's health isn't all that great these days. Shanti said that with Satchitta getting older, it was natural."

Leela frowned. "Natural? Hmmm..."

Pathen stood up and said, "Listen, Leela, I'm sorry but I promised Shanti I'd be right back after I delivered your food. Today is Dad's birthday and I want to help with the party. Do you know what you're going to do?"

Leela stood. "All I know is, I feel better after talking with you."

Pathen threw his pack over his shoulders. "Does that mean you're going to stay?"

"I... really… don't know."

Pathen nodded. "I sort of understand why you might want to leave, but not really."

Leela nodded, smiled, and hugged Pathen.

Pathen climbed down the hemp ladder. He walked a hundred feet down the path towards Gazabha, when suddenly he heard Leela shout, “PATHEN!”

Pathen turned around.

“I’ve changed my mind,” Leela bellowed. “Tell Shanti about our talk. I’ll come by tomorrow after the noon Zahn meditation to talk with the Inner Circle in Buddha Hall.”

Pathen smiled, nodded, turned around, then disappeared down the path to Gazabha.

CHAPTER 6

After a hearty breakfast of three poached eggs, fried potatoes and onions, coffee and whole wheat toast at O'Doul's Pub, Mark strolled to the beach. He sat down on a redwood stump and began to write in his journal:

•

Lots of feelings... the fresh ocean air helps...

Missouri...

Two days after Floyd died, rain poured down in buckets as I rode my horse into town for the funeral. It would be a day which would drastically, utterly, change my life, set me on my path to India.

I arrived at the church about an hour before mass, went inside, took off my Macintosh raincoat and pants and draped them over a life-size wooden statue of Francis of Assisi. I sat alone in a pew at the back and stared at the wooden casket at the foot of the altar.

I'll never forget this, my mind chanted over and over.... *Never forget this.... Why did Floyd kill himself? He was a normal kid; no one had a clue he would ever do such a thing. Why?*

Sitting with trembling knees in the wooden pew, a few of Mom's last words to Floyd flashed across my mind: "That's a *sin!*"

Soon folks started coming inside. I opened my eyes and saw Floyd's casket at the altar. Dark shadows loomed everywhere. I looked up at the tormented faces of the people in the crude paintings of the twelve stations of the cross hanging on the walls.

I wondered, *What happened to Floyd after he died? Did he go anywhere - heaven, hell - or did he just disappear?*

Nothing made sense. Guilt screamed from the depths of my heart. I felt terrible for not letting Floyd go with us to Six Boys Woods and for ignoring my feeling to console him after he was sent to his room.

But nothing mattered really. Floyd was dead.

Then I heard my parents' voices coming from outside the church door. I was surprised to hear Hank's voice, for I had never seen him in church.

Hank.... It was hard for everyone in my family after my natural father died when I was five. Mom was a wreck. But the strangest thing happened a year after Dad's funeral, when Mom suddenly married Hank Ketchim, a surly farmhand from down the road.

Hank was short, stocky and handsome in a macho sort of way. But one look in his steely grey eyes and one could tell he had no room for anyone but himself. He was a heavy drinker and shortly after he and Mom married, Hank began fighting with Mom and physically abusing us kids. I still have scars on my butt from Hank's leather belt. I didn't understand why Mom had married Hank until six months after the marriage when Mom gave birth to a baby girl. Life with Hank was hell, but Mom wouldn't talk about the situation or consider divorcing him for fear of being excommunicated by the Church. "After all," she once confided to a girlfriend, "that's a sin."

My eyes were closed there in the back pew when Mom, Hank, and my brother and sisters filed past me and sat in the front pew.

During Mass I was in my own world. I didn't know it then, but something in me had died, too. All the beliefs that had been given to me by the church, my parents, school... all the beliefs about heaven, hell and such... all those borrowed beliefs about what's good, bad, moral, immoral, true, false... all those beliefs just died, vanished, popped like a balloon.

All the beliefs looked like a dark road. The beliefs I had been given were lies, empty promises of some La-la Land after death.

I could see the lies in the eyes of the adults who had come to console me during the two days before the funeral. I could see in their eyes that their beliefs were a cover-up for hidden fear and doubt about the reality of heaven and hell. The gripping doubt in their eyes said it all: the beliefs that the church had given them were a cover-up for their doubts about what happens after death, doubts that gnawed at their guts. Their beliefs were on the circumference, doubts were at their very center, and it was the doubts that ran their lives, had run my own life till then.

I vaguely knew that everyone had meant well trying to console me, but consolations weren't good enough for me anymore. Fact was, I was in too much pain to know what I wanted in place of the consolations. I only knew what I didn't want: *No more lies,* I thought during the funeral mass. *No more lies.*

Somehow an inner light shone through the dark clouds of my mind, and a quiet inner voice said, *I've got to know the truth as an experience, and trust that...*

...I didn't know what...

The contrast between the shocked faces of the adults and their empty consolations was too obvious. The contrast spoke for itself: clearly no one in that church - including my mother's brother, Father McGynn - knew the truth about life after death from their personal experience.

At the sweet age of seventeen I made a promise to Floyd, a promise to myself: *I'll never forget this, Floyd.*

Since then, I've been walking an unmarked footpath into the unknown. All the crutches of the borrowed religious beliefs, unverifiable dogma, and self-righteous authorities had been cast away. All the consolations were too painful, too heavy to carry anymore. I had to discover the truth for myself, as an experience, not as a belief.

My need to know the truth felt like an actual hunger. I had been like a hungry man who had read books and theories about nutrition but remained hungry. Now my hunger for truth could only be satisfied through experience, not by any "holy" books or empty promises.

Since then, my heart's been whispering, *Thank you, Floyd. Thank you.*

•

Mark looked up from his journal at the Bay before him. He shook the sand out of his boots, put the boots on, laced them, and closed the journal. He walked from the beach back to *The Emerald Queen*. He was emotionally drained from writing about Floyd, so he jumped into his hammock below deck, closed his eyes, and fell into a deep sleep.

CHAPTER 7

Leela tossed and turned in her sleep all night long in Bodhi Cave. When she finally awoke, all she could do was watch her mind argue both sides of the burning question: *Should I go to Srinagar to be with Satchi or stay here and meditate alone?*

She had broken her vows of silence and aloneness and thought that she would probably not be allowed to continue as a Prasad. But today at noon she would meet with Gazabha's Inner Circle to discuss the matter, and now as she lay in bed agonizing over her situation, she remembered Satchitta once saying, "Utter helplessness is the only prayer." And with that understanding, she thought, *Let the Inner Circle decide.*

Leela threw off her yak rug blankets, dressed, and stirred the embers in the fire pit to get the fire going again. Then she ate a light breakfast of fruit and nuts and sat silently by the fire in the morning sun until it was time to leave for Gazabha.

The eight-mile hike to the commune was a sensual feast of fragrant meadows, gurgling streams, and curious animals darting across her path. Several of the animals were already Leela's friends: Bol the Bear, Sol the Eagle, and Tol the Turtle.

Leela heard the noon Zahn bell ring in the distance as she approached the outskirts of Gazabha. In her mind's eye she saw everyone sitting silently with closed eyes in meditation as she arrived.

It was so… on her way to the village center, Leela strolled by meditator after meditator sitting silently alongside the road. She marveled at how rare Gazabha was: for two thousand years the community had existed without any police and with little crime.

The main reason for this, Leela thought, *is our commitment to the ghotul and the Zahn meditations. Also, because of our remote location, we don't have neighboring terrorists like Rakan.*

Over the centuries the combination of Zahn and the ghotul had supported folks in Gazabha to mature in such a way that mutual respect and cooperation were the norm. Crime and power-politics were virtually non-existent because the ghotul supported young adults to consciously feel power during sex. They experienced *real* power within themselves and had no need to seek false substitutes for power through accumulating money, possessions, prestige, or power over others. There were still disagreements and judgments of course - egos are egos - but most ego issues quickly vanished in the light of choiceless awareness.

On her way to the center of the village, Leela strolled past many of the multi-colored pebble roads leading to the residential bungalows. Each road was lined with evergreen trees and the bungalows were barely visible to Leela. The commune had a total of 60 residential bungalows which housed 242 residents, excluding the 40 teenagers in the ghotul. Each bungalow was self-contained with indoor plumbing and an iron wood stove for heat. There were central farming and dairy warehouses as well as a huge art studio which produced exquisitely painted pottery, Gazabha's main source of external income.

Leela reached the center of Gazabha just as the Zahn bell rang and the ten-minute meditation ended. A large circular golden bamboo and red tile bungalow, Buddha Hall, loomed before her. She opened the tall elegantly engraved bamboo front door, entered quietly, and sat among the Inner Circle of eleven women and ten men, all dressed in the full-length white woolen robes they wore during their meetings.

Pathen's mother, Shanti, was the Circle's spokesperson, a woman who emanated ageless charm and grace and was loved by everyone in the community. A former Prasad, Shanti had a regal presence, keen intelligence, loving heart, and compassionate understanding of herself and others. Her youthful beauty had faded somewhat over the years - she had gained considerable weight recently - but she still radiated an other-worldly beauty through her shining eyes and warm smile. Sitting in the circle before Leela now, Shanti nodded to her niece to speak.

Leela nodded in return and said, "I've come to talk with you because I've broken my vows of silence and aloneness."

A tangible silence filled the hall, then Shanti spoke: "And...?"

Leela took a deep breath. Tears welled up and coursed down her high cheekbones. "And that happened because I've been confused for several months now. I had to speak to someone, Pathen, about which path is right for me now, meditation or love."

Most of the adults nodded knowingly, and true to her intuitive and spontaneous nature, Shanti stood, walked to Leela and wiped her tears with a white cashmere scarf. "No problem, beloved," Shanti said. "Existence is still breathing you. You may be confused, but Existence isn't."

Leela roared with laughter and wiped her tears. "*Thank you!* I needed that! Breathing is about all I'm capable of now. I don't know what to do. I was sure my path was meditation, and you all must have felt so too, or you wouldn't have voted me to be a Prasad. But now I don't know..."

Everyone nodded.

Rajen, Shanti's jolly partner, nodded, adjusted his rainbow-colored headband, and stroked his long white beard. "We knew it was risky when we voted for you," he said, "but you had the most promise and authenticity."

Leela drank in Rajen's shiny eyes. She smiled and said, "After the last two years in Bodhi cave, I'm not so sure."

"What *are* you sure about?" Shanti asked.

Leela closed her eyes for a moment. Then she opened them and said, "My experience? In a way, love and meditation are the same. Both happen in the present moment. In meditation I'm alone, in love I'm with a lover or nature. Meditation and loving happen when I'm conscious in the present moment."

Everyone nodded.

Leela laughed aloud. "But you know what? I realized on my way here today that if love is really my path, and if I'm ever to be with a man whose path is meditation, I will have had to have experienced meditation to understand and love him, won't I?

"So maybe continuing to meditate in Bodhi Cave is preparing me for love, if love is my path. Maybe I'm meant to be a Prasad. I don't know. I'm confused," and she began to weep again.

A loud murmuring and nodding of heads rippled through the Inner Circle.

Leela finally wiped her tears and said, "My confusion and helplessness have intensified the last few months and I'm lonely as hell. My mind tells me I've even gone backwards. I feel guilty because I fantasize about old love affairs and pleasure myself, masturbate. I thought I was over that but I'm not."

Shanti held up her right hand. "Maybe that's not guilt in the ordinary sense. There is a subtle knowing in every sensitive but unenlightened human that he or she is not fulfilled yet. Maybe what you feel is the frustration from longing to be enlightened and not being there yet, the frustration of your desire to be enlightened. Pleasuring yourself is not a problem unless it becomes an unconscious habit. Maybe you unconsciously pleasure yourself to relieve the tension of frustration. Just be aware of that desire. Remember: you're not the mind or body; you're the consciousness which watches the mind and body."

"Or pleasure yourself consciously!" Rajen added with a flair.

"Like you!" Shanti said.

Everyone roared with laughter.

"What do you expect?" Rajen countered. "Old age is when getting it up gets you down. Now I get it any way I can!"

Wave upon wave of laughter rippled through the Circle for a full minute, and that changed the energy in the hall; there were smiles on everyone's face after the laughter subsided.

Laughter heals.

When everyone finally settled down, Shanti said, "Perhaps pleasuring yourself is just a symptom of a deeper need, beloved. Your body has a build-up of energy, and your mind wants to release it. The real issue is, what to do with that build-up of energy? Energy is always moving, changing. It can be transformed, raised, through meditation, watching the energy change, or by expressing the energy creatively. Living isolated in Bodhi Cave hasn't offered you a chance to express the energy creatively. Maybe we should consider providing you with whatever you need to express your creativity there."

Leela folded her hands over her heart and exclaimed, "Oh, thank you! That's my experience with creativity, too! And you said Existence is breathing me, taking care of me. I have glimpses of that when I silently watch my breathing. And about love... hmmm..."

Leela paused, took a deep breath, and said, "Maybe Existence knows better than me what I need to wake up. Maybe the issue is about trust: trusting that if a lover is needed to help me be more conscious, a lover will show up in Bodhi Cave."

She paused, took another deep breath, and added. "I feel better talking with you all. Thank you. Whatever you decide is fine with me. I want to remain a Prasad if you still feel it's right."

Leela closed her eyes and everyone in the Inner Circle closed their eyes and sat in silence. Soon the entire space was vibrating with loving presence.

Twenty minutes later Shanti opened her eyes, looked around, turned to Leela and said, "Please, Leela, we need to talk privately among ourselves. Wait in my house and I'll be by shortly to tell you what we decide. Thank you for your honesty."

Leela nodded, smiled, left the hall, and walked to Shanti's bungalow.

CHAPTER 8

It was early evening when Mark awoke from his nap on *The Emerald Queen.* He lit a candle, picked up his journal, skimmed over what he had written about Floyd's suicide, sighed, and laid the journal on his hammock.

Oh no! he thought. *Wo Lin! I promised her!*

Mark ran to Dr. Chang's office and found Wo Lin leaning against the storefront with her head hung low and tears in her eyes.

"Sorry I'm late," he said. "I fell asleep and... sorry..."

Wo Lin looked up, nodded, wiped her tears, and took a deep breath. She smiled weakly then took Mark by the hand and walked with him to O'Doul's.

They were about to enter the pub when the body of a crusty old Memphis gambler, Snake Gillis, sailed through the swinging French doors and onto the muddy street.

"And don't come back!" roared Casey O'Doul to the bag of bones lying in a heap in a puddle.

Casey puffed his chest, and with a gracious sweep of his hand, invited Mark and Wo Lin inside: "Sir, madam, welcome to O'Doul's, a harbor for kind and gentle souls."

"Trouble?" Mark asked.

"Ask him," replied Casey, nodding towards the crumpled old card shark. "Playing tonight, Mark?"

"We'll see."

"Come on," Casey implored, "play 'Stepping Out Tonight'."

"We'll see. Ethan here?"

"Um, talk about trouble. He's with a new flame."

Mark nodded. "Nothing new." Then he entered the noisy pub with Wo Lin. They wove through the ruckus and past a duo playing accordion and harmonica onstage. Mark's shipmate, Ethan McDonegal, was sitting at a back table, hunched over and devouring the neck of a drunken *senorita bonita.*

Mark had met Ethan two weeks before, when Mark first walked onboard *The Emerald Queen* to look for passage to India. Ethan was Quartermaster of *The Queen,* a tall, lanky, devilishly handsome sailor's sailor with pitch-black curly hair and beard. The black patch over his left eye added a mysterious charm to his macho demeanor, as did his black clothes. Many women found him irresistibly attractive.

Mark felt the black patch reflected a sinister quality in Ethan, for he was a compulsive womanizer, gambler and drinker, a sensitive but lost soul who woke up hung-over in some strange wench's bed or in a gutter most mornings. It was Ethan's charisma and bundle of contradictions that endeared Mark to Ethan, an endearment which was to be challenged to the hilt tonight...

Mark and Wo Lin stood over Ethan and his *senorita.*

"Ahem!" Mark interrupted. "Ethan?"

Ethan looked up and roared with laughter: "Mark! Blimey, sit down! Meet Rosa!" Then he waved to Casey, "Another round! No, make that two!"

Ethan grabbed Wo Lin's right hand and slobbered, "When are you going to leave this landlubber for me, eh?"

Wo Lin blushed and pulled away.

Mark had never seen Ethan this drunk. He sat down with Wo Lin and chided Ethan: "Let her go."

Ethan huffed and let go of Wo Lin's hand. He glared at Mark. "Say, where's your white horse, gallant knight?"

Ethan quickly steadied himself and slurred, “Okay, okay, I’ll behave. Sit down, *mahatma.* Casey, where’s that round, dammit?” Then he turned to Rosa, and said, “Yeah, Mark here’s a regular *mahatma,* honey. Going to India to snatch the gold ring of enlightenment. Right, Mark?”

Mark shook his head. “You’re drunk.”

“Am I? Well, blame Casey here for that, right Casey?”

Casey stood over the table, rolled his eyes, then set down a pitcher of beer and two empty porcelain steins on the table.

“This is for Mark and Wo Lin,” Casey said. “No more trouble from you tonight, Ethan. You’re cut off!”

Ethan hit the roof! He jumped up and shouted, “AM I? Blimey, do you know who I’m drinking with, Casey? Mark here’s got God on his side. A meditator! Yeah, made a pile of dough panning gold, too! Don’t that mean something, eh, Casey? No? Well, Mark here’s got... HE’S GOT THE POWER! Don’t you, Mark?”

Ethan picked up Mark and Wo Lin’s pitcher and drank it straight down, pouring a quarter of the golden liquid on his chest and shirt. He slammed the pitcher on the table and demanded, “Another round!”

Mark felt his belly contract. He stood, put a gentle hand on Ethan’s shoulder, and said, “Let’s go, Ethan, before Casey--”

Ethan slapped Mark’s hand off his shoulder and shouted, “Leave me alone!” Then he grabbed Mark by his flannel shirt-pocket and pulled him towards himself, ripping off the pocket. Ethan took a swing at Mark, who ducked.

Mark grabbed Ethan’s right wrist, twisted his arm behind his back, and forced the cussing sailor outside to the middle of the muddy street.

The moment Mark let go, Ethan shouted, “Bilge rat!” and took another drunken swing at Mark.

Mark ducked. Then with a lightning left, he popped Ethan in his good right eye and sent him sprawling into a puddle. Mark slowly backed away towards the entrance where Casey, Wo Lin, and a cheering crowd had gathered.

Ethan shook his fist then stood up. "You're done, swine, you hear? Finished! You'll not sail on my ship!" Then he staggered down the street and into The Bawdy Toddy Pub.

Casey patted Mark on the shoulder. "Think he means it?"

Mark casually shrugged his shoulders. "Me, fired? Who knows, he's drunk. Besides, he's just Quartermaster. The Captain hires and fires. We'll see." Mark turned to Wo Lin and said, "Let's go." He took her by the hand and started to walk down the street.

"Come on, Mark," Casey pleaded, "drinks on the house if you play."

Mark hesitated, smiled, then looked at Wo Lin. She nodded. So, Mark took her by the hand and led her back inside. Casey cleared off a front row table then set them up with a pitcher of beer and two steins. After a couple of beers Mark climbed onto the stage, picked up the house guitar and tuned it. Two other musicians joined in with a harmonica and accordion and they all began to hoedown. Within seconds everyone in the pub was dancing to Mark's original tune, "Stepping Out Tonight".

Mark and Wo Lin left O'Doul's at midnight, went back to Wo Lin's hut and made love, slowly, tenderly, like children playing.

Precious...

Wo Lin had a silent, delicate beauty and sensuality which helped Mark relax and be more vulnerable than he ever had been with a woman before. His first experiences of sex with Kay Ellen and Shelly in Missouri were innocently beautiful, but it was altogether different with Wo Lin. She and Mark had a strong silent connection which nurtured their love and helped them deal with the limitations of the language barrier between them.

After Mark and Wo Lin made love that night, Wo Lin couldn't understand when Mark tried to explain that earlier that day Captain McDonegal had imposed a curfew on his crew.

"The Captain wants everyone back onboard and in their hammocks by three." Mark said. "No more overnights. We're sailing soon and the Captain wants more discipline. You know, discipline?"

Wo Lin shook her head.

"That's okay. Anyway, I need to leave at two-thirty."

Wo Lin nodded. "Tooth hurtee? Me fixee." And she tenderly kissed Mark's cheek.

"No, tooth no hurtee," Mark corrected. "Two-thirty."

"Tooth hurtee or no hurtee?"

"Don't worry. Two-thirty I'll get up."

"No worry? If tooth hurtee, I worry. Get up."

"Don't get up. Don't worry about two-thirty. I'm sorry."

"So solly? About tooth hurtee?"

"Okay, forget it. I'll get up at two-thirty."

Wo Lin began to cry.

Mark gently stroked her cheek. "Please, Lin, don't cry."

But she kept crying.

Soon Wo Lin stopped crying and she and Mark fell asleep in each other's arms.

At "tooth hurtee" Mark left Wo Lin's hut in a downpour and sloshed his way back to *The Emerald Queen.* On the way he thought about Ethan and wondered if he would be fired. Then he remembered when he first met Ethan two weeks before...

It was on a sunny afternoon - three days after Mark had arrived in San Francisco with 900 ounces of gold - that he walked down a wharf and onto *The Emerald Queen.*

Ethan was the first sailor Mark saw when he climbed aboard. Eight other sailors were hauling provisions from the deck to the lazaret below.

Ethan addressed Mark suspiciously, "Ahoy, swabbie! Who goes there?"

"Ahoy," Mark echoed.

Ethan's Irish father, Captain McDonegal, stood behind Ethan dressed in white pants and a white shirt with a merchant captain's epaulettes on each shoulder. At sixty-three, the old salt was thirty-one years Ethan's senior. The Captain pulled on his long snow-white beard, scratched his bald head, and studied Mark carefully.

"Ahoy! Looking for work?"

Mark grinned. "Yes, sir."

The Captain smiled. "Half our crew abandoned ship. Gold in the hills, you know! Your hands, callused. Where have you been working?" He turned to Ethan. "An able-bodied sailor."

"No more landlubbers!" Ethan growled.

"Quiet!" the Captain snapped. "*I* do the hiring!"

"I'm from Missouri," Mark said. "Worked on a farm most of my life. Been logging and mining in the Sierras most of this last year. Panning gold too."

"Gold? Where?" Ethan asked.

"In the hills near Colina. Rumor has it that you may be sailing to India."

"True," the Captain said, turning around and nodding towards a copper-skinned sailor carrying a box of fruit. "India is where we got that gem, Vedant."

Swami Prem Vedant turned when he heard the Captain call his name. Dressed in faded blue serge work pants and shirt, the wizened old Mumbai sailor set the box of dried fruit he was carrying on the deck and responded, "Captain?"

"Nothing, Vedant," the Captain said. "Carry on. A possible swabbie here."

Vedant smiled and nodded at Mark.

Strange, Mark thought, *I know him. But from where? When?*

Vedant picked up the box and took it to the lazaret.

Ethan's tone softened. "Why India?"

"An enlightened Master, Gopal."

Ethan frowned. "Master?"

"Yeah," Mark confirmed. "Anyway, I worked on a farm my whole life. Carpentry, farming, hauling this and that."

The Captain squinted and said, "India, eh?" Then he scratched his head and said, "No matter, you're hired! Mumbai's our final port west. We sail as soon as I get my crew together. Bunch of thieves out there! A good swabbie is scarce. My son, Ethan, here's the Quartermaster, and--"

"Quartermaster?" Mark asked.

"Um, Quartermaster. Pretty much my equal," the Captain replied. "In charge of everything except hiring and firing. Settles quarrels, starts them, too! Keeps the crew in order; that is, when he's not galivanting around town and I can't get a lick of work from him."

The Captain paused, then said, "Gold, eh? Ethan takes care of the strongbox in my cabin. Give him your valuables."

"You strike it rich?" Ethan asked curiously.

"I did okay," Mark answered guardedly.

"I'll take care of your booty," Ethan said.

Mark studied the Captain closely. *I can trust him*, he thought. Then he looked at Ethan, felt a knot in his belly. *But not him.*

Mark remembered one of the heart meditations that Merschel had taught him in Missouri: "Seeing as a Whole". He expanded his field of vision, gazed at Ethan as a whole, took a deep breath, and his belly relaxed.

"Okay," Mark said, "I banked some money in town but kept the rest for India. I need to--"

"Keep it safe with us," Ethan completed.

"Yeah."

Ethan grinned mischievously. "Don't worry, you'll get some of it back."

Mark winced. *"Some?"*

The Captain clipped Ethan's right shoulder. "Don't tease him! Now mate, get your gear onboard."

"What about wages?" Mark asked.

"Right," the Captain said. "Come below and I'll sign you up. Meanwhile Ethan, you have these provisions to store."

At a little past "tooth hurtee", and drenched from the driving rain, Mark climbed aboard *The Emerald Queen* and was shocked to find all his gear lying soaking wet on deck! He cursed Ethan under his breath, went directly to the Captain's quarters, and knocked hard on the door.

No response.

He knocked again, louder!

Finally, he heard rumbling inside and bleary-eyed Captain McDonegal opened the door. The Captain studied Mark for a moment, then roared, "YOU! OFF MY SHIP! I saw what you did to Ethan's eye! Practically blind now! And he told me you said you hated my guts."

"I... I... NO!" Mark stammered. "I said nothing about you! And Ethan attacked *me!* You got it wrong, sir. I, I--"

Captain McDonegal wasn't listening. While Mark stammered, he stomped over to the unlocked strongbox, took out the large leather bag of gold coins that Mark had given Ethan for safe-keeping, and tossed the bag to Mark.

Mark tried desperately to explain: "Ethan was drunk! I was trying to protect him from himself! Casey was going to--"

The Captain stood eye-to-eye with Mark and shouted, "Get out, swine!" Then he shoved Mark outside the cabin and slammed the door.

Shocked, Mark stood for a moment in utter disbelief, his bag of coins dangling from his hand. Frustrated, furious, he took a deep breath, stormed over to Ethan's cabin and pounded on the door: "Ethan, goddammit, open up! Ethan! Open up!"

No response.

Mark tried to pry the door open with his large hunting knife, but the thick solid-oak door was locked shut and wouldn't budge.

"Shit!" he cursed, then pounded on the door again.

Suddenly, he heard the Captain shout menacingly from behind, "Leave now or you'll be food for Davy Jones' Locker!"

Mark cringed. He slowly turned around and saw the Captain pointing a Colt revolver at his head.

My God!

Mark shook his head in disbelief. He slowly edged back, turned around, ran up the stairs to the deck, gathered up his wet gear, ran down the wharf and checked into a small room on the top floor of the Knob Hill Inn.

Mark hung his wet clothes and other gear on the bed posts and the backs of two chairs to dry. He walked to the bathroom, stood naked in front of the full-length mirror, and gazed at his body.

That's it, I've had it! he thought. *Going back to Missouri tomorrow! Enough is enough! Thieves everywhere! New Orleans, here, everywhere! Can't trust anyone. Goddamn you, Merschel! Why did I ever meet you?*

Mark took a step closer to the mirror and studied his face. His boyish face had broken out with a rash of blemishes soon after Floyd's death, and a few scars remained from picking at the blemishes. He loathed what he saw in the mirror.

Then he remembered: Seeing as a Whole.

Mark took a deep breath, unfocused his eyes, and for several minutes gazed at his face as a whole without blinking.

Slowly, slowly, his face began to mutate: first, into the face of a battle-scarred Aztec warrior; then into the face of a homely

Welsh washerwoman. Then into a sequence of faces: a righteous minister, beautiful female ballet dancer, a leper, a frightened little girl, the wrinkled and bearded face of a Taoist monk, and finally into the face of a young male Baul mystic.

Time passed... there was a silent gap in consciousness…

Then... weird... for a moment Mark wasn't sure what had happened. He stared at his face in disbelief.

Um… did I… disappear?… but here I am again...

In wonder, Mark took a deep breath, stepped back, and looked at his body as a whole for ten minutes. Finally, feeling centered, he crawled into bed and fell asleep within a minute after his exhausted body had curled up under the covers.

A rooster's crow woke Mark from his deep sleep. He got out of bed and walked over to his money pouch on the seat of a wooden chair. He opened the pouch and counted the gold coins.

About $500 was missing from the money he had given Ethan!

Mark's blood began to boil. He threw on some clothes and ran to the police station. Chief O'Reilly recognized Mark and greeted him, "Top of the morning! The Emperor with you?"

Mark shook his head and blurted out his story.

The Chief said, "Do I know Ethan? A brawler! Spent several nights here in the clink. Do you have a receipt for the money you gave him? And a receipt for the money the Captain gave you back?"

This took the wind out of Mark's sails. "No, I, ah... no."

"Then forget about it, sonny," O'Reilly said. "It's your word against theirs. Sorry."

Mark left in a huff. Fuming, he stormed towards O'Doul's, where he intended to drown his sorrows in a barrel of stout.

On the way he suddenly stopped dead in his tracks. He couldn't believe his eyes. On the street corner before him stood the Lord Emperor George Bull Goose Beatty in front of a wooden outhouse: a five-foot-square by seven-foot-high sloped roof redwood structure with a hinged front door and the words "SHOUT HOUSE" painted in white on a black shingle above the door.

A large crowd stood around the Emperor and the bizarre structure.

Mark squinted. *Shout House? What the...?*

The Emperor saw Mark inching towards him through the crowd and shouted, "Ah, what have we here, my first customer? Yes, I can see by your aura that you're ripe for the experience."

Mark wondered, *Aura? What experience?*

Like a seasoned barker, the Emperor shouted, "Yes, step inside, my friend, step inside. And all of you, please move aside so my friend here can have a taste of the latest, yes, the greatest, most modern device yet created to assist in one's transformation."

Mark chuckled to himself. *Transformation?* He slowly edged his way through the crowd till he stood face to face with the Emperor.

"Yes," the Emperor said, "step inside. Let it all go!" Then he leaned over and whispered into Mark's right ear: "You want to kill, need to kill someone, anyone. Right, friend?"

Mark knew the Emperor was right but didn't reply.

Then Bull Goose smiled, leaned over, and whispered in Mark's left ear: "Let it go before you hurt yourself or others. What do you say? There are four kinds of horses."

Mark's face lit up. *Four kinds of horses?*

He got it.

Blushing, Mark began to step into the Shout House, when the Emperor stopped him with his right hand.

Mark laughed. *Oh, four kinds of horses!* He took a gold coin from his pocket, flipped it to the Emperor, then stepped inside the Shout House. He closed the door and began to blow his top!

Furious, Mark screamed with every cell of his being! He cursed Ethan, cursed the Captain, his parents, the priests, nuns! He cursed the man-made God he was taught to love! Cursed everything and everybody he could think of for thirty minutes, until finally, utterly exhausted, he dropped to the floor dripping with sweat and tears.

At that very instant the crowd sensed a tangible silence inside the Shout House which caused them, too, to be silent. The entire street became a living temple of the Divine.

Grace had descended upon Havoc...

Ten minutes later the door of the Shout House slowly opened. A radiant, transformed Mark Trimble looked out upon the crowd. The first person he saw was the Emperor, whose face, too, reflected an inner luminosity.

With tears of joy in his eyes, and his heart overflowing with gratitude, Mark walked up to the Emperor and hugged him.

The two embraced in silent communion for several minutes, while the crowd of laborers, beggars, housewives, miscreants and shopkeepers remained respectfully silent.

Mark and the Emperor each smiled, then separated. Mark walked back to The Knob Hill Inn to take a nap, and the Emperor didn't lose a beat. The moment Mark disappeared around the corner, he bellowed, "Now friends, who's next to experience the magic, yes, the wonder, yes, the mystery and majesty of the Shout House?"

Within seconds, twenty eager customers lined up for a chance to experience the Shout House, a sight which was to become common on the streets of San Francisco during the next twenty-three years. At the peak of the phenomenon in 1868, a total of forty-five Shout Houses dotted the hilly landscape of the city.

CHAPTER 9

Bunny thought of Leela and in the wink of an eye found herself invisible to others in the center of the Gazabha commune.

She looked around and thought, *Ah, the place hasn't changed much.* Then she whisked over to Shanti's bungalow and into the living room. There she saw Leela sitting on a cushion on the floor with closed eyes. Just then Shanti walked in the door and strode into the living room.

Leela stood.

Bunny watched.

Shanti said, "Please sit."

Leela sat on a cushion.

Shanti sat on a cushion facing Leela, and asked, "How are you?"

"Okay, I guess," Leela said nervously. "I've never been in this position before."

"How would you describe your position?"

"Open."

Shanti nodded. "The only way to be. There are three conditions for you to remain a Prasad if you still want to continue."

"I do."

Shanti smiled. "Okay. First: you must spend your nights in Bodhi Cave. If you ever need to talk with the Circle again, let Pathen know a day or so ahead of time and we'll meet. But you must return to Bodhi Cave each evening. Agreed?"

"Yes."

"Two: no guests other than Pathen."

"Agreed."

"And three we need to discuss, because it has never been done with a Prasad before."

Shanti took Leela by both hands, gazed softly into her eyes and continued: "You've been dealt a challenging hand, beloved. Your father is no ordinary father; your mother, too; your path no ordinary path. Love or meditation? Or both? Who knows?

"No one in the Inner Circle pretends to know what another person needs to wake up. Gopal is gone now and none of us are enlightened. But one thing was clear to us when you shared today. You are identified with your mind, with the past, and are projecting your past into the future. You remember the good old days with Satchitta and his commune in Srinagar and want them back.

"The past and future are basically dreams, and there you sit in Bodhi Cave watching the dreams over and over with no one to distract you from watching the mind and its cunning ways.

"Well, that's why you're there! To become more conscious by watching the mind and feelings! When we voted for you to be a Prasad, we felt that you were already meditative, conscious enough to know what you were getting into. And we still feel that way.

"The whole point of meditation is to bring you into the present moment. You've obviously had the experience of being present with meditation *and* love. Now what to do? Which path is right for you? And is there another way for you to be in the present moment?

"Everybody's different, and we took that fact into consideration during our discussion just now. Your father was a potter, your mother a master gardener. You are a born artist, painter, singer, dancer. So, we decided that for you - for *you!* - creativity can be a meditation by bringing you into the present moment. Creativity is an overflow of meditative and love energy, a melting and merging of your subjectivity and the object of your expression.

"We decided to supply you with all you need to be creative in Bodhi Cave: paints and paper, flute and drum - whatever you need. Be creative and have fun! Allow meditation, awareness, to be your focus, and be creative. Paint, sing, dance your way to *nirvana!* If you feel the need to, it's okay to briefly share your experiences with Pathen when he comes once a week. Otherwise, be silent and watch the mind. What do you say?"

Leela's heart soared with gratitude and tears flowed. "GREAT!" she cried with joy. "Thank you! It was best to tell the truth."

Shanti smiled knowingly and joked, "We women only lie about our age, dearie."

Bunny listened for a few moments more, thought of Lloyd, and immediately whisked back to Lloyd's cloud.

Lloyd looked surprised. "Where did you go?"

"To Gazabha."

"With Leela? Oh, how was it?"

"Awesome! The Circle gave her permission to continue as a Prasad and let her paint, sing and dance!"

Lloyd clapped his hands. "Great! What will they think of next?"

"Well, I read Leela's mind while Shanti talked with her."

"And...?"

"And Leela thought, 'A masseuse would be nice, too.'"

After their dialog, Shanti and Leela stood and hugged. Shanti said, "You still have quite a hike if want to get back before sunset. Want some pea soup before you go?"

Leela's eyes lit up. "Oh, yes!"

Just then Pathen walked in the door and was surprised to find Leela there. His eyes silently asked, *What happened?*

"Ah, Pathen!" Shanti said. "I have to go back to the Circle now. Have some soup with Leela before she goes back, and--"

"Goes *back?*" Pathen said. "You mean back to Bodhi Cave?"

"Yes," Leela said. "I'm going back."

"YES!" Pathen shouted, then ran and hugged Leela.

The two danced around the room until finally, Shanti said, "Leela, let Pathen know what painting and music materials you need." Then she quietly slipped out the door.

"What materials?" Pathen asked.

"Soup first," Leela said, "then I'll fill you in."

Pathen nodded, then dished out Shanti's famous soup for Leela and himself: a homegrown culinary masterpiece of split peas, barley, garlic, onion, celery, carrots and potatoes, all delicately seasoned with basil and thyme, and flavored with curry, a little salt, and honey.

They sat on cushions at the low dinner table and slurped Shanti's pea soup while Leela shared the Inner Circle's new conditions for remaining a Prasad. Then Leela wrote a list of the materials she wanted Pathen to bring to her.

After Leela had finished writing, Pathen said, "Amazing!"

Leela said, "I never would have dreamed they would let me play there. I've got to get back before it gets too dark."

Pathen frowned. "I have some questions."

Leela looked out the window and saw that she had time to get back to Bodhi Cave before the sun set. "Okay."

"I'm in love with Punya."

Leela smiled. "And...?"

"And I'm scared."

"That's love alright."

"Well," Pathen said, "hearing what you've been through, I have my doubts about... well, the path of love."

"Join the club."

"No, I mean it!" Pathen said seriously.

"Me, too," Leela agreed.

"Okay… then what I mean is, I think my path is meditation. Meditating in Gopal's presence before he died a few years ago was so natural. I want to be with a Master again, Satchitta."

Leela nodded. "Oh, in Srinagar, not here."

"Yes."

"Um, then it's a different story. You may want to leave home. When?"

Pathen shook his head. "I don't know. You were about my age when you left Srinagar and came back here, weren't you?"

Leela shrugged her shoulders. "Yes, but everybody's different. The point is, why would you want to stay home, or why would you want to leave?"

Pathen closed his eyes, hung his head, and sat silently for a moment. Then he said, "One reason I may not leave is that it may be more peaceful, more supportive here for meditation. Rakan nearly destroyed the ashram when he had Satchitta arrested. Except for Rakan, I would probably go now. What was your experience of Rakan?"

Leela raised her eyebrows. "He's brilliant, shrewd, terrified, vengeful, totally identified with his criminal mind. I can't imagine he's ever had any experience of love or meditation, of a silent blissful energy beyond the mind, or he wouldn't try to control everything and everyone like he does in order to feel safe and powerful."

Pathen nodded.

Leela continued, "But you wonder if it would be easier to be conscious in Srinagar than here? I can't say one way or the other."

She looked out the window, stood, and said, "Basically, you have to decide for yourself. You're in love with Punya? Great, go into it, totally! Surrender to her. Then maybe you'll know if love is your path or not. But really, what do I know? I have to go."

Pathen stood, hugged Leela, and said, "I'm in no hurry to decide. I'll bring the supplies tomorrow. Meanwhile, here's some paper, something to write with, and a flute."

Leela smiled and accepted the gifts. "Thank you," she said, then walked out the door and back to Bodhi Cave.

CHAPTER 10

Mark walked back to his room in the Knob Hill Inn after his wild experience in the Shout House. He flopped into bed and took a long nap, slept like a rock despite the din of the construction noise which banged, screamed, and throbbed outside his room.

Emotionally exhausted, he slept till 4 AM and awoke feeling weak. He lit a candle, slowly dressed, washed the sleep from his eyes, sat on a wooden chair, and began the Conscious Breathing Meditation that Merschel had taught him a few years back.

He closed his eyes and breathed fully, deeply, into the body's seven energy centers: at the base of the spine; just below the navel; below the ribs; into the heart; the throat; in the middle of the forehead between the eyes; and the top of the head.

After a half-hour of conscious breathing, Mark sat silently for another hour and just watched his breath go in and out, in and out his navel center.

After the meditation, Mark felt centered, energized, and gazed out the window. The sun sat on the horizon. It was still quite early, but he wanted to be with Wo Lin. So, he walked to Dr. Chang's office and around back to Wo Lin's hut.

He slowly opened her door and WHAM! - was shocked to see Wo Lin and her fiancé, Wei Ding, asleep in bed together!

Wo Lin sat up with a jerk. Wei Ding kept sleeping. Mark and Wo Lin locked eyes for a few moments. Mark felt his heart sink. The delicate bridge between himself and Wo Lin crumbled in an instant, dropped into a fathomless abyss. The space in Mark's heart that Wo Lin had occupied immediately filled with pain.

Utterly shocked, Mark slowly turned around, shut the door, and trudged his way to the beach in a daze. He took off his boots and stood barefoot at the edge of the bay. He stared blankly at the waves while his mind wreaked havoc with his emotions. Finally, he gathered himself and slowly walked down the beach as his mind continued to spin a web of futile thoughts:

What did you expect, dummy? Wo Lin knew you were leaving for India, and you knew Wei Ding was coming back any day. You don't deserve her anyway! Trust no one! Camille in New Orleans! Ethan here! Go back to Missouri! The hell with love, enlightenment! Why live? For what...?

On and on Mark's mind rambled like tumbleweed blown by a fickle, callous wind.

Watching and hearing all this from a cloud above, Bunny finally said, "Okay, I'm going down there. *Now!*"

Lloyd shrugged his shoulders and said, "Well, as long as you don't advise Mark. It's against the rules."

"Angelic Rules? Rules are tools," Bunny countered, "useful when they help, harmful when they keep me from trusting my inner guide."

"I hope you know what you're doing," Lloyd said.

"I'm going," Bunny insisted, and she projected the thought of going to Mark through her third eye center and in an instant was hovering invisibly next to Mark.

She's always right but you never know why, Lloyd thought.

Then he projected himself to Bunny'a side.

Bunny whispered into Mark's left ear: "Remember, you're not your body-mind, not your feelings. You're the consciousness inside watching the mind and feelings. So just be a witness."

Mark took a deep breath and witnessed his mind and feelings for a few moments. It helped. But after 10 minutes of witnessing, he became lost again in the muck of his dark emotions and rambling mind.

"See?!" Lloyd said. "He's back where he started!"

Bunny scolded Lloyd: "Hush!" Then she turned and whispered into Mark's left ear: "Turn around and walk back."

Mark turned around and began to backtrack his steps up the beach. A minute later he looked up and saw Bull Goose Beatty 200 feet ahead, nude and balancing on something as he rode a wave to shore.

Once on shore, the Emperor turned and saw Mark. He waved, picked up the long, tapered object he had used to ride the wave, then trotted to within a few feet of Mark.

Mark stared in amazement at the Emperor's solid muscular body. *Like an oak tree!*

"Wanna try?" the Emperor said casually.

Mark studied the sleek tapered eight-foot wooden board which the Emperor was carrying, and noticed a small fixed curved wooden rudder on one side of the board.

"Try what?" Mark asked.

"Surfing."

"I, ah... don't know how," Mark said weakly.

The Emperor saw the tortured look on Mark's face. He carefully laid his board on the sand and asked, "What's wrong?"

Mark felt naked before the Emperor's penetrating gaze. He blushed and said, "Wo Lin's fiancé is back."

The Emperor nodded. "Oh... tough."

"I... don't know any more," Mark sighed. "I mean, why..."

The Emperor took a deep breath. "Why go on?"

"Yeah."

George nodded. "I understand."

"I mean what's the point?" Mark grunted.

The Emperor silently gazed at Mark's tear-stained cheeks and bloodshot eyes. He shrugged his shoulders, and said, "Maybe there is and maybe there isn't a point. Take off your clothes and follow me."

The Emperor strode purposefully into the bay.

Mark stood in disbelief as the Emperor walked up to his waist in water then turned and waved for Mark to join him. Mark stripped naked and began to walk towards the Emperor, shivering in the frigid water. *Damn, this water's freezing!*

Bull Goose Beatty walked further out until he was up to his chest in foamy brine. Mark followed until he stood facing the Emperor in the strong current.

In a flash the Emperor grabbed Mark's head in a vise-grip and ducked him under the water! He twisted his right leg behind Mark's knees and swept him off his feet.

Mark floundered helplessly in a desperate attempt to find his footing, but the Emperor had him in a death-grip. Black thoughts of certain death immediately swelled up in Mark's mind as he punched, clawed, and kicked the Emperor in a futile effort to get free. A searing pain quickly spread throughout his chest. Death's greedy paws clawed at his throat. For what seemed like an eternity, he panicked and felt his being shrink and slip down, down, down into a deep dark tunnel...

...until suddenly... the Emperor let go...

Mark thrashed his arms and legs about and finally raised his head above water. He opened his eyes and gasped for breath after precious breath until he felt revived. He stared in utter horror at the Emperor.

"Wha-what the--!" Mark stammered. "Why did you--?"

Bull Goose calmly looked at Mark and said nothing.

Mark shoved the Emperor and cursed, "Bastard! Why did you try to kill me?"

"When you want Truth as much as you wanted to breathe now," the Emperor said, "you will find Truth."

Mark was stunned. "Truth?"

"Truth," the Emperor concluded, "beyond death. And maybe with Truth you'll find meaning in life."

Mark blinked incredulously as he tried to grasp the Emperor's meaning. Then, in a flash, he silently *felt* the meaning, and his face softened…

"Wo Lin gave you a gift," the Emperor continued. "Sex and love are a good beginning but not the end."

"Not the...?"

"A seed in itself has no meaning. Meaning comes when a seed dies, becomes a tree. And a tree in itself is just a name until it flowers. And a flower is meaningless until it releases its fragrance. Beyond the fragrance, who knows? The Unknowable?"

Mark nodded.

"Meaning always comes from evolving into a higher state," the Emperor concluded, "from sex into love, love into creativity, into silence, meditation, no-mind and beyond. Learn from Wo Lin, evolve, mature consciously. It's up to you."

Mark considered the Emperor's words for a moment: *Learn, evolve....* Then he nodded and softly said, "Um... thank you." And through shivering purple lips, he added, "I'm *freezing!*"

The Emperor nodded, then turned and began to walk towards shore. Mark followed. Once on shore he quickly dressed and stood facing the Emperor. They smiled at each other.

The Emperor picked up his surfboard and began to walk away. After a few steps, he turned around and said, "Speaking of women, I traveled the whole world looking for a perfect woman."

Surprised, Mark asked, "Did you find her?"

"Yes, I did," the Emperor replied. "But it's a sad story."

"Why?"

"Because... she was looking for a perfect man."

Mark roared with laughter.

The Emperor turned and walked away.

Lloyd threw his hands up in exasperation and said, "The Emperor almost killed him!"

"Almost," Bunny said, "but look what happened! Mark got it! Anyway, we're done here for now. Let's get back up there before you-know-who finds out we broke the Angelic Rule!"

In an instant Bunny and Lloyd were sitting on a cloud, smiling down at Mark.

"You'll be the death of me yet," Lloyd sighed.

"Promise?" Bunny quipped.

On the way back to his hotel room, Mark looked across the street and saw Vedant, the white-bearded old Indian sailor from the Emerald Queen.

Vedant saw Mark, too. He waved and shouted, "Mark!"

Mark waved then walked across the street.

Vedant looked concerned. "What happened? The Captain said you quit."

"Quit, eh? More like robbed and fired."

"Robbed? Fired? Um, I thought there was more to it than the Captain said. You don't seem like the quitting type. Look," he pointed, "there's a *chai wallah* on the corner. Want some chai?"

"Tea? Sure."

The two walked to the corner and ordered chai. After the *chai wallah* poured tea, they sat on the back of a broken-down wooden cart while Mark shared his side of the story about what had happened with Ethan and the Captain.

After Mark had finished, Vedant said, "I believe you. I've worked on *The Queen* for three years. The Captain trusts me. Let's see what he thinks after I tell him your story."

Mark shook Vedant's leathery hand. "Thanks."

The two stood and Vedant asked, "Where are you staying?"

"The Knob Hill Inn."

Vedant smiled. "I'll let you know what the Captain says."

Then the Swamiji walked towards the wharfs and Mark had another cup of chai.

CHAPTER 11

Rakan Kailin adjusted the jewel-studded golden crown on his deformed bald head as he sat on the black marble Holy Commode of the High Honchah in the dark dank basement of Rufus Temple in Srinagar.

In the center of the circular chamber before him, a single candle flickered over the skeleton of a former acolyte of the Sacred Order of Rufus, a young man who had been burned alive for betraying his oath of secrecy to the Order. Forty-one acolytes, or Pauhns, stood in a circle facing the candle and the skeleton, the large hoods of their black cloaks hiding the somber looks on their faces.

This was a special day for Rakan. Today each member of the largest class of Pauhns ever was to graduate from the five-year initiation program to the status of Idiyok, priest.

Each Pauhn had gone through a rigorous indoctrination to prepare him to perform essential duties in Rakan's home-grown religion, Rufism. The duties included the kidnapping of children to work in Rakan's ore mines and weapons factories, managing Rufism's orphanages, facilitating religious ceremonies, and publishing *The Kashmir Beacon*, the newspaper Rakan used to communicate and justify his religious, economic, political, criminal and social agenda for Kashmir and beyond.

Rakan's black silk garments and robe draped over his massive belly as he perused the circle of Pauhns and spoke in a deep bellowing voice:

"Behold, Pauhns, for though ye are born in sin, today is the first day of the rest of your life, or something like that. Today you will have the opportunity to cleanse yourself of twelve percent of the original sin you inherited from Eve the Sorceress in the Garden of Eden. Are you ready, Pauhns?"

The Pauhns roared "YES!" in unison.

Gollash, a young Pauhn with a wooden right leg and green glass right eye, whispered, "No," but no one heard him amidst the roar of the crowd.

Gollash had been kidnapped by Rakan's agents in Bengal when he was eight. For the next nine years he had worked sixteen hours a day in one of Rakan's munitions factories. When Gollash was seventeen, his right leg was amputated, and his right eye removed and replaced with green glass after he had tried to escape from Rakan's service. As fate would have it, a few weeks later Rakan captured Asanga and imprisoned him in Rufus Temple with Gollash.

Rakan prided himself as a master strategist, and his egoistic strategy for reforming his rebellious son and Gollash was simple: "Feed their greed and they will obey."

He soon appointed Gollash to be chief caregiver for Asanga and ordered him to "shower Asanga with all the luxuries that wealth can offer." Rakan's understanding was that living in luxury would reform *both* Asanga *and* Gollash. But it didn't happen that way. Over the years Gollash and Asanga became close friends without anyone becoming aware of the fact.

Now, as Gollash stood within the circle of Pauhns, he vowed to pay back Rakan for the suffering that Rakan had caused himself and Asanga. He seethed, *Someday, Rakan... someday...*

Rakan finished the ceremony by shouting, "Welcome to the Sacred Order of Rufus!" and read from the Sacred Book of Rufus:

"As was evidenced by Eve the Sorceress in the Garden of Eden, women's empowerment and self-determination pose a threat to God, Rufus. Women are inferior to men, incarnations of Peekaboo, the devil.

"It is our duty to suppress women and the female principles of receptivity and caring in every way. Have as many wives as possible, use women as you would use your donkey because none of them, including your own mother, is good enough to be cherished. Misogyny is ecstasy!"

Rakan looked up from the Book of Rufus.

"AGOK AL-HOOPALOO!" he cried.

"AGOK AL-HOOPALOO!" the Idiyoks roared in unison.

And so it was: all men in Rufism became cut off from developing any feminine qualities like openness, receptivity and love. Rakan needed such repressed men to achieve his diabolical plans for world domination. He needed insensitive shamed savages who felt a psychological abandonment of their mothers and who were ripe for kidnapping, terror and suicide missions.

And why did the women of Rufism tolerate this inhumane treatment by men? Fear, and the resulting desire for physical security. Spiritual greed was another reason the women tolerated abuse by men. The Sacred Book of Rufus guaranteed "eternal bliss in Whoopidoo Heaven if a woman behaves like a sheep and obediently serves the men of Rufism with pious guilt and shame."

Thus, the women of Rufism became cut off from developing any masculine qualities of their own, like courage, risk-taking and creativity.

Neither the men nor the women of Rufism ever developed into natural human beings because each sex repressed positive qualities of the opposite sex *within themselves!*

The irony of all this was that the Sacred Book of Rufus stated that "Rufus created everything in Existence." But in the same book, Rufites were instructed to reject and repress much of what Rufus had created in the Rufites themselves, thereby placing a Rufite on a higher level than their supposed God, Rufus!

In essence, the Sacred Book of Rufus was a collection of primitive childish superstitions and dogma, channeled through the criminal mind of its author, Rakan's grandfather, Jakal.

Rakan closed the Sacred Book of Rufus. And now with the ceremony complete, he felt a strong urge to return to his luxurious chambers and drown himself in carnal pleasures with one or more of his nine "holy nuns", his mistresses, his Vestas.

Rakan ended the ceremony by shouting, "We shall meet here this evening at 6 PM. AGOK AL-HOOPALOO!"

The Idiyoks roared, "AGOK AL-HOOPALOO!"

And the crowd dispersed.

Three hours later, Rakan lay naked in bed, sexually satiated by several Vestas, bathed and oiled, a king of kings, the High Honchah of Rufism.

He thought, *No woman can reject me. My Vestas are all obedient. I am in total control of my universe.*

Then he wondered, *Hmmm, total control?*

With that, he closed his eyes and a memory appeared...

It was his son, Asanga's, fifth birthday. He and Asanga were standing in the center of the Grand Hall of Rufus Temple surrounded by an adoring crowd. Next to them was his own father, Bezuhl, at that time the High Honchah of Rufism.

As a child playing with Leela, Asanga had demonstrated a rebelliousness which had challenged Rakan's absolute authority, and in his vision now, Rakan watched himself try to bribe Asanga into obedient submission with a huge pile of birthday presents.

At first Asanga blushed and seemed flattered when he was shown the presents. Then he innocently picked up each present, and without removing the paper wrapping, handed each gift to one of the other children in the crowd.

Rakan was embarrassed, enraged! *Such a selfless son is beyond my control!*

But before the crowd Rakan was helpless to do anything. To rebuke Asanga before the crowd would remove the mask of pious generosity that Rakan wore in public. And if there was any feeling that Rakan abhorred, it was helplessness.

After the ceremony, Rakan forced Asanga into the torture chamber in the basement of the temple.

"I'll teach you to make a mockery of my generosity!" he roared. He ordered Asanga to strip naked then mercilessly whipped him with a leather strap. Little Asanga finally fainted and had to be revived by several Vestas.

Now, as Rakan lay on his silk sheets and pillows, he thought, *Do I really have total control? No, even after spoiling Asanga for the last six years, I can never be sure that he is under my control. And it's that damn Satchitta's fault! And Leela's fault!*

Leela was gone, but Satchitta was still alive in Srinagar. And although Satchitta was small fry in relation to others who threatened the expansion of his empire, Rakan knew that eventually Satchitta and his ashram had to be dealt with. He decided that his inner circle of fifty senior Idiyoks, the Hassas priests, would advise him how. He immediately called for an emergency meeting of the Hassas in the Tomb Room of Rufus Temple.

CHAPTER 12

Lloyd sat on the edge of Cloud Nine lusting over the luscious nude centerfold photo of Lola Hubbahubba in the May 1848 issue of Fun Time Magazine. Suddenly he looked up, turned to Bunny and said, “Satchitta should rub Rakan out. An eye for an eye, tooth for a tooth.”

Bunny gasped, “Are you *nuts?!*”

“Give Rakan a little of his own medicine,” Lloyd insisted. “Who would know?”

“Satchitta would know, bozo!” Bunny exclaimed. “Put the magazine down when you talk with me! You had some sense when we were on Earth, but now I don’t know...”

Lloyd lowered the magazine. “How do you think I got to be a devil?”

Bunny huffed. “Violence only creates more violence. Eventually a murderer dies and is reborn and is murdered by another bozo who dies and is reborn and so forth and so on.”

Lloyd took a deep breath. “Take it easy. So what if I think like a politician sometimes?”

“You’re incorrigible!” Bunny said. “Really, you remind me.... In one past life I was shopping and walked into a store full of bizarre antiques. There was a shelf with glass jars full of different kinds of brains. I asked the shopkeeper how much each jar cost.

“‘Well,’ the man said, ‘housewife brains are $2 a pound, engineer brains are $4 a pound, and politician brains are $200 a pound.’

“‘$200 a pound!’ I said. ‘Why so much?’

“He said, ’Do you know how many politicians it takes to get a pound of brains?’”

Lloyd chuckled, "*Touche'*. You're a tough cookie." Then he picked up Fun Time magazine and began to read the articles.

Ten minutes later, Lloyd said, "Here's an article about a hotshot women's liberation activist who spoke at a cement contractors' convention. She addressed the all-male audience and claimed that women were the foundation of the American republic. And some guy in the back of the room shouted, 'Maybe so, but remember who laid the foundation!'"

Bunny shook her head. "Euwwww… *incorrigible!"*

CHAPTER 13

Leela sat at the mouth of Bodhi Cave and watched the sun set behind the mountains to the west. The day had been glorious. Her dialogs with the Inner Circle, Shanti and Pathen, had given her a positive context for being a Prasad.

Now she just needed to Be.

Slowly, slowly, night descended. Stars twinkled and Leela felt a surge of energy within her heart. She took a deep breath, picked up her flute and began to play, played until she was not and only the music was. Then she put the flute down, picked up her writing materials and scribbled lyrics to the melody she had just played:

My heart waits patiently, here, my love, for you.
Alone, silently, there's nothing to do,
but feel this silent longing
to disappear into you.

Tonight, stars shine bright as diamonds do.
With morning light they'll disappear
into the blue, blue sky.
But why, why do I feel this way?
I just know I do.
I feel this silent longing to disappear into you.

Leela knew the words were not hers. They had come from a space beyond. The song had written itself. She had been a hollow bamboo, a vehicle for the Beyond to express itself. She knelt, bowed, and touched her forehead to the ground. Then she stood, walked to a pile of yak rugs, crawled between two layers, and fell into a deep sleep.

The next morning the orange sun peeked over the mountains and fell on Leela's face. She opened her eyes, tossed the yak rug covers aside, then glanced at Dilai Dalai's original sutras on yak skins near her bedding.

She recalled one favorite sutra: "A true artist becomes one with his work, which in time may require ego surgery."

Good reminder...

She stood, slipped on a beige cashmere robe, strapped sandals on her feet, and hiked to the nearby hot springs. There she undressed, slid into the soothing, bubbling water, closed her eyes, and watched her breathing: in and out, around and around...

Soon, a clear vision appeared: Satchitta giving a public discourse on creativity before she left Srinagar:

"Creativity is non-doing," the Master said. "Like breathing and meditation, creativity is a happening. You don't do it and certainly you are not what you do. You are a vehicle for an unknown energy to express itself through form. Existence flows through you.

"Let the consciousness that arises through meditation be expressed creatively. Let creativity be a celebration of consciousness. Meditate, yes, but allow the pearls you gather in your inner world to beautify the outer world.

"I was a potter. This was my meditation for many, many years. Touching the clay, the water, shaping a pot, curing the pot in the fire, painting the pot, gave me joy beyond words.

"But remember, everyone is unique. Whatever brings you into the present moment is meditation. And don't worry about what anyone one else thinks about your creative expression. If it brings joy, do it! It may be preparing a meal, planting a garden, sweeping a floor. Do it lovingly. Your loving energy is creative, not what you create."

In the hot spring, Leela opened her eyes, took a deep breath, and playfully blew bubbles in the warm water. Finally, she climbed out of the pool, dried with a towel, dressed, then went back to the cave and ate breakfast.

Around noon Leela heard someone climbing up the ladder to the cave. She walked to the entrance. It was Pathen carrying a full backpack. He climbed to the top of the ladder, crawled onto the landing, stood, walked to Leela and hugged her.

The silence in their hug was palatable.

Pathen laid the backpack onto one of the yak rugs. He took out fruit, nuts, vegetables, paints, brushes, rag paper, and a *tabla* drum.

"Thank you," Leela said. "Hungry?"

Pathen nodded.

Together they sat and silently ate dried fruit and nuts.

Finally, Leela stood and said, "I need to dance."

She handed the drum to Pathen and asked, "Can you play?"

Pathen nodded, sat before the drum and played an upbeat rhythm.

Leela closed her eyes, felt the music... then slowly, slowly, began to dance.

Fluidly, gracefully, she whirled and twirled around the cave like a dervish drunk on the Divine. Round and round she danced and pranced like a fawn in the woods, whirling and twirling like a juggler clown, unbound by rhyme or reason...

Gradually, Pathen's drumming and Leela's dancing became one energy of sound and movement that at its peak attracted an audience of birds and animals, including Bol, Sol and Tol.

Thirty minutes later, Pathen slowed the rhythm and stopped. He and Leela sat silently for twenty minutes.

Then Leela slowly stood and gazed at the paints and brushes that lay before her on the yak rug.

What do you want? She silently asked the materials.

Play! they replied.

Leela smiled and asked Pathen, "Do you want to paint?"

Pathen smiled and nodded.

"For now, though," Leela said, "just watch how I paint, okay?"

"Okay."

Leela set up her paints, brushes and paper, and bending over the rag paper, began to paint. Like a swan mating, a child waiting, a lover praying, Leela became the wind, the moon, a smile, lightning and roses in one endless flow of loving energy - pure ecstasy...

Suddenly Leela stopped painting...

There was a gap...

Still...

Silent...

Leela took a deep breath, opened her eyes, and gazed at the painting. *"In Wonder,"* she thought.

She silently asked the painting, *Who are you?*

You, the painting silently replied.

Leela laughed loudly, took a brush and feathered the edge of one of the colors, producing a tapered shading between two hues.

"Shading creates depth, the illusion of three-dimensional form on two-dimensional paper," she said to Pathen.

Pathen nodded. "I see."

"Now you do it," Leela said. "First the masculine, active part. Dance to get your energy moving from the head to the heart. Then paint and play with the colors till you feel to stop. FEEL to stop! Just be with the painting. This is the feminine part: wait, see, listen, feel the painting. Silently ask the colors and forms, Who are you? What do you want?

"Then move back and forth between the masculine and feminine energies for as many cycles as you feel to until you feel the painting is done. Silently ask the painting, Are you finished, complete yet?

Then Leela smiled and said, "Okay, now you enjoy! I'll do the drumming."

Leela began to drum and Pathen began to dance. After dancing for ten minutes, Pathen slowly, slowly repeated the painting process that Leela had shown him, and within twenty minutes a visual masterpiece of insight and delight was born from Pathen's playfulness and spontaneity.

Oneness, Leela thought as she gazed at Pathen's painting.

Pathen didn't think so. He stepped back, studied the painting, frowned, and said, "Not as beautiful as yours."

Leela took a deep breath, shook her head, then calmly, slowly stepped towards Pathen and playfully slapped him on the face!

Pathen was shocked!

He stood still for a moment, then began to tremble. "What? Why did you...?"

"Because you were asleep on your feet," Leela said. "I woke you up. Follow me."

She took Pathen by the hand and led him to the edge of the cave.

"Where are we going?" Pathen asked.

"This way," Leela said, and began to climb down the rope ladder.

Pathen followed Leela as she walked away from the cliff. She stopped before two trees, pointed to each one, then asked, "How would you describe each tree?"

Pathen pointed to the tree on the left and said, "This one is small, bushy, with dark green leaves." Then pointing to the one on the right, he said, "This one is tall, thin, with red leaves and pink flowers."

Leela nodded and said, "And which tree thinks it is more beautiful than the other?"

The question seemed ridiculous to Pathen. He chuckled and said, "More beautiful? Trees don't compare."

Leela just stood and gazed into Pathen's eyes. Her silence and presence unnerved Pathen, and he began to look nervously back and forth between the two trees - back and forth, back and forth - until, *Presto!* - he got it and laughed!

"Oh," Pathen said, "I see... comparison!"

"What do you see?"

"Comparison is silly. My painting is my painting, yours is yours."

Leela nodded and said, "Let's go back and see what's what."

Then she turned and walked back to the ladder. Pathen followed, and the two climbed up to the cave.

Standing before the two paintings, Leela said, "There's a difference between a creator and a producer. Each may call himself an artist, but a creator allows creating to happen in the present. It is Existence that creates *through* the artist. It's not a doing. There's no goal.

"A producer may look like an artist but is not an artist in the true sense. A producer is utilitarian and has a goal in mind when he or she creates. They use their knowledge of a certain technique to guide their senses to create something. The producer is there as an ego; the creator is there playing.

"Sometimes an artist can be a hybrid, an artist and a producer. A vision, sound, or feeling comes to the artist from the Beyond and the artist uses certain techniques to bring what he or she has experienced inside into the physical world.

"But remember: the artist is not better than the producer, just different. The artist is relaxed, empty; the producer focused, concentrated. Now look at your painting. Ask the painting, 'What do you want?'"

Pathen gazed at his painting and silently asked, *What do you want?*

Moments passed...

No answer came...

Finally, Pathen said, “She is silent.”

Leela nodded. “Beautiful. Maybe a response will come later, maybe not. For now, you can let it dry here if you’d like.”

“Thank you,” Pathen said.

Leela hugged Pathen and asked, “See you next week?”

Pathen nodded, then strapped the empty backpack on his shoulders, climbed down the ladder, and disappeared down the path to Gazabha.

CHAPTER 14

The day had been intense. Mark had lost Wo Lin and been dunked and debunked by the Emperor in the ocean. It was late afternoon now and he needed a nap. He jumped into bed in his snug little redwood-paneled Knob Hill Inn room, pulled a blanket from his feet to his neck, and closed his eyes...

In his mind's eye Mark saw Wo Lin in bed with her fiancé and it gnawed at his guts.

Wo Lin... gone...

Mark took a few deep breaths and tears flowed. Slowly, slowly, tears washed away grief about losing Wo Lin. Soon a feeling of utter helplessness swallowed up Mark and it was too much for him to bear consciously. He dozed off and slept through the night.

When the orange morning sun peeked through the window and fell on Mark's face, he tossed his blankets aside, stood, walked to the window, opened it, and took deep breaths of the salty air. A sparrow sang sweetly in a big-leaf maple tree outside. He took another deep breath, closed his eyes, and saw Wo Lin's angelic face. He opened his eyes and looked outside.

The sparrow was gone.

Tears flowed.

Mark picked up his journal from the night table and wrote:

Sitting on the sunrise side of broken dreams,
a breeze drying all my tears.
How was I to know that my love for you
was hiding in the shadow of my fear?

You sang your song of love so sweet my heart grew wings,
and flew with you through the sky.
But since your song is gone, I feel a heavy heart,
and all I do is sit and cry.

Drifting skies, railroad ties,
all that comes and goes,
my heart can feel your song.
These bones got no home
and here comes the dawn.
And the sparrow in my tree is gone.

You flew away to try to find sunny skies,
that never, ever rain.
But it's not the clouds in the sky that make me cry,
it's wishing love will never, ever change.

Mark laid the journal on the windowsill, slipped into bed, closed his eyes and saw Wo Lin's loving face. He felt an ache in his heart, and a yearning for the love he had known in Missouri swept over him like a nostalgic cloud...

He fell asleep and dreamt of old Colonel Winston Holgate standing in his vast library in an impeccable white vested suit, Panama hat, black string bowtie, white goatee, corncob pipe, and bamboo cane.

Born July 4, 1776, the Colonel exuded the strength of a peaceful warrior who had lost his innocence in the gore of war and regained it by trusting in the intelligence of his heart. It was the Colonel who had first introduced Mark to meditation after Floyd died and provided a safe refuge in his vast library from the constant harassment that Mark experienced from the priests and nuns at school and at home with Hank.

Then Mark dreamt of his mother, Bridget, and Merschel Whistle riding together into the barnyard of their farm on a buckboard. Mark was twenty when Merschel blew in like the wind that mid-October, leaves crimson and yellow on the oak trees. Merschel had been passing through town going West when Bridget had met him at Steinberg's General Store in town and hired him to help harvest the apple crop.

Merschel was a tall forty-year-old former Maine farmer with a great laugh, healthy tan, and genuine smile, someone you just wanted to be with. He had a full red-brown beard and long curly hair with hints of silver. But it was Merschel's eyes that first struck Mark: fathomless, magnetic eyes.

The synchronicity around Merschel showing up that day was amazing. Three days earlier, Hank had disappeared with the buckboard in the middle of the night. No one knew what had happened until a day later when one of Mark's friends, Shelly Turner, told Mark and Bridget that on the full moon night that Hank disappeared, she couldn't sleep and was sitting on her front porch swing when she saw Hank and young Stacy Simmons riding in a buckboard down the road in front of her house. Hank was never seen or heard of again. It was the peak of the harvest season and Bridget needed a foreman to run the farm. Merschel was the man she hired for the job.

The day after Merschel arrived, Mark and Merschel began to transform the run-down fifteen-by-fifteen-foot shack behind the barn into a comfortable space for Merschel to live. They tossed out all the junk and dead rats, re-shingled the roof, scrubbed the inside with soap and water, insulated the ceiling and walls with hay, paneled the inside with old barn wood, partially covered the rafters with clean white sheets, built a bed that could be raised and lowered on a pulley, added a couple of chairs, a table, a sofa, an old Persian rug and pillows, put candles and wildflowers around, and WOW! At night when Merschel burned sandalwood incense and lit a dozen candles, the inside looked, smelled, and felt like a temple. He even gave it a name, “the Taj”.

Sometime during the next ten months Bridget and Merschel became lovers. Although Merschel insisted on continuing to live alone in the Taj, he nurtured Bridget like the sun nurtures a flower, and in time Bridget blossomed into the “Wild Irish Rose” she naturally was. To her brother, Father McG’s dismay, she even stopped going to church. Mark had already dropped church after Floyd’s death.

Mark was amazed at his mother’s transformation. *Merschel is primarily responsible,* he thought. *He knows something about women.*

Mark had been in the dark about women for the previous four years that he had dated Kay Ellen Smith, the pretty brunette daughter of the village’s hell-and-brimstone preacher. Kay Ellen would only go so far in sex with Mark, always insisting, “I’m saving myself for marriage.”

Mark was frustrated to the hilt with Kay Ellen and one hot August day he let out his frustrations to Merschel...

Shortly after dawn that day, Mark and Merschel were shoveling horse manure in the corral, when Mark blurted out, “All I get is blue balls and excuses from Kay Ellen! Maybe it’s me, I don’t know. What’s it all about, sex and love?”

Merschel laughed. “I was born from sex! When sex is accepted as natural and played with consciously, it transforms into love and creativity. Seems like you and Kay Ellen have gone as far as you can. Maybe you’re ready for safe sex with another woman.”

“Safe sex?”

Merschel nodded. “No babies. You may want to find another girlfriend; or better yet, let her find you.”

Mark blushed. “I don’t know how to be with a woman that way - safe sex.”

"Ask her what she wants; let her lead," Merschel advised. "Be empty, open. Right now, you and I need to talk about safe sex."

So they did.

A week later Mark's wish came true...

During the previous two years, he had played guitar in a band every Saturday night at the hoedown in Goetter's barn. The night after his "safe sex" talk with Merschel, Mark had just stepped down from the stage at the hoedown when Shelly Turner walked up behind him and pinched his ass!

Mark whipped around and saw Kay Ellen with her mouth wide open standing behind Shelly. Kay Ellen turned beet red, huffed, then stomped away when she saw Shelly pinch Mark.

Shelly wiggled up to Mark and said, "You guys were great! Meet me tomorrow night at Dalton's Mill. Ten o'clock. I'll have a surprise."

"What kind of surprise?" Mark asked.

Shelly didn't answer. She smiled, winked, and wiggled away in her seductive red cotton dress.

The next night Mark beat his way through the cattails along Stony Creek, got to Dalton's Mill around ten.

Full moon night.

Hoot owls.

Late August.

Humid as hell.

Pesky mosquitoes biting.

Mark was so hot he wanted to jump out of his boots! Once at the mill though, he ducked under the cracked beam above the front door and stepped inside, full of jizum and rhythm.

Hay and fresh wheat, just cut...

Mark looked to his left... *nobody...*

He heard a sweet voice, "Mark, over here."

Mark looked to his right. The full moon shone through the window on Shelly, standing naked by a haystack.

Mark blinked a few times then slowly walked to her. Shelly's fiery red hair, full breasts, and slim body glowed in the moonlight. She reached out and took Mark's hands.

"Wow," Mark said.

"You're shaking," Shelly said softly. "It's okay."

Mark took a deep breath and relaxed.

He stepped back and drank up Shelly's body as a whole.

Recalling Merschel's advice, he asked, "What do you want?"

Shelly smiled, stepped to Mark and wrapped her arms around his neck. Mark put his hands around Shelly's slim waist. She kissed Mark on the lips and flicked her tongue in his mouth. Mark's *lingam* hardened. Shelly unbuttoned Mark's shirt, took off his socks and boots and pulled down his trousers and underwear. Then she knelt, put one hand around Mark's *lingam* and began to slowly, tenderly kiss his *lingam* - just a young adult playing with a friend.

Then Shelly stood, looked Mark in the eyes, and pushed him back into the hay. Mark was shocked at first, then Shelly purred, "I want to be on top."

Mark opened his arms.

Shelly straddled his hips with her legs, eased his *lingam* into her *yoni*, and began gyrating ecstatically.

"Let her lead," Merschel had said, and Mark did.

Within minutes neither Shelly nor Mark knew who or where they were. They just panted, sweated, groaned, and loved every second of lovemaking!

Then Shelly whispered, "Slow... slower..."

Did I hurt her? Mark thought.

He slowed down...

...then slower still...

...and slower still...

...until the boundary between them dissolved and got dreamy as they melted into each other....

Then "AHHHHHHHHHHHH!" Shelly screamed!

She arched her back, flailed her arms, and let go in ecstatic full body orgasm! Her shrieking and moaning became quieter and quieter until both she and Mark lay still in the hay, breathing gently and gazing into each other's eyes for several minutes.

"Wow," Mark whispered.

"Wow," Shelly smiled. Then she rolled off Mark and began to dress.

Mark dressed too, and the couple slowly walked hand in hand out of the mill and across the Colonel's hay field, finally climbing into a hay wagon out of breath and giggling like kids.

They hugged for a while, then Shelly whispered: "I heard Father McG lecturing little kids about sex, sin, and eternal hellfire. He asked the kids, 'Where do little boys and girls go when they do bad things?'

"Do you know what Tommy said?"

"No."

"Tommy said, 'They go in the bushes.'"

Mark and Shelly laughed till they cried.

Finally, Mark hugged Shelly, and said, "Thank you. Are you okay?"

Shelly smiled, nodded, pecked Mark on the lips, then got up and dressed.

Mark dressed, too, then walked her home.

Lloyd and Bunny watched Mark as he lay dreaming in bed in the Knob Hill Inn. They, too, kissed.

"Kissing's not the same, is it?" Bunny said.

"Without a physical body? No way," Lloyd agreed.

"The relating game..." Bunny reflected.

"What about it?"

"Oh, you know," Bunny mused, "wanting to feel complete, whole, through another person."

Lloyd nodded. "You and I played the game many lifetimes."

"True," Bunny agreed. "Two bank robbers run into a bank and order the customers and clerks to get behind the counter. They tell everyone to take off all their clothes and lie face down on the floor. One nervous female clerk pulls off her dress and lies on her back.

"'Turn over, Gloria!' whispers her friend. 'This is a robbery, not the office party.'"

Lloyd laughed. "What's that have to do with relating?"

"Nothing," Bunny said, "except humor keeps the relating game fun."

Secretly - so as not to stir up too much gossip within their small conservative community - Mark and Shelly were lovers as often as possible after their tryst in Dalton Mill.

And Merschel?

One cold January morning, fifteen months after Merschel had entered Mark's life, Merschel let the cat out of the bag...

Mark was an early bird and often heard Merschel singing in a strange language before sunrise. One frosty morning, Mark peeked through one of the Taj's glass windows to see what Merschel was doing, and was shocked to see Merschel staring right back at him!

Mark jumped back.

Merschel smiled and waved, "Come in."

Mark went in and sat on a cushion on the faded old Persian rug by the warm potbelly stove. Merschel brought over a pot of chai tea, sat on another cushion facing Mark, then poured two cups of tea.

"Why are you snooping around?" Merschel asked playfully.

Mark blushed. "What's that song you sing every morning?"

"A mantra: *Om Muni Padme Hum*. Relaxes me, gets me in the space for meditation."

"I *knew* it!" Mark exclaimed. "I knew you were a meditator! The Colonel's a meditator, too!"

For the previous four years, Mark had been playing with some of the 112 *Vigyan Bhairav Tantra* meditations that he had learned from a rare book in the Colonel's library. The Colonel had also talked with Mark about chanting Sanskrit mantras, but Mark had never heard anyone chanting a mantra.

The strange thing was that Merschel had rarely talked about his past. He was a man of few words, and whenever Mark had mentioned anything about meditation or mantras in the past, Merschel seemed uninterested.

Now though, Merschel laughed at Mark's excitement. Then he said, "Some folks call chanting and yoga postures meditating. I don't. Meditation is being, not doing or chanting. You can't *do* meditation. It's our nature, already the case inside. Just watch, be conscious, aware of what's happening inside and out, that's all. But chanting and stretching relaxes me till I feel open to watching what's happening inside. That's where the juice is."

Mark looked puzzled. "Juice?"

"A figure of speech," Merschel explained. "I spent ten years traveling the world before I was lucky enough to stumble upon an enlightened Master, Gopal, in Northwest India. Somehow I got lost in a remote part of the Swat Valley and stumbled upon a small ancient community, Gazabha, a tight-knit group of mystics. They usually didn't accept strangers, but I was invited to live there. Stayed for a year, became a disciple of Gopal."

"A disciple?" Mark said. "What's that like?"

"Later," Merschel said. "The point is, through a young interpreter, Deva Leela, Gopal helped me become aware of the gross and subtle energetic layers of our nature, and the significance that our Center, Being, plays in being able to witness what is happening in our subtle bodies."

"Witness... subtle bodies?"

"We're not just a physical body," Merschel said. "As infants we're also pure feeling, heart, energy without thought. Our Center is a mystery, but for discussion purposes we can call the Center a spiritual Being, consciousness, energy without form. Our Center pulses subtle energy which activates our breathing, giving life to the body even when we are asleep."

"I never thought of that!" Mark said. "Who breathes me when I'm asleep?"

Merschel nodded. "Exactly. Gopal said our Center is transcendental to our spiritual heart, mind and body. Essential qualities like love, trust, and courage, and our talents and strengths naturally become available to us when we are relaxed in our Center. At our Center is a witness, a watcher, consciousness, a seer of all the peripheral centers. That's what I mean when I say watching happens, meditation happens, when we are centered. Watching or witnessing is not something we can do, it's who we already are deep inside. Watching happens when we are conscious of what is so."

Mark looked puzzled. "But how, ah...?"

"I doubt that I would have experientially understood this on my own," Merschel said. "It's too subtle. I needed to be with a living Master. Once Gopal explained the Center and witnessing - being choicelessly aware of the body-mind - I began to experiment and understand the duality of the mind - good-bad, happy-sad - and not be identified. I'm not the mind and feelings! I'm the *witness* of my body, thoughts, positive and negative emotions, talents, and essential qualities! I became more playful, began to relax and feel that I am already who I need to be at my Center. I realized that the sacred is hidden within the mundane. My body is a temple which houses the divine. Spirituality is being dis-identified with everything that you experience, everything that is an object to your witnessing consciousness. It is one's pure subjectivity."

Mark got excited and asked, "How did you end up in India?"

"I was raised in the West like you, and the utter poverty of the West is that there is basically no such thing as a Master-disciple relationship here. Much of the West is rich materially but utterly poor spiritually. Phony really! That's why it has progressed so much technologically. The West has largely ignored authentic spiritual exploration and embraced materialism. True religion is rare in the West; there are only moralities pretending to be religion. Morality is created and enforced by others, religion you must seek and search for yourself. Religion can only flower from within."

"But how did I end up in India? I was miserable in the West and thirsty for the real deal. I *had* to meet a Master! My advice to anyone who wants to understand meditation and love? Find a *living* Master! It takes guts, because in the West we are taught to develop a strong mind and ego, and a Master's job is to guide one to drop the ego through meditation. A Master guides us from the head to the heart and finally to our Center. And loving is the only bridge I know of from the head to the Center."

Mark hung his head then looked up. "Love... you know, Kay Ellen drove me crazy, and now Shelly drives me crazy. I really don't know what love is. And you and Mom.... Well, Mom has really changed..."

Merschel smiled. "Ultimately it's not about men and women. It's about the male principle - the mind - and the female principle - the heart: feeling, openness, receptivity. And finally, it's about our Center.

"Listening to Gopal and experimenting on my own, I began to understand that men tend to be mental creatures. I sure was. And women tend to be feeling creatures. Gopal said there are two paths to realizing the truth of one's own nature - meditation and love."

"Two?"

"For two different types of people: feeling types and mental types. The path of love is for the feeling type and the path of meditation is for the mental type. But some men are feeling types and some women are thinking types, so it's not all that simple. The only way to know which path is most natural for you is to experiment with both paths and determine for yourself.

"Gopal said that 99% of mystics reach enlightenment through meditation because love brings in all the problems of another person. He said great awareness is needed on the path of love and great love is needed on the path of awareness. In fact, love and awareness are two sides of the same coin. He said that either path can lead to enlightenment.

"You've been experimenting with meditation. Great! Another way to find your true self is to lose yourself in love: surrender. Surrendering to Shelly, being with her *as she is*, might give you a good foundation if you ever have a chance to surrender to a Master."

"Is that possible?"

"Depends on you. You mentioned the *Vigyan Bhairav Tantra* meditations before. There are techniques for both mental and heart types in those 112 meditations. Gopal advised me to try both types of techniques, but to only stick with one *type* of technique at a time. Don't mix love and meditation techniques in the beginning. So, I did that, and slowly, slowly, I began to drop from the head to the heart and relate more consciously with women, and now with Bridget. Play with meditation and love techniques, then decide which path is more natural... for *you!*"

Merschel sipped the last of his tea, then lay his cup on the table.

"We're in a good space now, have work to do," Merschel said. "The stock need feeding. But if you want, we can experiment with heart meditations and then you can see if they help you relate with Shelly better. What do you say?"

"Sure, but I'm still confused."

"Let's shovel horse shit. That may dissolve the confusion."

Mark laughed. "Sure."

So, they walked to the corral and silently shoveled horse shit, then fed the stock.

CHAPTER 15

Rakan stormed into the office of Kashmir's most highly circulated weekly newspaper, *The Kashmir Beacon.* The Editor-in-Chief, Visiog, was at his desk going over the following week's edition with four members of his Hassas editorial staff. Everyone stood the second Rakan burst into the room.

"All of you out!" Rakan commanded. "Not you, Visiog. We need to talk." Visiog's staff left immediately.

Visiog was Chief of the Hassas, a former Bengal orphan who carried out the High Honchah's diabolical orders with deadly precision. Visiog had a keen analytical mind, penetrating brown eyes and powerful physique; and his intelligent, bearded face and booming voice gave him a commanding presence. But he had known mostly heartbreak since he was dragged from his home at age five and put to work in one of Rakan's munitions plants. Since then, he'd dedicated his substantial talents to Rakan's service and in Rakan's presence behaved more like a contrite lamb than the lion he knew he was inside.

Rakan barked at Visiog: "Call a meeting of the Hassas for tomorrow! It's time we got rid of Satchitta and his crowd. But for now, what have you found out about Saint Faykin's tomb in Pahalgam?"

"I still haven't heard word from our man in Pahalgam," Visiog replied.

Rakan shrugged his shoulders. "Okay then, forget about it for now. I want you to work on a special edition of *The Beacon* to celebrate my father's and grandfather's birthdays next month. It's been forty years since Jakal died and ten years since Bezuhl passed away."

"What angle?" Visiog asked.

"The usual flattery," Rakan said. "Jakal and Bezuhl created orphanages and food banks for the poor all over Kashmir. They were generous industrialists, bankers, fathers, grandfathers, and so on - saints who lived among us, humble servants of the people. Got it?"

"Okay," Visiog said.

"Good. I want to see a draft first thing in the morning."

Then Rakan pounded the table, stood and shouted, "AGOK AL-HOOPALOO!"

Visiog jumped up and shouted, "AGOK AL-HOOPALOO!"

Rakan rushed out of the office.

Visiog took a deep breath. It was past midnight and now he was going to be up all night again trying to meet another of Rakan's impossible deadlines. He rubbed his bloodshot eyes and sighed aloud as he considered writing an article portraying Rakan's deceased father, Bezuhl, and his grandfather, Jakal, as "saints who lived among us".

He glanced at the colorful oil painting on the wall in front of him. It showed a white-bearded Jakal with a golden halo around his head, surrounded by a throng of smiling orphans in front of the Srinagar orphanage that Jakal had built.

Okay, Visiog thought, *now all I must do is re-write history so people who don't know the truth will think Jakal and Bezuhl - and by association, Rakan - are saints.*

Visiog closed his eyes, sat back in his chair, and mentally reviewed Rakan's family's history as he knew it...

There were four generations to consider, beginning with Jakal who was born in 1730 in Bengal. Jakal begat Bezuhl who begat Rakan who begat Asanga.

Jakal's family had been part of a criminal tribe, Thuggees, for seven generations. Thuggees were a group of cutthroats who survived by attacking and looting caravans as they traveled through isolated mountain regions of Bengal.

Jakal was twenty-nine when most of his Thuggee tribe were killed in a skirmish with British soldiers. He was captured and languished in Fort William's prison for two months before he had an "awakening" – actually, he imagined that he heard the voice of God, "Rufus" say, "Escape and go to Srinagar, where your destiny as a prophet and leader of men will be fulfilled!"

That very night Jakal escaped from prison through a tunnel which several inmates had spent months digging. He took this unexpected stroke of good luck to be an omen that he was "The Blessed One".

He traveled to a nearby mountain cave where his Thuggee tribe had stored treasures from their conquests. He murdered the two guards, loaded gold, silver, diamonds and other valuables into a bullock cart and drove to Srinagar, where he intended to start over as an unknown and very rich man.

Within a week Jakal had another "awakening" in which he heard Rufus give him detailed instructions on "how to live a pious, rich, and morally righteous life, thus gaining eternal pleasure in Whoopidoo Heaven." Jakal wrote down the instructions in what was to become "The Sacred Book of Rufus", the foundation of the Rufus religion, with Jakal as the "moral and spiritual leader, the High Honchah".

During his first month in Srinagar, Jakal bought a beautiful Bengali teenager, Sheeba, from the slave market. He married her in grand ceremony to sustain his public image as a pious householder. The next year Sheeba bore Jakal his only son, Bezuhl. Four female babies were later born to Sheeba, but each one mysteriously disappeared immediately after birth.

During the next 28 years Jakal worked hard and surrounded himself with mediocre obedient minds. By 1788 he had built a rich empire which extended far beyond Srinagar. How he did this was twofold:

He purchased great tracts of land south of Srinagar in Jammu, land rich in copper, zinc, lead and iron. Then he hired Roger Oliver - a greedy British mining engineer and metallurgist - to supervise the mining of these natural resources and refine and mold them into end products to be assembled in Jakal's highly profitable weapons factories.

Concurrently, Thuggees were paid to kidnap children in remote villages of Kashmir and Bengal. The children were forced to work in Jakal's mines and metallurgical treatment plants. Not only did the children provide cheap labor for industry, but they also formed the foundation of his other profitable business: the Rufus religion, Rufism.

The kidnapped orphans were housed in high-security compounds around the mines and factories and were brainwashed from an early age on the principles of Rufism. Over the years Jakal's congregation grew in leaps and bounds.

As High Honchah of Rufism, Jakal wasn't satisfied with the fortune he made from exploiting kidnapped children. He was determined to make Rufism the only religion in the world. To this end, over the years he used one of the byproducts of the zinc and lead smelting processes, maegin (later "thallium" in English) - a soft, gray, water-soluble, highly toxic, tasteless metal - to poison several charismatic religious and political leaders in Kashmir and thus expand his empire.

Jakal built a huge Rufus temple in Srinagar - and using the time-honored method of converting people to pseudo-religions through feeding the poor, starting schools, and providing shelter for orphans - by 1788 his congregation grew to include a large percentage of Kashmir's population.

As High Honchah of Rufism, Jakal declared himself an infallible authority, and one of his perks included having nine female Vestas at his service around the clock. Each Vesta was personally selected by Jakal from among the teenage orphan girls in his congregation. Publicly, Vestas were portrayed as chaste virgins who fulfilled Jakal's practical needs and helped orchestrate Rufus religious ceremonies. Privately, they were his sex slaves.

Over the years, Jakal coddled his only son, Bezuhl, and kept him isolated from the outside world, grooming him to be heir to his industrial empire and world leader of Rufism. Bezuhl in turn married another Bengal beauty, Amata, who bore him their only son, Rakan. Bezuhl conditioned Rakan as he had been conditioned, and it looked like Jakal's dream of a continuous genetic line of despots was solidly intact...

...until Satchitta's ashram appeared on the scene....

It was then that Rakan's son, Asanga, became infected by Leela and her friends and began to rebel against Rakan. In Rakan's mind the future leadership of his empire was in jeopardy because of Satchitta, and as High Honchah, Rakan needed to do something about that.

Sitting slumped over in *The Kashmir Beacon* office, Visiog wondered, *How do I spin this implausible article?*

He huddled over his Pellegrino Turri typewriter and typed the heading of his article: "SAINTS WHO LIVED AMONG US".

Then he closed his eyes and fell asleep in his chair.

CHAPTER 16

Bunny sighed and shook her head. "I wouldn't mind if something bad happened to Rakan and the Hassas."

"Now you see my point!" Lloyd agreed. "Satchitta and Asanga never did Rakan any harm, only hurt his ego. It would be a disaster, but not a misfortune if an accident happened to them."

"What do you mean?"

Lloyd waved his hands and said, "Simple: a goat is walking across a bridge, loses its footing, falls into a river and drowns. That is a misfortune, not a disaster.

"But if Rakan and the Hassas are crossing the bridge and it collapses and they all drown, that is a disaster - but not a misfortune."

Bunny nodded. "All I know is, Rakan believes he is some sort of prophet and genius, but he has the intelligence of a sperm."

"Sperm?"

"You know, the sperm mind: 'I have to get there before the others, have to get Satchitta before he gets me.' But Satchitta isn't out to get him!"

"Paranoid ambition driven by fear," Lloyd surmised.

"I don't like where this is headed," Bunny said. "We should do something."

"*We?* What?"

"I don't know. Something."

"Sooner or later Rakan will get what he deserves," Lloyd said, "or wise up. You would think he would get the point after he had his portrait painted on that special edition of a postage stamp."

"Um" Bunny said, "the stamps didn't sell well, did they?"

"No," Lloyd said, "remember? When Rakan asked the Postmaster why the stamps didn't sell, the Postmaster said, 'Because the stamps wouldn't stick to the envelopes.'

"Rakan got furious and asked the Postmaster why he didn't use the right glue for the stamps.

"The Postmaster apologized, then said, 'I used the right glue, but most people spat on the wrong side of the stamp.'"

"Rakan may never get it," Bunny said. "Maybe we should do something. But what?"

Lloyd and Bunny contemplated for a few moments, then Lloyd's eyes lit up. "I have an idea!" he said excitedly. Then he whispered his plan into Bunny's ear.

"You gotta be crazy!" Bunny shouted.

"It takes a nut to crack a nut," Lloyd said.

Then, invisible, Lloyd whisked down from the cloud and whispered his plan into Visiog's right ear. Visiog, of course, thought the idea was his, and could hardly wait to tell Rakan his brilliant new plan to do away with Satchitta.

CHAPTER 17

Mark felt refreshed after a long night's sleep in his Knob Hill Inn room. He looked out his window and saw that it was a sunny and warm Spring Day by the San Francisco Bay.

Heaven.

He washed his face, dressed, then walked to O'Doul's for breakfast, ordered coffee and apple pie. Katie O'Doul served a large slice of pie, poured his coffee and asked, "Is it true you got fired from *The Queen?"*

Mark shrugged his shoulders and nodded.

Katie laid a gentle hand on Mark's left shoulder. "We need help here. Sweeping floors, tossing out drunks, washing dishes, playing music."

Mark smiled. "Thanks, Katie. I'll take you up on that."

"Start tonight at seven?"

"I'll be here."

"See you then."

Great day for a walk on the beach! Mark thought.

After breakfast he walked from O'Doul's towards the beach via the docks.

Suddenly Vedant crossed his path. Vedant cried, "Mark!" then hugged him.

"Wow!" Mark said. "Great to see you!"

"The Captain wants to see *you!"*

"Me? What did he say when you told him what happened?"

"You think he doesn't know Ethan? The Captain believed your version of the story! I was going to the inn now to tell you. Still want to sail with us?"

"Sure! Let's go!"

Vedant and Mark strode over to *The Emerald Queen,* and Mark knocked on Captain McDonegal's cabin door.

"Come in!" the Captain bellowed.

Mark and Vedant entered the cabin.

The Captain looked sad, subdued. He reached out and shook Mark's hand. "I'm sorry I didn't believe you the first time. Ethan's eye looked terrible and I'm his dad, wanted to protect him. Anyway, Ethan gave back the rest of your money. Here." He handed Mark the large leather bag of gold coins that was lying on his desk.

"Thanks," Mark said, and handed the bag back to the Captain. "Keep it till we get to Bombay."

The Captain smiled. "I felt you were that type. No hard feelings, eh?"

"No."

"Then welcome aboard, mate! But we have a problem."

Mark and Vedant looked at each other. Both chimed, "Ethan!"

"Right," the Captain sighed. He looked at Mark and said, "I fired him after he gave your gold back."

"Fired him?" Mark said.

The Captain nodded. "He's lucky I didn't make him walk the plank! He said he was sorry and would apologize to you, but I had had enough of his shenanigans. Fired him. It ripped my heart out, but I had to do it. He took his gear and left. Didn't sleep here last night. I've got a full crew now and we can sail as soon as we get a few more supplies. A good Quartermaster is hard to find though. Once Ethan is at sea, he's the best. Do either of you know where he is?"

Mark said, "The folks at The Bawdy Toddy Pub might know. Look, sir, Ethan is Ethan. He was drunk. I've been drunk plenty of times myself. It's fine with me if you want him back."

Vedant jumped between Mark and the Captain and said, "No, wait! Sorry, Captain, but I've known Ethan for three years, and maybe it's best to wait till Ethan comes back on his own - or not."

The Captain hung his head and considered the suggestion. Then he said, "Ultimately you're right." He turned to Mark and said, "Get your gear, mate. It will be a while before the supplies I ordered from Sacramento arrive and we can sail. You're free till then. I'll go to The Bawdy Toddy and deal with the Quartermaster issue myself."

Vedant and Mark left the Captain's quarters.

Mark got his gear from his hotel room, stowed it on board *The Queen*, then walked to O'Doul's. He strode up to Katie and said, "Things have changed. I'm sailing on *The Queen* in a couple of days. I don't need the work, but thanks anyway. I'd like to play tonight though, if that's alright."

Katie hugged him. "Any time."

That evening Mark went to O'Doul's, had a few beers, sang a few tunes, then went back to *The Queen* and slept through the night. Early the next morning before the fog lifted, Mark went to the beach and wrote in his journal:

•

Amazing how things work out. I'll be sailing on *The Queen* in a couple of days. Vedant told the Captain my side of the story with Ethan and I was hired back. I have mixed feelings about Ethan getting fired, but we'll see what happens...

Mark looked up and watched at the waves crashing on the shore. A feeling of nostalgia swept over him. Tears trickled down his cheeks. So much had happened since he had left Missouri, and now here he was on the verge of leaving his homeland for the unknown. He took a deep breath and continued to write:

Need to write Mom, Merschel, Shelly, Wayne, and other friends back home, let them know I'm alright and leaving for India soon.

Similar feelings now as when I left Missouri.

Seems like lifetimes ago...

Shelly and I were lovers and we had lots of fun together after Merschel came to live with my family. Merschel, Colonel Holgate and I experimented with the *Vigyan Bhairav Tantra* Meditations and meditating helped me relate with Shelly in a more relaxed, accepting way.

It was hard leaving Shelly and my family. But after my *satori* on the lake near the Colonel's cabin, there was no turning back. I needed to be with a live Master after that. Merschel, the Colonel, and my family had helped me immensely on my path, but after my experience on the lake I knew I was treading on dangerous ground. I needed a live Master to show me the rest of the way.

For the previous three years I had often consulted the *I Ching* in the Colonel's library. The readings gave me the sense that there were cosmic positive and negative energies that balanced each other in nature, causing creation and destruction.

I wondered, *Is the negative pole of this cosmic energy the source of evil? Or are the positive and negative energies one energy?*

I really didn't know.

It had been a cold and snowy winter. I was having fun with Shelly. Life was good. Mom and Merschel were in love. It sounds crazy now, but there was a gnawing thirst inside me to know what the source of evil was. Word was spreading that a Civil War was about to happen in the States. I wondered, *Why is there so much suffering, bigotry and people killing one another? Is there a God in the sky running the show? And maybe some devil pissing him off?*

I didn't think so, but I had to know for sure somehow.

I had dropped all the beliefs the Church had given me, had stopped going to church. I had to know the truth for myself, and felt I needed to be alone, meditate, and maybe the answer to my source-of-evil question would come.

It was late February, about sixteen months after Merschel had come to live with us, when I set off on my pilgrimage. There were three inches of snow at home, and I knew there would be a lot more snow at higher altitudes. I borrowed the Colonel's snowshoes, took some preserved peaches and pears, nuts, and an axe, and hiked twelve miles to the Colonel's old log hunting cabin by Lake Ozark.

A cougar stalked me during the last mile of the hike. I thought that once I got to the cabin and lit a fire, he would leave me alone. But I had my axe in case he attacked, which he didn't.

The accumulated snow had drifted high on the walls of the cabin, and I had to dig down through it to open the front door. It smelled musty inside. The Colonel hadn't been there in years, couldn't hike there because of his arthritis. I chased the rats out, swept the floor, dusted off the shelves, threw my bedding on the cot, chopped wood, kindled a fire in the potbelly stove, then hiked four miles along one side of the lake before sunset.

I meditated day and night for a week, then something amazing happened...

Twice a day during that week I walked slowly, consciously, across the vast snow-covered frozen lake in front of the cabin. And the day before I planned to leave, I was silently walking across the lake when BOOM! - I had an insight which hit me like I had run into a brick wall! In a flash I knew the answer to the question, "What is the source of evil?"

It is man's mind!

It was the first time in my life that I had been totally alone for a week, had not seen another human being, only nature in her silent splendor: birds and trees, sky and virgin snow, a few critters. And then an unexpected awakening happened as I walked over the lake that day. I knew: The mind is the source of the concept of "evil".

Maybe it was because I had not seen or been influenced by another human being all week, or because the purity of nature had penetrated every pore. I didn't know. But walking across the snow-covered lake, I realized in an instant that in nature there is no evil, no "good" or "bad". Sure, animals kill other animals for food, but there is nothing evil about that. It's Nature's way. And what is the difference between an animal and man? In a flash I got it: the mind! Man's mind was the source of the concepts of good and evil - the source of imaginary realms like heaven and hell. Evil and good are just ideas, not a reality. Reality was pure, innocent Nature; as innocent as the virgin snow I was standing on; as innocent as birds flying in the sky, who leave no footprints, no history, no imprint of ego as they soar above.

I was ecstatic!

I jumped for joy in the middle of the lake, danced around and around! I couldn't believe it! So simple! I KNEW! Not intellectually, not in words. I really knew and didn't need anyone to confirm or deny my insight. There was no doubt, no borrowed belief to cover up any doubt.

I knew and that was that!

That night I tested my insight. After sunset I sat on the cot and said aloud, "Okay, devil, if you are real, come and get me."

I sweated and worried all night, and a badger snarled and growled like some demon outside the cabin for hours. My mind said, *It's the devil outside!* But I just sat detached in sweat and watched the mind - "a watcher on a hill", as Merschel would say. I breathed into my heart and watched the mind trying to spin its web. Watching, I just let the mind be so, and no devil came!

By morning I was free! Truth had set me free.

The sun was out in all its glory that morning as I snowshoed towards home, almost floating and gliding across the glimmering snow. I stopped at the Colonel's mansion and told the Colonel about my insight.

I said, "I'm going to India as soon as possible to be with Merschel's living enlightened Master, Gopal."

The Colonel nodded knowingly and said, "If I was younger, I'd go with you. But my legs.... So, listen, son, you're going to need some money for your trip. I need an extra hand around here. What do you say?"

"Great!" I said.

Mom and Merschel, my friends and family, were all shocked that I was so passionate about going to India, but they accepted it after a while. Also, Merschel knew about my fascination with Dilai Dalai's sutras and scribbled a detailed map to Dilai Valley and wrote directions to the cave where he had seen the original scrolls.

"The cave is near Gopal's village, Gazabha," Merschel said. "The original scrolls are in the cave. But be discrete! There is always someone meditating in the cave year-round, and they have taken a vow of silence. Be careful not to disturb them."

I probably put in twenty or more extra hours a week working for the Colonel after my *satori,* and by the following Fall I had saved enough money for the trip to India.

Or so I thought...

Mark closed his journal and went to O'Doul's for lunch. The last entry he had made in the journal nagged him during lunch:

"I had saved enough money for the trip to India. Or so I thought..." He couldn't get the debacle of losing all his money in New Orleans out of his mind. So, he went back to the beach and journaled about that:

It was hard saying good-bye to my family and friends in Missouri, but I thought I had saved enough money for the trip to India and looked forward to the adventure. I even found work as a steward on a riverboat, The Alton, in St. Louis.

Prostitutes and gamblers added spice to the trip down the Mississippi. We docked in New Orleans around nine on a Friday evening. The timing seemed perfect. The French Quarter was lit up and roaring with excitement. I felt like a fox in a hen house with all the beautiful friendly women walking the street and Dixieland music streaming from the bars. I had heard wild tales about "N'awlins" from the gamblers and crew on the Alton, and as I registered for a room in Miss Lily's "boarding house" on Bourbon Street, the tales came alive.

The seductive red velvet decor inside Miss Lily's, oil portraits of nude women on the walls, and musk incense in the lobby got my blood moving. Laughing and cussing came from the four back rooms on the ground floor. Men and women shuffled in and out of the rooms, looking drunk.

I was ready for a hot time. All the pent-up anxiety of leaving the safety of my home boiled inside me. Meditation and India were nowhere in mind. Only sex was. I was chewing at the bit for whatever Sin City had in store.

When I finished registering at Miss Lily's front desk, the clerk disappeared behind a curtain.

Suddenly, a pretty crimson-haired, fiery young tart in a slinky red silk dress walked in the front door. She looked around furtively, walked up to me and asked, "Looking for fun?"

Startled, I said, "You Miss Lily?"

"I am if you want me to be," the redhead purred. "Would you like to buy me a drink?"

"S-sure," I stuttered, "I'm Mark."

The redhead laughed and shook my hand. "Camille. Not from here, eh?"

"Missouri, and you?"

"Tonight, your room," Camille said confidently. She nodded towards the bar and said, "A bottle or two of champagne would be nice."

The rest of the story is painful to think about. That night was Lust Heaven, drinking champagne and fucking Camille four times. But hell would have been better than the miserable state I found myself in when I woke up at noon. I had a terrible hangover and found that Camille was gone, and along with her my backpack with all my money!

I quickly dressed and ran down to the front desk. A buxom old blonde with too much makeup and a mean disposition was talking with a young new female clerk behind the desk.

"I've been robbed!" I yelled. "Camille, where is she?"

The old blonde looked puzzled. "No Camille here. I'm Miss Lily. Are you staying another night?"

"No Camille?" I replied. "Redhead, red dress, green eyes? You know, Camille! Camille! Where is she?"

Miss Lily looked suspicious. "Sorry, no one here by that description. Are you staying another night?"

"No, I've been robbed! By Camille!"

Miss Lily turned to the clerk and warned, "See what you have to deal with? Still want the job?"

The woman nodded affirmatively.

"Look," I said, "I don't know what's going on but I'm going to get the police!"

Miss Lily said, "I have no way of proving what you say is true or not, but check-out time is eleven and you're an hour late. I'll let that oversight pass considering your situation. Please leave now or *I'll* get the police!"

I had everything I owned on me, so I ran to the police station, stormed into the front office during the Saturday morning chaos, and spotted the Chief, who happened to be one of the old men I had seen the night before in Miss Lily's!

I ran to the Chief and shouted, "I've been robbed at Miss Lily's! Last night I saw you there, too!"

The Chief nonchalantly said, "Miss Lily's? Not me, son."

Then he handed me a piece of paper. "As you can see, we're busy here. Write out your complaint and we'll look into it when we have time."

I saw that the Chief had a gold wedding band on. Perplexed, I blurted out, "What the hell's going on? A wedding ring! Son of a bitch, you're married!"

The Chief glared at me with contempt. He pointed to the crowded, noisy cells in the back and snarled, "How'd you like to spend the rest of your life there?"

I shut up and wrote down my complaint. Before I left, the Chief told me that I'd better not come back, or I'd be thrown in the clink. As I walked out of the police station, I turned around and saw the Chief throw my complaint into a trash can.

I strode up and down the streets of the French Quarter the rest of that rainy day, frustrated, angry, soaking wet, broke, hungry, hungover, and condemning myself for my stupidity.

That night I huddled like a wet slug underneath a bridge near the edge of town until I finally fell asleep exhausted.

I woke up early Sunday morning with a sore throat and throbbing head. I thought, *Camille used me, but I used her, too - to relieve my fear about being a stranger in a strange land. What am I doing? I deserve this. I'm a fake, fraud, phony. This India trip is foolish because I'm a fool, drinking and fucking till I pass out and waking up broke and abandoned, alone!*

Alone! That's what this is all about: being totally alone under this bridge in the pouring rain! Some meditator! I'm pissed and miserable. What am I doing? Who am I fooling? I had it good back home! Just go home!

•

Mark looked up from his journal and gazed at the vast expanse of the San Francisco Bay before him. Then he closed his journal and walked back to O'Doul's.

CHAPTER 18

In the twilight just before sunrise, the full moon glowed like a luminous pearl in the vast azure sky above Bodhi Cave. Leela's friends, Bol the Bear, Sol the Eagle, and Tol the Turtle sat at the mouth of the cave and watched Leela sleep.

"Doesn't she look peaceful?" Bol said.

"So beautiful," Sol agreed.

Tol nodded. "Looks like she's having sweet dreams."

It was true. Leela was dreaming about a time when she was five years old, one year after she and her family had moved from Gazabha to Srinagar to develop the new ashram by the Jhelum River. Leela's dream ended, and she fell into a dreamless sleep.

Tol, Sol and Bol sighed.

"Sweet dreams," mused Tol the Turtle. "I remember when I was four, too, being nuzzled by my mother."

Sol the Eagle said, "I remember when I was just an egg lying in a nest."

Bol the Bear said. "I remember being a sperm going to a picnic with my father and coming back to our den with my mother."

Just then Leela stirred in her sleep.

Bol said, "Let's go before she wakes up."

Leela's three friends quietly slipped away.

The orange morning sun rose slowly above the horizon and fell on Leela's face. She opened her eyes and smiled at the sun.

Thank you, beloved...

Suddenly, Leela heard the scratching of footsteps on the stone path below the cave. Then she heard someone climbing the rope ladder.

Leela tossed off her yak rug, crawled ten feet to the edge of the cave and leaned over. She saw Pathen climbing up the ladder. Once at the top, Pathen pulled himself up and over and sat on the ledge.

"So early?" Leela asked.

Pathen nodded, then turned and gazed at the full moon glowing on the horizon. "I couldn't sleep, and the hike here is beautiful in a full moon."

Leela studied Pathen's face. He had just hiked eight miles, but oddly enough, his tearstained face looked pale. "But you're back so soon," Leela said curiously.

Pathen sighed. "Uh, Punya and I had a big fight after I got home yesterday. I need to talk with you."

Leela nodded. "How long have you been with her?"

"A year. When I got home yesterday, I told her I was thinking about going to be with Satchitta. She started crying, yelled at me, then ran away, said she never wants to see me again."

"Did you talk with your parents?"

"They don't want me to go either. Can we just talk?

"About...?"

"Same as before: I'm finished with love, want to be with a Master again."

Leela laughed. "Sorry, but when you stop breathing, you're finished with love, not before."

Pathen shrugged his shoulders. "Well, maybe... but love comes and goes; it's painful! I've been with lots of other girls, too, but with Punya it's different, deeper, and it hurts when she rejects me. I don't like being dependent on her. I want to be happy for no reason at all."

"Don't we all," Leela agreed. "But what do you expect? She probably felt hurt, too, when you said you were thinking of going to Srinagar."

Pathen's eyes widened. "Um... true. Damn! Leaving someone you love is painful."

"Feeling attached then separating can be painful," Leela said.

Pathen threw his hands into the air in frustration. "What to do?"

Leela shrugged her shoulders. "Do? I had the same - well, I don't know if it's the same - but I had similar feelings when Satchi and Asanga were imprisoned. Satchi almost died. I was miserable. And Asanga and I had connected so deeply. It was horrible! But that's why I'm here: to stick it out and see if being alone can help free me from attachment to the mind."

Pathen glanced at the bowl of dried apricots beside Leela.

"Mind if I have a few?" he asked.

"Sure."

Pathen nibbled on a few apricots and mused, "Aloneness..."

Leela sucked on a dried apricot then said, "Well I don't know about you, but I am alone, was born alone, will die alone. No pie-in-the-sky-God or after-life fantasy to keep me company.

"I remember once Satchi was approached by two old men who asked about *sannyas*. One old man said, 'My friend and I have known each other for seventy years and we have always argued over whether or not there is a God. I believe there is a God, and he believes there is no God. Now we are thinking about surrendering to you as *sannyasins*. But then, won't we be making you into some sort of God, too?'

"Satchi asked the theist, 'Have you seen God?'

"'No,' the old man answered, 'but I believe God exists.'

"Then Satchi asked his atheist friend, 'Have you looked all around the universe and seen that there is no God?'

"'No,' he said, 'but I believe there is no God.'

"Satchi laughed and said, 'Then there's no problem, no argument! Both of you are believers! Neither of you know from your own experience whether or not there is a God!'

"The two old men looked at each other and laughed.

"Satchi said, 'I am here, real, but there is no one inside me to believe or not believe, no one here to relate to. Any relationship with me can only be on your part. Look into my eyes - empty, and totally content in my aloneness. You have both been in a relationship with an imaginary God or no God in order to avoid aloneness. I know from my experience that aloneness is a positive state of being, but you don't. Surrendering to me is surrendering to your aloneness, inner reality. I'm only a mirror of your potential destiny.'

"Both old men nodded and became *sannyasins.*"

Pathen nodded. "But you... you left Satchitta..."

Leela shrugged her shoulders. "I was unconscious, jealous of Satchi. He tried to point that out to me the day I left him, but I was in too much pain to listen."

"Jealous?"

Leela nodded. "Like most kids, I developed a mind, ego. But as I grew, I had listened to Satchi long enough to understand that who I am is not the mind; my nature is consciousness, the watcher of the mind, the consciousness that's in everything: rocks, trees, birds, people.

"I spent lots of time in nature when I was little, sitting silently by Dal Lake, in the forests, trees. I felt a silent communion with nature, when there was no 'I', only nature was, and I was one with it.

"But the older I got, the less I felt this sense of oneness. And without my noticing it, my ego became more and more crystalized: 'I'm creative! I'm mischievous! I'm fearless! I'm sexy! I'm independent! I! I! I!'

"I was showered with love and freedom but became more and more suffocated by my ego, alone on my 'Island of Self'. Emotionally, I remained immature because I tried to reclaim the feeling of oneness through sex, through.... Well, I tried *everything* to get it back! But basically, I tried to find a permanent feeling of oneness on the outside and it can only be found on the inside! I tried to do the impossible and failed! I felt guilty because I failed, and jealous of Satchi because I could see he was fulfilled! I felt a oneness with him as a child, tried to be him on some level, and failed. Natural. I had to leave him to find myself."

"I see what you mean," Pathen said. "I'm still looking on the outside - Punya or Satchitta - for something that can only be found on the inside."

"It's natural." Leela said softly. "As a teenager I unconsciously still wanted what every child wants: someone to take care of me, be responsible for fulfilling my needs, give me undivided attention and protect me. I hadn't matured emotionally. I wanted others to fulfill my childish demands. And unconsciously, I felt jealous of Satchi because I could see that he had what I felt I lacked: a permanent connection with Existence. Leaving Satchi was a reaction, but natural because of my unconsciousness."

Pathen looked puzzled. "But why haven't you gone back?"

Leela took a deep breath and replied, "Other Sanes in our Srinagar ghotul and newer sannyasins mirrored my jealousy of Satchi by being jealous of *me*, 'The Master's Daughter'! I resented it, could see their phoniness, and became mischievous and revengeful. My beautiful world began to shrink, so slowly that I didn't notice that it was happening, like a frog sitting comfortably at the bottom of a pot of water, then the water's heated to a boil slowly, slowly, until the frog jumps out to save its life!

"Being around Satchi only made me thirstier to experience the oneness I unconsciously felt I'd lost, the oneness I'd experienced as a child with Nature. I left home to break the psychic umbilical cord with Satchi and the others. Natural! It's taken me years of meditation and contemplation to realize this, but I did realize it, and now I feel like a mountain of guilt and jealousy has been lifted from my heart. I could go back, but what's the point now? I know there's nowhere to go but inside myself to rediscover oneness... for me.... For you... you have to decide for yourself what's best."

Leela studied Pathen closely, then said, "You know, there's another way to be with Satchi here now, until you know for sure what you want to do."

"Another way? What's that?"

"Watch the Master breathing you inside the navel."

Pathen squinted. "Watch *what?*"

"You know the *Vigyan Bhairav Tantra* meditations you practice during Zahn?"

"Yes."

"Well, during all these years I've been physically away from Satchi, I discovered a variation of one of the meditations which help me feel connected to him: I watch Satchi breathing me in the navel."

Pathen's eyes lit up. "Oh, I get it! It's not me who is breathing; Existence is breathing me, even when I'm asleep! I've been with Gopal. Gopal and Satchitta are one with Existence, so imagine that the Master is breathing me in the navel!"

"Not only imagine, FEEL THE ENERGY!" Leela offered. "Then let go of the feeling. Just be and watch. Want to play with the meditation before you go back?"

"Yes!"

"Okay then," Leela said, "close your eyes... that's right... and focus your awareness between your eyebrows... that's right.... Focus your awareness in your third eye center in the middle of your forehead, and be there for a few minutes..."

Leela closed her eyes, and after a few minutes continued: "Now... remaining aware at your third eye... expand your awareness to include your heart… that's right… and slowly allow your awareness to expand to your navel center.... Just be there and watch...watch...

Leela was silent for a couple of minutes, then continued:

"Remember a time when you were with Gopal and feel each breath... that's right... feel each breath, in and out, as if the Master is breathing you: the Master is breathing you in the navel.... Relax and watch the Master breathing you..."

Leela closed her eyes and meditated with Pathen. They sat watching their breathing in the navel center for almost an hour. Then Leela opened her eyes and saw that Pathen was blissfully gazing at her.

Leela smiled and said, "It's up to you what to do or not do about being with Satchi. Meanwhile relax, be patient, then decide."

Pathen stood, held his hands in *namaste,* and said, "That was helpful. Thanks. I've got to go back now."

Leela nodded then closed her eyes.

Pathen climbed down the ladder to the path and hiked back to Gazabha.

CHAPTER 19

A power struggle had existed for the previous five hundred years between two pseudo-religious sects in Northern India, the Loofah and the Lunni. The Holy Gooft of the Loofah sect was a nervous, controlled prelate named Doedoh. The Archdoppe of the Lunni sect was a pious, effeminate ecclesiastic named Dildoh. As the High Honchah of Rufism, Rakan saw it as his duty to destroy both sects and solidify his empire.

This was the situation as fifty Hassas nervously awaited Rakan's entry in the large soundproof office next to the torture chamber in the basement of Rufus Temple. This "Tomb Room" was Rakan's central meeting room.

Suddenly the door slammed open and Rakan burst inside. Asanga slowly walked in behind him, dressed in the full-length black hooded cape of the Hassas.

The senior Idioyks were shocked and stared silently in amazement. For the previous six years, Asanga had been guarded by four armed Hassas around the clock inside his luxurious living quarters in Rufus Temple. This was the first time that anyone had seen him outside his quarters.

Now twenty-three, Asanga had taken a meditative attitude towards his imprisonment. He had surrendered to his impossible situation and taken the attitude that Rakan was playing a game, albeit a fanatical one. Asanga decided to enjoy the game as played and remain open to the fate that Existence had bestowed upon him, while embracing the freedom he felt privately in meditation. Over time, Rakan became convinced that Asanga had outgrown his rebellious ways and was ready to embrace his destiny as the future High Honchah of the Rufus religion.

"What are you gawking at?" Rakan roared. "Asanga is finally ready to join us, aren't you, son?"

Asanga nodded.

"Sit down!" Rakan demanded. "We have work to do."

The Hassas scrambled to their chairs around the long rectangular wooden table, and Rakan plopped down in the tall wooden replica of the Holy Commode.

Rakan turned to Asanga and said, "Sit on my right."

Asanga sat on the chair to Rakan's right. Rakan remained standing and said, "Asanga will get no special treatment. He will go through the same seven-year advanced Idioyk training as everyone else. Understand?"

The Hassas all bellowed, "YES!"

Rakan looked at the empty chair to his left, and demanded, "Where is Visiog?"

"He's, ah, coming," Snakji said.

Several of the Hassas snickered, for they knew that Visiog was late was because had been in the arms of one of the Vestas he was "training".

"Silence!" Rakan roared. "Okay then, your report, Snakji."

Snakji was a short, fat, bespectacled, scholarly type whose attention to detail and workaholic fervor greatly impressed Rakan. He rose to his maximum sitting height in his chair, puffed his chest, and read his report: "Due to increased demand for our new Stealtz Rifle, we--"

"The improved Brunswick Rifle imitation?" Rakan asked.

"Yes," Snakji said. "Due to the increased demand, twenty of the orphans from Bardhaman and Purulia have been reassigned to work at our weapons factory in Bandipur. Three young boys died from toxic fumes in our Bijbiara factory. The Sir Henry Lawrence assassination was successful. The--"

"Lawrence, the lout!" Rakan exclaimed. "Meddle in my affairs, eh? Maegin did the trick?"

"Yes," Snakji confirmed, "no one suspected poison."

Rakan scowled. "Too bad maegin didn't finish Satchitta when we had him in chains."

Snakji's face flushed. "Our chemists have perfected maegin since then, but rumor has it that Satchitta's health has been deteriorating steadily."

The door slammed open again, and Visiog bolted into the room sweating profusely under his black hooded cape. He saluted Rakan - "AGOK AL-HOOPALOO!" - and sat next to him.

Rakan nodded. "AGOK AL-HOOPALOO! What did you discover?"

Visiog pulled the black hood off his bald head and said, "About this so-called Lunni saint, Faykin: it's possible that his tomb is 96 kilometers from here, in Pahalgam. The building there is like one here in Srinagar, a circular wooden structure that encloses a grave. It's painted white and blue and has a carved wooden door and window panel with the Star of Measles filigree. According to our experts, the inscriptions in the tomb are in Sanskrit and indicate that Saint Faykin is buried there. He lived to be over a hundred years old. The site has two levels: a chamber below street level with the actual body of the deceased, and a mock grave built on top."

"Like the Taj Mahal," Snakji offered.

"Yes," Visiog continued, "the grave is laid out in the east-west direction facing Brooklyn - a Lunni tradition. And another thing: the Phalagam tomb has footprints in it of someone wearing galoshes, etched in stone in the sepulcher."

The Hassas gasped!

"Then it *is* Saint Faykin!" Snakji exclaimed.

"It's possible," Rakan said. "Lunni scriptures state that Saint Faykin died from water torture in Egypt at age 33. If Faykin survived the water torture and lived in Pahalgam to be over a hundred years old as the inscriptions on the tomb indicate, we have a scandal on our hands! No death from drowning in Egypt, no resurrection, no saint! Let's run with this one. How can we spin this in *The Beacon?*"

The Hassas mumbled aloud among themselves, then Rakan shouted, "QUIET! Visiog?"

Visiog squinted, then said, "Loofah militants disagree with these facts. They insist that the tomb in Pahalgam is that of a local Loofah saint, Saint Baykin, that there is no one called Saint Faykin buried there."

"Ah-ha!" Rakan exclaimed. "Then simple! Divide and conquer! Pit the Loofah and Lunni against each other! They're used to it! Snakji, get another supply of Stealtz Rifles to the Holy Gooft and Archdoppe."

"Doedoh and Dildoh?" Snakji asked.

"Yes," Rakan said, "and no paperwork. We must keep our hands clean. Now about Satchitta..."

Rakan paused, his face red with anger at the thought of Satchitta. "I want him out of the way! You say his health is failing. Maybe the maegin we put in his food did the job in the long run. But I want him gone as soon and as cleanly as possible - no traces of foul play. Any ideas?"

This was Visiog's opportunity to offer the plan that Lloyd had whispered in his ear. "Let me handle this," he pleaded. "I have a plan."

"Okay," Rakan said, "Sakaj Day is in two days. Let's talk about your plan then. We have so much to do to prepare for the celebration. Now I want a rough draft of an article on the alleged Saint Faykin tomb site on my desk by tomorrow evening. Headline: 'SAINT FAYKIN OR SAINT BAYKIN'S TOMB?' Dress it up with the usual: reliable sources report this and that. Include photos of the Pahalgam tomb. That Englishman, Rodgers, is your man for that. Also, Visiog, I read your article on Jakal and

Bezuhl's birthdays. Rubbish! Rewrite it and have it on my desk tomorrow morning - *or else!* Got it?"

Sweat immediately broke out on Visiog's forehead. He felt a lump in his throat as the word, "Yes," quietly slipped out his mouth.

Rakan pounded the table, then stood and shouted, "AGOK AL-HOOPALOO!"

The Hassas jumped up in unison and shouted, "AGOK AL-HOOPALOO!"

The meeting ended.

CHAPTER 20

O'Doul's Pub was packed to the gills and the audience clapped loudly as Mark and four other musicians stepped down from the stage after playing their first set.

Mark laid the house guitar in its case behind the stage then sat at a table with the other musicians. Casey set two pitchers of beer and five steins on the table, then said, "That got everyone dancing, men!" He turned to Mark and said, "Heard you're leaving. We'll miss your music."

Red Hughes raised his stein in a toast. "Here, here! To Mark! It won't be the same without you." Everyone drank up.

"That goes for me, too," rang a familiar voice behind Mark.

Mark turned around and saw Ethan, looking clear-eyed and clean-shaven in loose-fitting beige pants and a white hemp shirt.

Ethan seemed subdued and contrite. "I came to apologize. I was an ass. Time in the clink gave me time to think."

"You were in jail all this time?" Mark asked.

"Yeah."

Mark didn't need to ask why.

"My dad found me in jail, and I told him how sorry I was. He bailed me out and hired me back," Ethan said. "I stole your money because I was jealous of you. Can you forgive me?"

Mark was surprised at how sober Ethan looked. "Sure, I forgive you. What do you mean, jealous?"

"I've been around the world many times, thought I was hot stuff, but somehow I didn't feel that way around you. I don't know what you have but I want some of it and don't know how to get it."

"Forget it," Mark said. "I got lucky, lived with folks who helped me mature a little."

"Bloody hell, that's what I mean!" Ethan exclaimed. "You don't even know what I'm talking about! Anyway, thanks. I just came from *The Queen* and need to get some sleep. See you tomorrow?"

Mark stood, hugged Ethan, and said, "You bet. We have another set to do. See you tomorrow."

Ethan smiled, nodded, and left O'Doul's.

Mark and the other musicians had the whole pub dancing by the time their second set was over. By midnight Mark was sound asleep in his hammock on *The Emerald Queen.*

The sun shone brightly when Mark met with the Captain, Ethan, and the other thirty-five ragtag crew members on deck the next morning.

"We're sailing tomorrow!" Captain McDonegal bellowed. "No fighting during the trip or you'll walk the bloody plank! Agreed?"

The whole crew shouted, "Agreed!"

"From now on, settle your differences with me," the Captain said. "Ethan's on probation. Right, Ethan?"

Ethan lowered his head and nodded.

"Good," the Captain said. "Everyone has the rest of the day off! Back here by midnight or you're off the ship. *The Queen* is royalty and I aim to keep her so. Back by midnight or else!"

Everyone whooped and slapped each other's shoulders, then each sailor headed in a different direction.

Mark walked to the beach, sat on the sand, and continued to journal about losing all his money in New Orleans:

•

After spending a miserable Saturday night huddled underneath a bridge near the French Quarter in New Orleans, the next morning I got up and lumbered over to Miss Lily's. The same female clerk who had been at the front desk on Friday night was there. I asked her if she had seen Camille.

"I remember you!" she snapped. "Miss Lily never heard of Camille. You best leave or I'll call the police."

Then I went across the street to the Blue Note Cafe and sat by the front door to beg for food with my empty hat on my lap. That's when I first saw "Rev", as Dilai Dalai Jai priests are called.

Reverend Saul Beecher was an ordained minister of the Dilai Dalai Jai, the religion that had been formed over the centuries around Dilai Dalai's sutras.

I had heard rumors about Dilai Dalai Jai priests but had never seen one before. I couldn't believe my eyes! Walking towards me was a clown in full regalia: a tall, gangly clean shaven middle-aged man wearing colorful spangled tights and a flowery polka dot shirt and carrying a thick copy of the Dilai Dalai Jai scripture, "The Word".

"The Word" had evolved over the thirteen centuries after Dilai Dalai's death. It included Dilai Dalai's 99 sutras and 1,284 pages of interpretations of the sutras by pundits and self-proclaimed messengers of Dilai Dalai.

In my wretched state I must have looked like a potential lamb for Rev's flock because he stopped right in front of me. Rev temptingly jangled some coins in front of my nose then spoke with a pious air of arrogance: "The Lord giveth and the Lord taketh away."

"Right now, 'giveth' would be just great," I said in a weak, raspy voice.

Rev puffed out his chest and rebuked, "Have you no humility, young man?"

I looked down at my empty hat and said, “What I have is a headache. And I’m hungry.”

Rev straightened up and looked at me. “What you need is guidance.”

“Okay, where’s the bread and coffee?” I said sarcastically.

“You pitiful wreck!” Rev sneered.

“I agree,” I said. “Look at me.”

Rev opened “The Word” and quoted Dilai Dalai: “Every human is doing the best they can to be conscious, to spiritually wake up here now, including me.”

Then he closed the book and said, “You can be forgiven your trespasses. Repent and come with us. Some friends and I are going to the West Coast to bring the heathens there his message.”

“Whose message?” I asked.

“Dilai Dalai’s.”

“What’s his message?”

“Freedom. Freedom to believe what Dilai Dalai wrote.”

“Believe? Where’s the freedom in that?” I asked.

Rev changed the subject. “Repent your sins and you’ll be saved. I see a flicker of understanding in you. My mission is to bring souls like yours to the light.”

A small crowd gathered, and several folks cried, “Amen! Amen! Amen!”

Rev was on a roll. He rose to his full height, clutched “The Word”, raised his eyes towards the cloudy sky, and fervently prayed: “Yes, Dilai Dalai, one of your flock has gone astray. Forgive him. I see a glimmer of light in him, and I implore you to help him.”

Then Rev held out “The Word” and said, “It’s up to you now. Put your hand on ‘The Word’. Repent and come with us to the promised land. We have twenty-one wagons. Seven of us are devotees of Dilai Dalai. We have plenty of food and provisions.”

The word “food” perked my interest.

Rev looked ridiculous. But I did too. I felt as deluded as he looked in his silly clown outfit. Fact was, I was angry, hungry, and lonely as hell, far from home and destitute in New Orleans.

I thought, *Rev wants to use me as a pawn in his religious game. Why not use him to get to the West Coast?*

So, I put one hand on "The Word", closed my eyes, and said, "I repent my sins."

Then I opened my eyes and looked up at Rev. He was beaming with pride and said, "With Dilai Dalai as my witness, your conversion is complete. Join us humble servants on our journey to the promised land and help us spread 'The Word' to the distant shores of our great country."

I stood and said, "I'm ready when you are."

Rev dropped a few coins into my hat. "Great!" he said, then furtively looked across the street at Miss Lily's.

"I've, ah, got to go now," he concluded. "I'll meet you here in an hour and take you to our camp."

I shook Rev's hand. "Thanks!" I said, then turned and walked into the Blue Note Cafe, which was just opening.

As I closed the front door behind me, I looked across the street and saw Rev walking into Miss Lily's.

I thought, *This is going to be interesting!*

"What are you doing with that fool?"

I turned around and saw an elegant black man with a white goatee and fuchsia beret sitting by a piano. He had spoken with an African accent, had the presence of royalty, and was dressed in a brightly colored African robe, brown pants, and leather sandals.

He smoothed his robe and continued, "Shakespeare wrote, 'The devil cites scriptures for his own purpose.' I dig Dilai Dalai's sutras, too, but that man's a fool. Moralists like him fuck sheep then forgive them. What are you doing with that hypocrite?"

I walked over to him and said, "I'm broke and hungry."

"Ripe for the pickin's!" the black man said. "Feed 'em then bleed 'em - that's how the pseudo-religions get converts. Anyway, that's your business, son! The name's Obo."

"Mark," I said, and shook his hand. "Never heard the name, Obo."

"Common name in the Central African Republic."

I nodded towards the piano and asked, "You play?"

He glanced at the piano and smiled. "Meet Lucy," he said. Then he pointed to three other black musicians at a table near the bar. "Leroy, Henry, Cornbread. Men, meet Mark."

The three musicians came over and shook my hand.

"So how did you end up with Rev?" Obo asked.

"I got here Friday from Missouri," I said, "had everything stolen at Miss Lily's. Tried to get the police to help me. One of the cops, the Chief, had been at Miss Lily's in plain clothes the night I was there. But at the police station I saw that he had a wedding ring on. He was married and wanted no part of me."

Cornbread, an old, bearded country gentleman in blue overalls, became animated. He waved his arms around and slapped his thigh. "Dat's right!" he crowed. "Dat's de situation, yes, yes! Da fox was in da henhouse, and da fox got beat up in da henhouse, yes, yes! And dat Chief ain't gonna help da fox 'cause he be a roosta who shudda been in his own henhouse but wasn't! No, no! He was in de other henhouse *wit* da fox! Yes, yes! Dey brothas in crime bidin' their time! Yes, yes!"

Everyone roared with laughter!

I looked at Obo and said, "Rev said he'd meet me here in an hour."

"What you do with him is your business," Obo said.

Cornbread asked me, "You play Blues?"

"Guitar," I said. "Don't know Blues."

"Over here," one of the other musicians said. He walked over to a guitar case, opened it, and brought a new Martin guitar over to me.

"Wow!" I said, as he handed me the guitar. I marveled at the exquisite workmanship and said, "Beautiful."

"Now the Blues," Cornbread said, "is a feelin', yes, yes, a feelin'! Most Blues begin, 'Woke up this mornin'. Ain't that right, fellas?"

The other three musicians laughed and chimed, "Yes, yes!"

"Blues is not about choice," Cornbread said. "No, you stuck in a ditch, you stuck in a ditch, ain't no way out. Yes, and you can have the Blues in New York City, but not in Hawaii or anywhere in Canada, no, no. And breakin' your leg at work ain't the Blues. But breakin' your leg 'cause a gator be chompin' on it is! Yes, yes!

"So, Mister Mark, do you have the *right* to sing the Blues? The *right!?*

"You do if you older than dirt, you blind, you shot a man in Memphis, or can't be satisfied. Then you can sing the Blues!

"But you don't have the right if you have all your teeth, were blind but now see, dat man in Memphis lived, or you *can* be satisfied! Yes, Yes!"

Everyone laughed. Obo said, "Mark looks like he's had enough Blues for today. Let's try something inspirational. How about 'Rise Above the Storm'?"

The other musicians said, "Yes."

I quickly tuned the Martin guitar while the other musicians grabbed their instruments: a standing bass, saxophone, and clarinet. Then the four of us joined Obo as he played piano and sang his upbeat Dixieland tune, "Rise Above the Storm":

There's a light pure and bright
shining in my heart.
Feeling my heart opening,
I rise above the storm.

Have you seen the new woman
whose heart is free and strong?
She has courage to speak the truth.
She'll rise above the storm.

Have you seen the new-born man
whose heart is true and warm?
His love is stronger than the sword.
He'll rise above the storm.

There's a storm of ignorance
raging in the mind.
Through the wisdom of the heart,
we rise above the storm.

There's a light pure and bright
shining in our hearts.
Feeling our hearts opening,
we rise above the storm.

We played tune after tune for an hour. The music and singing cheered me up. When Rev came back, I hugged and thanked all the musicians. Then Rev and I rode on his horse out of town to a camp beside Lake Pontchartrain.

As we rode there, I thought about the promise I'd made to myself at Floyd's funeral - "No more lies" - and a tinge of guilt rushed through my veins. True, I had lied to Rev about wanting to be saved, but survival was the only truth I knew in the moment, so I let the guilt be so and settled into being a penitent debaucher on his way to salvation. That was the truth of that moment, and the moment was all I had…

At Rev's camp by the lake, I saw twenty-one wagons full of ragged idealists, escaped criminals, deserted soldiers, and frightened women and children. I shared a wagon with a matronly old woman and three married Dilai Dalai Jai couples, including Rev and Rachel, Rev's beautiful young raven-haired wife. The Dilai Dalai Jai men were dressed in different brightly colored clown outfits, and the women in violet low-cut robes and peacock-feathered headbands.

Our wagon train left New Orleans the next morning. For the first few weeks I kept to myself, meditating as much as possible. I avoided Rev and his constant sermons and made myself busy by helping with the cooking, cleaning up, and other chores.

For some reason Rachel kept flirting with me the whole way, even in front of Rev. I could tell Rev didn't like it, and I didn't want to jeopardize my free ride to the Coast, so I tried to ignore Rachel. But she persisted: the more I tried to withdraw, the more she came on to me.

Finally, one evening when we were camped at Horsehead Crossing near Girvin, where the Pecos and Rio Grande rivers meet, I felt like writing a letter to my family and friends back home. I didn't have any writing paper, so I asked Rachel, "Do you keep stationery?"

"At first, yes," she said, "then when I get hot and wet and start to climax, I go completely wild!"

I was so stunned I left her and got paper from Rev.

I was attracted to Rachel, too, maybe because she was a little cuckoo. During the previous weeks she had said crazy things:

"See your reflection in a dewdrop. Paint the dewdrop. Burn the painting. Give the ashes to a snail."

"You can't have everything. Where would you put it?"

"I started out with nothing, and I still have most of it."

Rachel was crazy in a sane way. Rev on the other hand, was drunk most of the time and ignored Rachel the whole trip.

What made the trip tolerable were the nightly laughing meditations, when all the Dilai Dalai Jai's and me sat in a circle and laughed for an hour, then sat in silence for a while.

Also, for one hour after lunch each day the Dilai Dalai Jai women and men performed their sacred "Cha-cha Ceremony". They formed a circle and spun yo-yo's up and down on a string while chanting, "Dilai cha-cha, Dalai cha-cha, Jai! Pass the mustard!"

Our wagon train took the Texas-California Cattle Trail through Houston, San Antonio, El Paso, Tucson, Yuma and finally San Diego. It was no picnic. The War with Mexico was broiling on both sides of the Trail, there were constant rumors about Indian massacres, and good water was hard to find at times.

One full moon night on the eastern edge of the Sonoran Desert, I was climbing over a four-foot ridge in a dry creek bed when a big rattlesnake bit my right calf.

I hobbled back towards the wagons and met Rachel on the way. "What's the matter?" she asked.

I grimaced. "Rattler bit me."

"You have a knife?"

I pulled my hunting knife from its sheath.

"Give it to me, take off your pants and lie down," she said.

I took off my boots, pants and underwear, then put a stick between my teeth and said, "Go ahead."

Rachel cut open the fang marks, sucked the venom out, and spat it on the ground. The pain from the procedure was so bad that I almost cracked my teeth biting the stick.

When Rachel finished draining my wound, she washed out her mouth with water from my canteen. Then she asked me to take off my shirt and hand it to her. I did and Rachel ripped strips of cloth from the shirt to make a tourniquet to stop the bleeding.

I was left there sitting nude.

Rachel paused and looked at my body for a few moments. Then she threw back her long black hair, bent over, and slowly, seductively, began to kiss the thigh that had been bitten. Then she kissed my *lingam* and within a minute I was inside her and we fucked like wild pigs.

After we finished, we lay there gazing at each other.

Rachel chuckled and quoted Dilai Dalai:

"Banana peels are made for wedding aisles. What does law have to do with love?"

She waited a moment for me to respond, but I said nothing.

"Rev and I are finished," she said. "You must know that by now."

I kept silent.

Rachel fidgeted a bit, then quoted Dilai Dalai again: "'Love is overwhelming if it's love, over-the-hill if it's business.' It's been business between Rev and me for quite a while now."

I knew where Rachel was going with this kind of talk, so I didn't reply. I stood up, pulled my trousers up, buckled my belt, gathered up my shredded shirt, and said, "Thank you for this. You may have saved my life. I'm sure you and Rev will work it out. But we'd better get back to camp before it starts raining."

Rachel frowned. "Is that all you have to say?"

I shrugged my shoulders, then reached out to give Rachel a hand to stand up. But she just sat there and said, "No, you go on. I've got some thinking to do."

I left Rachel and went back to camp alone. Rachel and I never got together again during the rest of the trip, and the closer we got to San Diego, things got nastier and nastier between her and Rev. They argued all the time.

After our wagon train settled near a beach that first sunny afternoon in San Diego, I knew it was time to be on my own. With a clear sense of wholeness, I walked up to Rev and Rachel as they sat by their wagon among the other Dilai Dalai Jai's.

I looked at the pair and said, "I've got to talk with you two... alone."

Rev and Rachel looked surprised. "About what?" Rev asked.

"I need to talk with you... alone," I repeated.

They stood and walked with me to the shoreline.

As the three of us stood watching the waves breaking on the beach, I remembered one of Merschel's heart meditations - Speaking From The Heart.

I put one hand on my heart, looked back and forth between Rev and Rachel, and said, "I'm sorry for using you to get to the West Coast."

Rev was dumbfounded. "*Using?* S-sorry? For what?"

I took a deep breath, looked into Rev's eyes, and said, "I needed to get to the West Coast, so I pretended to repent my sins and believe in things you believe in, so you'd take me with you."

Rev's eyes flashed in anger. *"Son-of-a-bitch!* You--"

Rachel stopped Rev short by jumping between him and me. She stared at me and said, "Go on, say what you have to say."

"I can't pretend anymore," I said. "Heaven and hell I've lived, don't need to believe in salvation. Belief is irrelevant. It's fine with me if you want to believe whatever. Not my business. I'm sorry if I hurt you, but I've got to go now."

Rev still looked shocked, but Rachel's eyes softened. "What are you going to do?" she asked sympathetically. "You have no money."

"Doesn't matter," I said. "Got this far without any money."

I tapped my heart and added, "Seems all I really need is this. I'll get to India somehow."

Rev's eyes widened. *"India?* Why?"

"To be with a live Master, Gopal. In New Orleans and during our trip I realized how spiritually asleep, how unconscious I am. At least now I know it. I need to be with a live Master. But anyway, good-bye, take care, and thank you."

Rev and Rachel seemed too stunned to say anything.

I hugged them, then walked north along the beach.

Telling the truth was so healing that I felt like I had bathed my soul in the ocean. So I did: I walked several miles up the beach to a cove, stripped naked and waded into the sea. I swam around for a while and let the chilly saltwater wash away layers of guilt and grit.

Two days later, three Mormon soldiers let me join their wagon, and together we worked our way north, finding odd jobs along the way and taking two months to reach the Sierra Mountains. The soldiers and I parted company in the Sierras, and I found work for five months as a logger with a rough-neck crew. Then I went off on my own and made a bundle panning gold near Sutter's Mill. All the rest of my trip till now seems like some dream, a dream I hope to wake up from in India.

•

Mark put his journal down and stared at the San Francisco Bay. Then he laid on the warm sand and took a nap.

CHAPTER 21

Lloyd puffed on a big Havana cigar in the Zebra Lounge on Cloud Nine. He shook his head and said, "Clown outfits? Yo-yo ceremonies? The Dilai Dalai Jai priests and nuns have turned playful sutras into a fanatical religion!"

Bunny sipped on her margarita. "Sad," she said. "Hueng Tsiang was dilly-dallying, just having fun when he wrote the sutras. Now the folks who are clinging to Dilai Dalai's words have used the sutras to postpone going in to discover their being.

"But how was Hueng Tsiang to know that would happen? Most pseudo-religions have evolved the same way. Some mystic *experiences* spiritual Truth inside; then later, people who have no experience of Truth misinterpret the mystic's words and create moralistic dogma to live by which has nothing to do with spiritual Truth! Stupid!

"Lao Tzu said, 'The truth that can be said is not the Ultimate Truth.' But his words weren't turned into a religion because he spoke in paradox, the language of mystics. Intellectuals couldn't understand him so they couldn't exploit his words and create an organized religion."

Lloyd nodded. "At least Mark is looking for the real deal, a live Master."

Bunny nodded. "Even with an alive Master there are no guarantees. Remember what Gopal said? 'Even an alive Master can't give you Truth. Truth is untransferable. One must discover Truth inside oneself. And so-called holy scriptures are only words, dead symbols. Truth is an alive phenomenon.'"

Lloyd nodded. "Being in the presence of an alive Master can inspire Mark to go within himself to discover Truth. Reading dead scriptures gives one the illusion that one already knows the Truth and the search for Truth stops there. One remains childish - emotionally, mentally and spiritually immature.

"Anyway, I agree with Gopal," Lloyd concluded. "But the path to Truth is dangerous. Who wants to let go of their ego?"

"Right!" Bunny concurred. "Like the lifetime you and I were disciples of Mahananda and contracted the Bee Colony Collapse Disorder."

"Horrible disease!" Lloyd said.

"Horrible!" Bunny agreed. "I remember I went to a doctor for a cure. He told me to take off my clothes. I was only eighteen and a little shy, so I asked him to extinguish the candle in the room.

"'Don't be shy,' he said, 'after all I am a doctor.'

"But I insisted, so he squashed the flame with his fingers.

"After I took off my clothes in the dark room, I asked him, 'Doctor, where shall I put my clothes?'

"'Over here,' he said, 'on top of mine.'"

CHAPTER 22

Leela's day had been pleasant: meditating before dawn; soaking in the hot springs near Bodhi Cave; eating, singing, dancing, painting; an afternoon nap.

An hour after sunset, Leela was silently walking along Khidir Creek in the full moon light, when suddenly she felt an intense pressure within her chest and could hardly breathe. She felt an overwhelming sense of dread, and within minutes the pressure became unbearable. She felt as if all her life energy became condensed within her chest. Fear gripped her and she sat down on the bank of the creek to compose herself.

For almost an hour Leela sat in shock by the side of the gurgling creek, wondering, *What is happening?*

She couldn't tell. All she knew was that she was very afraid, and wondered, *Should I go to Gazabha for help?*

She wanted to escape, to hide from herself somehow. Her mind beat like a loud drum. Thoughts of hopelessness, futility, and suicide attacked her from every direction. The mind wanted out - *End it now!*

She felt crazy, mad, but was too afraid to move.

With whatever awareness Leela could muster, she closed her eyes and saw a small flame in the middle of her chest. Over the next hour the flame kept getting smaller and smaller. The totality of her awareness went inward towards the flame, towards the tiny inner light and away from the outer madness of the mind. She felt like she was dying, and the inner flame felt like it was the only thing keeping her alive.

The flame *was* life!

She felt totally helpless; the fear was so intense. For protection she held on tightly to the sandalwood necklace, the *mala*, that her father, Satchitta, had given her when she became his sannyasin.

Then slowly, slowly, something relaxed, shifted, as Leela accepted the pain, gave space to the pain she experienced. She let go and consciously surrendered to dying. Meanwhile, the flame had dwindled down to the size of a pinhead. She lay back on the damp grass and took a deep breath.

Okay, whatever is happening is natural somehow... let go...

Time crept by as she lay waiting for death's clammy hands to finish her. After a while she opened her eyes and looked up at the full moon.

Ah, beloved, thank you.

Leela felt herself trembling, as if she could go mad any moment, felt that each precious breath could be her last. Then she remembered one of Satchitta's discourses in which he described a similar experience of his own before he became enlightened.

She found consolation in the Master's words: "You are not the mind, not the body or feelings. At your center is a witness - consciousness - of all you experience. Just watch..."

As much as humanly possible, Leela just watched each moment crawl by in what seemed like an eternity. Meanwhile, she languished in her state of dread. Somewhere deep inside she understood that what was happening was a mysterious energy phenomenon, and that the mind was useless in this situation. The most she could do was to watch the moon creep slowly across the night sky and let go, watch what was happening inside herself.

As twilight began to appear, Leela felt a shift inside. Her whole life flashed before her eyes. She saw people she had loved and thought how she was helpless to reach out to them and how much she missed them - hopes, fears, longing. With tears streaming down her cheeks, she visualized her dead body lying by the creek.

Finally, Leela could no longer just watch and be with her sense of dread. Her navel center was in absolute turmoil. And as she had done many times, she expressed the truth of the moment. She rolled over and began to pound the ground with both fists.

She screamed aloud, "HELP ME, SATCHI, HELP! I don't want to die now! Help me!"

Over and over, she screamed until she felt drained and collapsed face down on the grass.

Minutes later, Leela turned her head to the right and saw Bol the Bear, Sol the Eagle, and Tol the Turtle about ten feet away. Then she heard Satchitta's strong clear voice coming from the direction of her animal friends: "Let go, beloved! You are safe in my hands. Let go!"

Leela was shocked!

What the...? Satchi?

Instinctively she sat up, took a deep breath, and watched her animal friends disappear into the twilight.

Leela blinked her eyes. *Were my friends real? Did I hear Satchi's voice?*

But whatever the truth was, Leela couldn't deny that the energy within her had changed after her catharsis.

Twenty minutes passed and Leela realized that something had shifted. A smile slowly spread across her face. She stood and let out a deep belly laugh.

Then another... and another...

With a song of gratitude in her heart, Leela took a few steps to the edge of the creek, knelt, scooped up handfuls of cold water, and splashed her face again and again. Then she stood, took a deep breath, and noticed that... *Huh...?*

Leela blinked... *What...?*

She felt... *bliss* is the only way to describe it: a soft, silent, subtle, tranquil energy that had come in the back door and now enveloped her whole Being. She closed her eyes and heard a voice inside say, *Heaven,* and that's how she felt: in *Heaven*.

The sun slowly rose above the horizon and Leela heard birds singing more beautifully than she had never heard them before. A soft luminosity shone everywhere. She looked around and saw, *felt*, the energy in the trees shimmering, in the flowers laughing, in the birds celebrating. The sky glowed violet and orange, all very natural, the way things are, the way she was... natural...

She wondered, *Am I... enlightened?*

She walked around like a child in wonder, sometimes skipping along, touching the delicate flowers as if for the first time, delighting in the song of Existence. She danced through the rest of the day like a newborn fawn innocently prancing through the forest.

That evening Leela sat at the mouth of Bodhi Cave and watched the sun dip behind the mountains to the West. Soon the bliss began to fade, and slowly, slowly, she settled into her "normal" self: relaxed, present and open...

She began to understand that the bliss had come and gone like a gentle breeze, and that during this time, she had been identified with the bliss, felt she *was* the bliss, just as she had been identified with agony before that.

The agony and bliss came and went and I'm still here!

Who is this "I" who was watching all this?

Who was seeing, watching the agony and the bliss?

Leela didn't know...

She had heard Satchitta say that enlightenment is a state where the experiencer and the experience, the knower and the known, are one - no duality. But she knew that SHE had been there identified with the agony and bliss! The observer and the observed had been separate. She knew that the "I" was still there and felt her heart longing to dance without the heavy chains of the "I". She felt a longing for the dancer to disappear into the dance.

She took a deep breath and felt she had no understanding of who she really was. Again, she felt utterly helpless, and thought, *Maybe this Prasad situation is too much!*

She took several deeper breaths, then crawled over to a pile of yak rugs, slipped between several rugs and fell asleep.

Bunny and Lloyd hovered above Leela, watched her curled up, a long lump under the furry rugs.

"Leela's doing great," Lloyd said. "It's hard being dis-identified with what we experience. Choiceless awareness is so subtle."

Bunny glanced at the pile of rolled-up yak scrolls next to Leela. She quoted one of Dilai Dalai's sutras:

Love is a rose with thorns,
consciousness the fragrance."

"True," Lloyd said, "it's hard not to prefer a rose flower over its thorns.

Bunny nodded. "Preference invites paradox. Everyone wants to live long, but no one wants the pain and limited lifestyle that comes with old age."

Lloyd laughed. "We want to be rich but don't want the hassles that come along with being wealthy."

"Um," Bunny mused, "there are two ways to be rich: to have all you want or to be content with all you have."

"There's a third way," Lloyd offered.

"What's that?"

"Not knowing the difference."

Bunny laughed. "Not knowing works."

CHAPTER 23

You can usually tell a man's nationality by introducing him to a beautiful woman. A proper Englishman shakes her hand, a Frenchman kisses her hand, an American asks her for a date, and a Russian writes to Moscow for instructions.

Rakan had no nationality. True, he had declared Sakaj Day to be an Indian national holiday, but only in name was it national. For Rakan it was a day to celebrate himself.

On this particular Sakaj Day, Rakan waddled through the throng of cheering Rufites outside Rufus Temple, and silently congratulated himself on creating such an ardent following for his misogyny.

The ruckus crowd was proof that he had pulled the wool over not only his own eyes, but over the eyes of everyone outside the temple.

Everyone in the crowd, including Rakan himself, was wearing traditional Sakaj Day faux donkey ears and tail, and horse blinders - two pieces of leather tack that restricted their vision to the rear and side.

Rakan stood at the top step to the temple, turned, and gave one last humble bow. Then he triumphantly entered and saluted the cheering throng of Rufites inside.

"AGOK AL-HOOPALOO! Hee-Haw!" Rakan shouted.

"AGOK AL-HOOPALOO! Hee-Haw!" the crowd roared.

"Hee-Haw!" Visiog cried, as Rakan passed by him.

"Hee-Haw!" Rakan replied. "Follow me."

Visiog followed Rakan down the stairs to the basement of the temple and into the Tomb Room.

"Hee-Haw!" was the traditional greeting during Sakaj Day. According to Jakal, the founder of Rufism, Sakaj was the day - the June full moon - that God, Rufus, took the form of a Divine Donkey, "Sakaj", and declared Jakal to be the "Head Honchah" of Rufism.

Jakal's grandson, Rakan, knew how to throw a party, and Sakaj Day was the *creme de la creme* of his parties. There were balloons, cake, ice cream, and donkey costumes for the kids, as well as the promise of heaven after death for the grownups.

The word around Kashmir was that the kids got the better part of the deal.

Visiog opened the door and bowed as Rakan entered the Tomb Room. The large rectangular conference table spanned the center space of the room. The table was covered with a black silk cloth which hung to the floor. Rakan adjusted the tablecloth then sat on the replica of the Holy Commode.

He waved to Visiog to sit down, then got right to the point. "Tell me what you've come up with for Satchitta," he said.

Visiog sat to Rakan's left and exuberantly explained in detail his plan for Satchitta's demise.

Rakan had been worried all week. The plan to eliminate Satchitta was going to have to be a clever one because Satchitta had not stepped outside his ashram since Rakan had imprisoned him six years before. Now there were twelve-foot walls around the ashram and a dozen armed security guards patrolling the walls day and night. In addition, as corrupt and controllable as the Srinagar police were, Rakan knew that the general populace would not tolerate another outright attack on the ashram. In the long run such an attack would undermine the public's false sense of trust that Rakan and his ancestors had so carefully cultivated. But by the time Visiog had finished his presentation, Rakan was convinced that the plan that Lloyd had whispered into Visiog's ear was brilliant.

"Superb! So be it!" Rakan declared. "Make it a priority. The precautions you described are necessary for the plan to be foolproof."

"I'll get my team together," Visiog beamed.

"Hee-Haw!" Rakan shouted.

"Hee-Haw!" Visiog replied.

The two left the Tomb Room.

Ten minutes later, Gollash, the young Idiyok with one wooden leg and a green glass right eye, quietly crawled from under the low-hanging tablecloth. He slipped out the door, limped back to Asanga's room and explained the essence of Rakan's plan to Asanga.

Bunny looked down at the scene and huffed. "I hope you know what you're doing," she said to Lloyd. "Rakan is a mean customer."

Lloyd looked surprised and said, "You don't think my plan is great? Rakan and Visiog seem to think so."

Bunny knitted her eyebrows. "Maybe..."

Lloyd looked into Bunny's eyes. She had that, *Maybe a little mischief is in order* look in her eyes.

Lloyd recognized the look and said, "Uh-oh. What are you up to?"

Bunny chuckled. "Nothing... much..."

Lloyd winced. "Nothing means something. Come on, spill the beans."

"Well-l-l..." Leela drawled, "suppose.... No, follow me!"

And Leela immediately whisked down to a deserted garden behind Rufus Temple. Lloyd followed her.

"Here we go!" Lloyd exclaimed once they landed.

Bunny rolled around in the dirt and immediately her body became flesh and blood and her gown material.

"You, too," she said to Lloyd.

Lloyd followed suit.

"We're human again... till this dirt rubs off," Bunny said. "See those two donkey outfits over there? I don't know who left them there, but suppose we just, you know, *borrow* them..."

"I knew it!" Lloyd protested. "Look, we're walking on thin ice with the Angelic Council. If we--"

"Relax!" Bunny insisted. "Take a risk. Even a turtle gets nowhere until he sticks his neck out."

Then she pulled down the low neck of her gown and exposed her full bosom. "How do you like them apples?"

Lloyd's eyes almost popped out of his head. "More like melons. A convincing argument. What'll we do?"

"Come on," Bunny said.

Bunny and Lloyd put on the donkey costumes, replete with faux donkey ears, tail and horse blinders; then Lloyd followed Bunny as she entered Rufus Temple and stood at the back of the large auditorium.

Rakan sat on the Holy Commode at the altar in front of several thousand Rufus faithful, delivering his standard Sakaj Day sermon.

"And I say to you, brethren," he bellowed, "trust in Rufus and the kingdom of Hoopaloo will be yours eternally. Repent your sins and--"

"WHO'S RUFUS?" Bunny shouted from the back.

Rakan was startled. He strained to see who had caused the disturbance, then regained his composure and tried to continue: "Repent your sins. Offer up your--"

"WHO'S RUFUS?" Bunny shouted even louder. "DOES RUFUS SLEEP IN THE NUDE?"

Rakan was flabbergasted. "Wha...?" he said weakly. No one had ever interrupted him before! He motioned to the Hassas to deal with the disturbance.

Then he tried to go on: "I, ah--"

But Bunny shouted even louder: "IS RUFUS A SHE? OR IS RUFUS A HE *AND* A SHE? IF SO, WHO WEARS THE PANTS IN THE FAMILY?"

The children and teenagers in the congregation laughed hysterically, but Rakan and most of the adults were outraged.

Lloyd saw ten scary Hassas hurtling through the crowd towards them. He grabbed onto Bunny's costume and dragged her out of the temple and around back to the garden before the Hassas could reach them.

Bunny and Lloyd quickly removed their faux donkey ears, tails and horse blinders, slipped out of the costumes, jumped into a fountain to wash off the dirt, and were immediately transformed into a transparent angel and devil just as several Hassas ran into the garden, and staring wildly around, saw no one.

The two rebellious deities safely transported themselves back onto a cloud. Lloyd turned to Bunny and said, "I know who wears the pants in our family," and kissed Bunny on the lips.

Bunny snuggled up to Lloyd and said, "I still don't feel anything. But... want to play doctor?"

CHAPTER 24

Mark woke up from an afternoon nap on a Bay beach and remembered that he was leaving for India the next day. He picked up his journal, walked to Dr. Chang's office and around to the back. He found Wo Lin alone in her shack weighing herbs. Wo Lin turned around and saw Mark standing in the doorway. She nodded and smiled.

Mark smiled and walked up to her. "Hello and *Ciao*."

Wo Lin's eyes widened in surprise. "You coming or going?"

Mark laughed. "Sometimes I don't know if I'm coming or going."

Wo Lin laughed. "You go to India?"

Mark nodded. "Yes. I love you."

Tears welled up in Wo Lin's eyes. She hugged Mark and they stood in silence until her tears subsided. Finally, she dropped her arms from around Mark's waist, pulled a hanky from her apron pocket and blew her nose.

"I rove you, too," she said.

"No tooth hurtee?" Mark asked.

Wo Lin chuckled. "No tooth hurtee.

Mark took a deep breath, turned and walked away.

Relieved, renewed, he strolled to his bank, withdrew ten pounds of gold coins and put them into a leather bag. He walked to a beach where he saw the Emperor and a young black woman kneeling in the sand.

Mark was flabbergasted. The Emperor had changed drastically since he'd last seen him. Gone was his ragged old military outfit. His hair and beard had been neatly trimmed, his eyes sparkled brightly, and new light brown hemp pants and shirt hung loosely on his solid frame.

The Emperor looked up. “Mark... Lisha. Lisha... Mark.”

Lisha looked up from the large figure she had been drawing in the sand. Her long black braids and bright violet robe framed her lovely face.

“Hello,” she said with a resonant Brazilian accent.

Mark was immediately stuck by the joy which shone from Lisha’s large brown eyes.

“Hello,” he said, then pointed to the figure in the sand.

“What’s that?”

Lisha shrugged her shoulders. “Don’t know.”

The Emperor laughed. “She never knows what she’s going to draw or paint till she does it.”

Lisha asked Mark, “What does it look like to you?”

Mark studied the figure in the golden sand. “A bridge, sort of. But I’ve never seen one like it.”

Lisha smiled. “A bridge? Okay, a bridge.”

The Emperor looked across the bay at the north shore, then back to the south shore where they stood. With a sweep of his left arm, he pointed back and forth between the two shores and said, “A golden gate suspension bridge from this shore to that!”

Mark looked at the vast expanse between the two shores, then at the figure in the golden sand.

He smiled and said, “Anything’s possible.”

“Anything?” the Emperor asked. “Then join us.” He took Lisha by the hand and began to walk towards a group of nine sea lions lounging by the shore.

Mark followed.

The Emperor and Lisha sat down on the sand near the sea lions and closed their eyes. The mammals closed their eyes as well. They all sat in silence for a minute or so.

Mark wondered, *Are the sea lions meditating?* Somewhat amused, he sat silently with the group and closed his eyes.

The crashing of the waves...

The scent of the salty air...

Soon they were all one with Nature...

The group sat for almost an hour, then the sea lions slowly waddled into the ocean and disappeared.

Lisha, the Emperor, and Mark all opened their eyes at the same time. Lisha smiled at Mark. She stood, and without a word, walked down the beach.

Mark and the Emperor sat in silence for a few moments.

"I'm leaving tomorrow," Mark said to the Emperor. "I'll miss you. Please take this." Mark handed the Emperor a leather pouch containing gold coins.

"What's this?" the Emperor asked. Then he opened the pouch, saw the coins, and his eyes widened.

"For another Shout House or two or three," Mark said.

The Emperor smiled. "Will do. *Bon voyage!* India, eh? Gopal? Anyway, here, I have something for you, too."

The Emperor pulled a leather pouch from his mail bag and handed it to Mark.

Mark looked inside and saw a pipe, some dried green leaves, stems and seeds. "What's this?"

"Pifka, marijuana, whatever you want to call it. To loosen you up. You're somewhat of a spiritual idealist, wound a little tight. A little silliness on your serious sacred journey might help."

"Silliness? What do I do with this?"

"Smoke it. Try it once, then again if you feel to. It'll give you another perspective on the mind, that's all. But don't smoke it till you get to India, okay? I don't want you sliding off the ship somewhere near Japan."

"What about Lisha?" Mark asked.

"What about her?" the Emperor asked.

"Is she the one?"

"The one what?"

"For you?"

"For me or for you?"

Mark laughed. "I love you, man."

"I love you, too," the Emperor said.

The two friends hugged, then Mark turned around and walked towards O'Doul's. He still had the rest of the day to enjoy before he had to be back on board *The Queen* and he wanted to say goodbye to a few other friends.

Halfway to O'Doul's, Mark rounded a street corner and bumped solidly into a man walking the opposite way. Both men fell backwards onto the muddy street. Mark sat up and was shocked to see... Reverend Beecher in rags, sitting in the mud in front of him!

Gone was Rev's clown outfit. He was dressed in a ragged dark blue cotton shirt and pants. His hair was matted, eyes bloodshot. He was a shell of his former self.

"Rev!" Mark said.

Rev squinted. "Mark?" he said weakly.

"What happened to you?" Mark asked.

Rev hung his head, paused, then replied, "She left me."

"Rachel?"

"Yeah. She said she had had enough bullshit."

"Bullshit?"

Both Rev and Mark stood up. "Yeah," Rev said. "When you left that day on the beach, what you said, the way you said it, got to both of us. Rachel especially. She told me she fucked you. But her leaving wasn't about that. We both knew the fraud was over, imitating somebody else's idea of what spirituality is and isn't. All our doubts bubbled up and we were afraid, scared to death what to do about it. Preaching had been our livelihood. I started drinking even more than before, crocked every waking moment.

"Rachel crumbled in her own way, too. Not by drinking, but by blaming me for the mess she'd gotten herself into. She never looked at her own self - and she *knew!* She knew the fraud was over, but she looked the other way, away from herself and towards me. I was her scapegoat. Then she caught me with another woman. Yeah, Dilai Dalai Jai is strict about monogamy, but I've been with other women, many times in fact."

"I saw you go into Miss Lily's," Mark said.

"You saw? Rachel saw, too, in Los Angeles. Then she left me. And look at me now."

Rev studied Mark carefully. "And look at you!" he said. "You look great! A grown man now. You were a young buck when I met you in New Orleans."

"I was in as bad a shape as you are now," Mark said.

Rev nodded. "Um... yeah."

"Meditation helped," Mark said. "It's a mystery how it works, but somehow I got here okay and tomorrow we sail for India."

"Tomorrow? We?"

"Yeah," Mark said. Then he paused and said, "Wait a minute. Maybe we could use another hand onboard. You ever work on a ship?"

"No. You think there's work for me?"

"Maybe. Come on, Rev. Let's see what the Captain says."

"I'm Saul now," Rev said.

"Okay, Saul, let's go."

Mark and Saul made their way to the wharf where *The Queen* was docked and walked up the gangplank.

"Who's that?" Captain McDonegal asked when he saw Mark with a stranger.

"Saul," Mark said.

"Saul Beecher," Saul said, extending his hand to the Captain. "Mark said maybe you could use another hand and I thought--"

"Think again!" the Captain interrupted. "Sorry, mate, but I over-hired, and you look terrible! Try another ship. Good luck."

The Captain looked at Mark and asked, "Done galivanting?"

"Yes," Mark said.

"Then give Ethan a hand with those crates. Vedant will have dinner ready soon." And the Captain disappeared below deck.

Mark turned to Saul. "Sorry."

"I feel better seeing you again," Saul said. "Maybe there's hope for me, too."

Ethan walked over to Mark. "Who's your friend, mate?"

"Oh," Mark said, "Ethan, this is Rev. I mean, Saul."

Ethan shook Saul's hand. "You looking for work?"

"Yes," Saul said. "The Captain said no more hiring."

"That's so," Ethan confirmed. "Try… um, wait a minute! Mark, didn't you say that Katie had some work for you at O'Doul's?"

Mark's face lit up. "Right! Saul, meet me at O'Doul's Pub around seven tonight and I'll put in a good word with Katie O'Doul for you. She might have some work."

"Great!" Saul said. "See you at seven. And thanks!"

"No problem," Mark said.

"Bye," Saul said. "Nice meeting you, Ethan." Then he hugged Mark and left *The Queen.*

Mark watched Saul make his slow way off the wharf, then helped Ethan carry crates of fruit, vegetables, and other supplies below deck.

That night at O'Doul's, Mark and Saul went up to Katie, and Mark said, "My friend, Saul, here needs some work. Great guy, hard worker. Came West from New Orleans with me."

Katie smiled, shook Saul's hand, and said, "If Mark says so, hired!" Then she gazed at Saul's shoddy condition and asked,

"Need a bath and a place to stay? There's a cot in the shed behind the pub."

Saul gave a whoop! "Thank you, Katie, Mark!"

Mark nodded to Katie and said, "You're a sweetheart."

"You're the sweetheart!" Katie said. "He'll work out fine."

The rest of the evening was bittersweet. A good time was had by all, and some sad good-byes were exchanged. Ethan played washboard in the band with Mark and the other musicians, and Saul danced until he was exhausted, and then went to sleep in the shed behind the pub.

Mark and Ethan were back onboard *The Emerald Queen* by midnight. The next morning, they sailed for India.

CHAPTER 25

The morning after Leela's *satori* at Khidir Creek, she hiked to Gazabha and met with the Inner Circle. She described her experiences of the previous day and concluded, "I'm frustrated. Yesterday was so amazing and today I feel have no understanding of who I really am. Maybe I... I don't know...." and she hung her head.

Shanti said, "Relax, beloved, you're doing great. There's no pressure to remain a Prasad. But again, your frustration comes from your desire to be enlightened and not being there yet."

"Maybe you need a lover," Rajen joked. "That'll take your mind off enlightenment!"

The Inner Circle laughed.

But Leela remained serious, somber. "A lover? I don't think I could handle it. But maybe--"

"THE GOOSE IS OUT!" Rajen shouted.

Rajen's sudden outburst struck Leela and everyone else like lightning! The whole space vibrated. Everyone took a deep breath and within seconds the tension in the room dissipated.

Leela stared wide-eyed at Rajen.

Finally, Shanti said, "I love that koan about the goose."

"Me, too," Leela said.

Rajen narrated the Zen story:

"Zen Master, Nansen, was asked by the official, Riko, to explain the problem of the goose in the bottle.

"Riko asked Nansen: 'Master, if a man puts a goose into a bottle and feeds him until he is full grown, how can he get the goose out without killing the goose or breaking the bottle?'

"Nansen clapped his hands loudly and shouted, 'RIKO!'

"'Yes, Master?' Riko asked with a start!

"'SEE!' Nansen shouted, 'THE GOOSE IS OUT!'"

Leela smiled and took a deep breath.

"Thank you," she said. "I needed that. When I'm watching the mind I'm disidentified from the mind. The goose is already out! But I forget."

"We all do," Rajen said. "Now what?"

"I feel better talking with you all," Leela said. "If it's okay with everyone, I'd like to go back to Bodhi Cave. Mind if I give the cave another name? How about 'Home'?"

Everyone in the Inner Circle laughed and nodded.

Shanti looked around and saw that there was consensus. "Go with our blessings. We're here whenever you need to talk."

"Thank you," Leela said.

Then she got up and walked out of Buddha Hall with the full intention of remaining a Prasad for the next five years.

But Existence had other plans for her...

CHAPTER 26

Bunny and Lloyd were shooting a game of pool on Cloud Nine. Bunny deftly stroked the cue ball into the 12-ball. The 12-ball rolled into the side pocket.

"Mark is on his way to India," Lloyd said.

Bunny nodded. "9-ball in the corner pocket."

Then she lined up her next shot. "And Leela seems settled in Bodhi Cave."

She pocketed the 9-ball.

"Nice shot. You're on today," Lloyd said. "Remember Leela longing for the source of love inside? We had trouble with that."

"True," Bunny said, "that lifetime in Fez, Morocco.

"We were in love and trying to have a baby, couldn't for a long time. Then who was it? That doctor who advised us to wait for the right moment to do it?

"11-ball in the corner."

Bunny pocketed the 11-ball.

"Yeah," Lloyd said. "When we finally got pregnant, my buddy asked me how we finally did it. I said, 'We were having a romantic candlelight dinner with fine wine and soft music, when suddenly our hands met, we looked deeply into each other's eyes and both of us knew! This was the right moment! We threw off our clothes and made mad passionate love then and there on the dinner table!'"

"'Wow!' my buddy said.

"'Yeah,' I said, "but we'll never get service at that restaurant again.'"

Bunny, meanwhile, had pocketed another ball.

"8-ball in the side pocket," she said.

She pocketed the 8-ball.

"Game," she said.

CHAPTER 27

India is an ancient country. In many parts of this beloved land, there is an ancient smell as well. People have reproduced like rabbits and have dumped human waste into stormwater drains which run like putrid streams through the cities. They are the dirtiest parts of most metropolitan areas.

Mid-nineteenth century Srinagar was no exception.

The main storm drain that ran through Srinagar passed through twelve acres of wasteland next to Satchitta's ashram. This land was a key to the plan that Visiog had laid out for Rakan in the Tomb Room.

Immediately after that initial meeting with Visiog, Rakan paid an exorbitant price for 27 acres of land that included the twelve acres of wasteland which bordered Satchitta's ashram. Visiog's plan for Satchitta's demise was set in motion.

Rakan lay oiled and rubbed down in the Tomb Room of Rufus Temple as he gloated over Visiog's "SAINTS WHO LIVED AMONG US" article in *The Kashmir Beacon.*

"Brilliant!" he cried to himself. "You did it, Visiog!"

The article's flowery portrayal of Rakan's two ancestors, Jakal and Bezuhl, lifted his spirits. He asked one of his Vestas to go fetch Visiog and she did.

Within minutes Visiog entered the Tomb Room.

"Would you like some good news?" Visiog asked.

"Of course," Rakan said.

Visiog puffed out his chest. "Archdoppe Dildoh and Holy Gooft Doedoh are at each other's throats after our articles on Saint Faykin's tomb in *The Beacon!* Twenty-two Loofahs were slaughtered by Lunnis near Pahalgam this morning. Hundreds more were injured.

"Doedoh wants revenge and has ordered a thousand more Stealtz rifles. The first lot we gave him was free. Now he's willing to pay."

"Wonderful!" Rakan said. "I want a front-page article in the next *Beacon* with all the gory details about the massacre. Also, the 'SAINTS WHO LIVED AMONG US' article was the best you've done."

Visiog blushed. "Thank you."

"Now," Rakan continued, "we need to start construction on the food bank once the storm-water drains are cleaned up and the bamboo and gardens are planted. 'The People's Bank' will be our gift to the poor of Srinagar. Who is most reliable to run the food bank?"

Visiog pulled on his beard as he considered the question.

Finally, he said, "Gollash."

Rakan pictured one-eyed Gollash limping around on his wooden leg. "Gollash? Hmmm... Asanga's aide... a talented man, and reliable now. So be it. "AGOK AL-HOOPALOO!"

"AGOK AL-HOOPALOO!" Visiog shouted.

CHAPTER 28

Dawn's light shone weakly though the mist as Mark gingerly hiked up the rocky trail to Bodhi Cave. He stopped and shifted the heavy backpack on his shoulders. Fluffy white snowflakes fell onto his nose and melted. He took three quick steps, twisted his right ankle on a slippery rock, then bent down and felt his ankle.

Ouch... slow down... Then he straightened up and limped as he continued his hike up the steep incline towards the cave.

Soon he stopped again, reached into his left leather jacket pocket and pulled out the paper with Merschel's directions to the mysterious cave. He unfolded the paper and studied the details for a moment. Then he heard faint drumming and an angelic voice singing in the distance.

He felt goosebumps.

Wow...

Enchanted, Mark continued the steady climb towards the celestial music.

Must be the meditator Merschel talked about. Don't disturb...

He limped along for a hundred yards; then as he rounded a bend, the drumming and singing suddenly stopped.

Mark, too, stopped... and waited...

...but nothing, the silence ever so poignant...

Mark hobbled around a bend and looked up towards the source of the singing. He walked another twenty yards then stopped and looked up to the right. Twenty-four feet above his head he saw a beautiful young raven-haired woman in a brown full-length cashmere robe standing at the mouth of a large cave.

The cave... the meditator...

Mark's eyes met with the woman's and chills went up his spine. With a wave of her hand, the woman beckoned Mark to come up. Mark waved back, then climbed the hemp-and-bamboo ladder to the cave. The woman reached out, took Mark's right hand, and pulled him up the last couple of feet to the cave's packed-earth platform.

Mark gazed into the woman's friendly opal eyes and felt like he was diving into a sea of emptiness. The woman's other features - especially her high cheekbones, full lips, and long black hair - looked like those of the nomadic herdsmen and villagers he had seen while he was hiking through the Swat Valley. But there was something different about this woman, something intriguingly Western. Her skin was lighter than the others', she was much taller, almost Mark's height, and she had a mysterious magnetic presence about her.

The woman smiled and glanced at Mark's foot. "Deva Leela," she said in English. "Um... your foot... please..."

With a wave of her hand, Leela motioned for Mark to sit down on a yak-skin rug near a small fire by the entrance. Mark sat and Leela unlaced his right boot and took it off. She closed her eyes and silently held his foot in her hands.

Ten minutes later Leela opened her eyes, smiled, turned around, sat on another yak-skin rug, and began to play a tabla and sing the same haunting mantra and rhythm that Mark had heard before.

Mark closed his eyes and listened.

Why was she singing and why did she introduce herself? he thought. *Merschel said the meditator was in silence.*

Leela's drumming and singing took Mark on a melodic journey into inner space. He was tired and the music felt like an invitation to go beyond sound, to relax into silence... so he did...

The next thing Mark knew, he was lying on his left side licking his parched lips. He opened his eyes and saw that Leela was gone! And to his utter amazement, his sprained right foot had stopped throbbing! The pain and the swelling were gone!

What the...? He couldn't believe it!

Mark put on his right boot, stood, and saw a brown leather bladder and Leela's tabla lying on the yak-skin rug which Leela had been sitting on. He picked the bladder up, shook it, and heard liquid sloshing inside. He untied the leather strap around the bladder's opening and sniffed the contents.

Water!

Mark's mouth craved the precious liquid, and he quickly drained the bladder. Then he walked to the mouth of the cave and looked around. Leela was nowhere in sight, so he turned and went inside the cave.

A large pile of 21 smooth rolled-up yak-skin scrolls lay near the back of the cave. He untied the leather string on one scroll, unrolled it, and looked at the calligraphy. The graceful Chinese calligraphy was unmistakable.

Dilai Dalai's original sutras!

Mark took a deep breath, rolled up the skin, retied the leather string, and placed the scroll on top of the others. Then he looked around and saw that there were a few other furry yak skins piled into what looked like a bed. There was also a large stash of dried fruit and nuts, a flute, a small pile of clothes, twenty exquisite paintings on rag paper, and art materials.

Mark walked back to the mouth of the cave and sat on a shaggy yak rug. It was still snowing lightly, but the sun was beginning to peek through the clouds to the west, and he gazed in wonder at the snow-covered valley below. Above, several large eagles majestically soared and surveyed their magical kingdom.

Ah, the silence...

Mark sat alone for more than an hour, sometimes getting up and pacing around the cave. Then he heard scraping on the footpath below. He looked around the bend to his left and saw Leela walking up the snow-covered path towards the cave. She came to the ladder, and like a graceful cat, swiftly climbed up to the platform.

She dragged a few yak rugs from the back of the cave to the front, and said, "You fell asleep, so I went to soak in the hot springs. These yak-skin rugs are your bed. You can stay if you'd like. We need to go to Gazabha tomorrow morning for a meeting."

Mark blinked his eyes. "Stay? Meeting?"

Leela nodded.

Mark's jaw dropped.

Leela nonchalantly shrugged her shoulders then sat on the yak-skin rug near the fire, closed her eyes, and remained in silence.

What does she mean? Mark wondered. *What's going on?*

My ankle has healed, and she invites me to stay?

Mark sat on another yak-skin rug, closed his eyes and meditated with Leela. Soon he felt a seductive cloud of forgetfulness, lay down and dozed off.

The sun was beginning to set when Mark finally woke up. He saw that it had stopped snowing. Leela sat on a yak rug to his left. The sinking sun peeked under a blanket of white clouds and shone on a yak-skin rug covered with a colorful display of dried fruit, nuts, and Winter flowers that Leela had laid out.

Amazed, Mark asked, "Your name, does it have a meaning?"

Leela nodded. "Deva means divine; Leela, play."

Mark smiled. "You speak English. Weren't you supposed to be in silence?"

"Who told you that?"

"Merschel... ah, Whistle."

"You know him?"

"Lived with him in the States. Do you know him?"

"We worked together in the tree nursery for a while."

"In Gazabha?"

"Yes," Leela said. "Did you go through there?"

"No, I took the trail around Gazabha, wanted to see Dilai Dalai's scrolls first. How did you learn English?"

"My mother," Leela said. "But if it's okay with you, let's enjoy our food in silence."

"Okay," Mark said, and they ate silently.

After the meal Leela stood up, stretched, then said, "I'm going for a short walk. Alone. Be back later. Make yourself at home."

Leela picked up the empty water bladder, tilted her head and smiled, as if to say, *So, you drank it all, eh!* Giggling to herself, Leela laid the bladder on a yak-skin rug, climbed down the ladder and disappeared.

Too much! Mark thought. *What's going on?*

He sat at the mouth of the cave and watched the sun disappear behind the snowcapped mountains in the distance.

Who is she...?

Doubts and more doubts spun around Mark's head for a while. Finally, a still small voice inside said, *Forget it! Enjoy!*

So, he sat silently at the mouth of the cave…

A few hours later Mark looked up and down the trail below the cave and saw that Leela was still nowhere in sight. The night sky was clear, and a full moon hung over the mountains. Mark yawned. The day before he had hiked thirty miles, including eight miles around the outskirts of Gazabha and up the steep path to the cave. He was physically and emotionally exhausted, so he slipped beneath the yak-skin rugs that Leela had laid out for him and fell asleep.

In the middle of the night Mark was awakened by the moon shining brightly on his face. He turned his head and saw Leela sleeping beneath another pile of rugs about five feet away.

Wide awake now, Mark sat up, wrapped one of the rugs around his shoulders, opened his backpack, took out his journal, stoked the fire with kindling, and began to write about what had happened after he sailed from San Francisco...

•

Amazing what's happened! It's winter now and I'm in India, living in the magical cave Merschel led me to! And Leela, the meditator in this cave, speaks English! And the original Dilai Dalai sutras are here on scrolls! And Leela invited me to stay here with her. I'm confused. Everything is happening so fast! Maybe things will get clearer at some meeting tomorrow in Gazabha.

Meanwhile, it feels good to write about what happened after I sailed from San Francisco...

The Emerald Queen left San Francisco at sunset in mid-June. As we left the harbor, Captain McDonegal shouted, "We have the winds at our back, lads, and we've got the fastest Clipper on the seas. West to the sunset and Tokyo, hi-ho!"

The Queen sailed sleek and fast. The winds and weather were ideal for sailing most of the way. I was sick as a dog the first three days out, but finally got my sea legs after that. Mostly I worked in the galley with Vedant, cleaning fish, preparing meals and cleaning up. Spent some time in the crow's nest, too. Incredible views!

Ethan was a different man at sea. He had a commanding presence as Quartermaster and joined Vedant and me when we had time to meditate.

We sailed into Mumbai in October, having stopped in Tokyo and Hong Kong, and in Singapore for repairs to *The Queen*. Ethan stayed sober the whole way.

Miracles happen...

The Captain was ecstatic when we anchored at Mumbai. On deck the first morning, he broke out the best rum I had ever tasted and lifted his glass for a toast: "Here's to the finest crew that's ever sailed the high seas! Hi-ho!"

"HI-HO!" the crew cheered, and we all drank up. It was a great feeling to be part of such a selfless crew.

During our trip I had mentioned to Vedant that the Emperor had given me pifka to smoke. Vedant said that when he was eighteen in India, a mystic named Vishnu Prem initiated him into using hashish and psychedelic mushrooms to experience states of consciousness higher than the sleepy norm.

Vedant quoted Vishnu Prem:

"Ordinarily religions and societies create insensitivity by setting idealistic moral standards which require a person to repress negative thoughts and feelings in order to maintain so-called peace, order and public safety. But that goal is impossible! Thoughts and feelings can't be repressed. When so-called negative feelings like anger and lust are repressed, like a jack-in-the-box they spring up and express themselves through war, destructiveness, and physical and emotional diseases. So, some people use drugs to feel sensitive again after their natural feelings have been repressed.

"Hypocrisy governs those societies. A repressive society or religion creates the need for drugs, then makes *faux* heroes out of police, social workers, politicians and priests who make respectable careers out of trying to cure the problems that taking drugs create.

"I support a few students to consciously use drugs to help them feel again and to explore different levels of consciousness. You are one of those students, Vedant.

"But using drugs should be like using a boat to cross a river. A boat is useful for crossing a river, but once you're on the other shore, do you continue to carry the boat as you travel further? No, you drop the boat and continue your journey without the burden of the boat.

"There are many rivers to cross on the journey to Truth. After crossing each river, you need to discard the boat you used to cross it if you want to travel onwards and upwards. And finally, when you discover Truth within yourself, you'll see that there was no outward journey at all, only an awakening to who you already are at the deepest core of your Being. Ego, mind, is the greatest drug. Meditation awakens you to a natural space within, which is beyond the mind."

Vedant continued: "After three months of experimentation with drugs and meditation, Vishnu Prem said to me, 'Now you've crossed the first river, Vedant, and you must choose. Do you want to continue using drugs to attain altered states of consciousness and possibly destroy your body in the process? Or are you ready to explore consciousness without the burden and damage that drugs do to your physical and subtle bodies? Are you ready to use the boat of Dhyana to cross the next river on your journey?'"

Vedant finished sharing by saying that he had chosen to drop the drugs and explore Dhyana.

Ethan came into the galley just as my conversation with Vedant ended. "Who's Dhyana?" he asked.

Vedant replied, "Dhyana? Meditation: being relaxed, watching the mind and feelings, trusting your consciousness."

"Whoa! That's a mouthful, Vedant!" Ethan said.

"Never mind," Vedant said, "you seem to enjoy meditating."

"True," Ethan joked, "keeps me out of trouble."

On deck the morning I left *The Queen* in Bombay, Vedant hugged me and said, "I'm sure we'll met again. Meanwhile, Ethan and I will carry on with meditation. Right, Ethan?"

"So far so good," Ethan said. "I'm not sure how it works but it does! Especially that chackra breathing meditation!"

"You look great," I said to Ethan. "Maybe we'll meet again."

Ethan teared up, then wiped his face and said, "Go before I get mushy!"

Vedant and I laughed, then I climbed off the ship.

I was excited, hopeful, when I first set foot on Indian soil. I soon discovered that I felt more at home in India than I did in the States. The pace was slower and most of the folks friendlier, even though I didn't speak a word of their language.

I went straightaway to the East India Company's Bank of Mumbai to open an account. Before I entered the bank's tall stately brown brick building, I gave an apple to a ragged, crippled little boy begging by the front door.

I took a deep breath as I entered the front door, confident and reassured that my journey to the feet of a live Master was finally nearing completion.

My banker's name was Mr. Dakshi. I handed over half of my gold coins and sat in a chair facing him. A lovely young Indian secretary in a violet sari placed a cup of chai on the desk in front of me. I sipped chai while I filled out the paperwork.

Dakshi asked, "Where will you be traveling?"

"I leave today for Gopal's ashram near the Swat Valley."

Dakshi seemed confused, then composed himself and said, "Oh, I see, Gazabha. I spent a month there listening to Gopal's discourses. Wonderful man, but *sannyas* wasn't for me. It must be different there now since Gopal left his body."

Dakshi might as well have hit me with a club! I felt one of the biggest shocks of my life.

I jumped up and shouted, "Left his *WHAT!*"

Dakshi fell back in his chair. Then he straightened up and said, "His... body."

Dakshi said no more. He could see from the shocked expression on my face that this was news to me.

Bad news.

"When, ah, did he leave his body?" I asked.

"Over three years ago."

I felt like I was drowning and couldn't breathe. My whole life flashed before my eyes.

Dakshi called over his secretary and said, "Please, more chai for Mr. Trimble."

The secretary poured chai into my cup.

After a few sips, I said, "I can't believe it. This, ah, changes my, ah, plans. Ah, thank you... I guess..."

Then I stood and said, "Good-bye, sir. I'll keep in touch by post."

"Please do that, Mr. Trimble," Dakshi said. "I wish you well on your journey... where-ah-ever that might be."

I left confused. I pushed away the beggars who swarmed around me outside the bank. In my gloomy tunnel-vision I was in no mood for beggars. Looking around, I felt lost on another planet: homeless again, with my condemning mind rattling on and on about how stupid I was for coming all the way to India to be with Gopal, only to find out he had been dead for over three years!

I hired a roofless rickshaw and rode around the city to cool off. The last of the monsoon rains began to pour down during the ride but I didn't care. The warm rain felt nurturing and washed away layers of confusion.

During the ride, I put my hands over my heart, watched the volcano of feelings inside and the beehive of people scampering around in the rain. Soon the chaos inside me subsided, and I went back to the bank and asked Dakshi if he could recommend a hotel for me until I figured out what my next step was.

"The Raja is an elegant hotel with an excellent courtyard and garden," he said. And with an amused look at my soaked clothing, he added, "I'm certain the hotel provides towels."

I walked out of the bank into the rain and closed my eyes. I tuned into my belly and heard a small voice inside say, "Go to Gopal's ashram anyway."

So, I took a rickshaw to the marketplace to purchase a boat ticket to Karachi - and all hell broke loose!

That's when I met Lalou.

•

Mark closed his journal and looked up at the night sky outside Bodhi Cave. He felt utterly exhausted. The fire in front of him was almost out. Once again sleep beckoned him to her velvety womb. He stood, walked over to the small pile of yak-skin rugs beside Leela, and crawled between the layers.

Good night, Leela.

CHAPTER 29

Satchitta sat on a cushioned high-back chair on the podium beneath the huge canvas and mosquito-net tensile structure enclosing Buddha Hall. Before him sat 297 disciples from 21 countries, all dressed in white robes and wearing sandalwood malas.

The Master spoke the final words of his morning English discourse: "You are all Buddhas, dreaming that you are this and that. Wake up!"

Just then a cuckoo sitting in a tree outside the hall made a hollow, plaintive call: "Coo-coo coo coo-coo-coo."

The disciples in the audience roared with laughter.

"You hear that?" Satchitta said with perfect timing. "Even the cuckoo knows she is already a Buddha! Enough for today?"

The disciples laughed even louder. The Master stood and lifted his hands in prayer. The disciples returned the gesture and within a few moments the laughter faded.

A tangible silence filled the hall.

The Master stood in *namaste* before the crowd of disciples as they bowed and touched their foreheads on the green-and-white marble floor. Three disciples in the Music Group began to softly play on the tabla, sitar, and flute. Taichia stood, walked to Satchitta, held his right arm and firmly supported him to walk out of the hall and back to his bedroom.

Due to his poor health, Satchitta spent most of his time propped up on pillows in his bedroom or soaking in a tub. He did, however, leave his bungalow to give morning discourses and evening Darshan, when he initiated new disciples.

The Master's white marble bedroom was his sanctuary. One wall of the bedroom was covered with semi-transparent mosquito netting, allowing a waterfall of light into the room. Beyond the netting was a lush garden, a jungle of flowers, a variety of deciduous trees, thick stalks of golden bamboo with flowering vines around them, and a cascading stream and waterfall which flowed into a pond. Several peacocks foraged for food around the pond. Two white swans swam among the lotus flowers on the eastern end, near a small white marble statue of Gautama the Buddha.

Inside, next to the Master's large, cushioned bed, was a writing table and two straight-back wooden chairs. On the table was a small brass Tibetan meditation bell, an oil lamp, writing instruments and paper, a small vial of ink, a green ceramic pitcher of water and a clear drinking glass.

One of the other walls in the room was covered with exotic plants and flowers suspended from the ceiling. There was also a door leading to the adjacent indoor bathroom.

Several minutes after the discourse, Taichia helped Satchitta settle into his bed. She adjusted the wool covers around him, then sat on one of the chairs next to his bed and began to cry.

"You are going to die before me," she weaped.

Satchitta gazed at her and nodded.

Taichia pounded her fist on the table and shouted, "I'M SO ANGRY AT RAKAN!"

Satchitta remained silent.

"I'm sorry," Taichia said.

"There is something you should know," Satchitta offered.

"You were my beloved Archa when we were both sixteen. In your last life you drowned in a freak accident in Khidir Creek."

Taichia stared at Satchitta in shock.

"Your... *beloved?*"

"Yes," Satchitta replied. "You and I have danced this dance before, only last time it was I who was left alone on this shore."

Taichia wiped her cheeks with a hanky. "Oh," she said softly.

"We're born alone and die alone," Satchitta concluded, "but love doesn't die."

Taichia crossed her hands over her heart. She smiled, stood up, bent over Satchitta and kissed him on the cheek. "Are you comfortable?"

Satchitta nodded. "What did you find?"

Taichia frowned. She sat down and said, "I don't like it. It's been six months since Rakan bought the property next to ours. Their conservation work is continuing rapidly. Rakan is no philanthropist. It's not like him to invest so much money and resources on such a project. And there are rumors that he is building a food bank there. I don't know what he has up his sleeve, but... I don't know..."

The Master nodded. "Let's wait and see. So far so good. If Existence is breathing him, who am I to question his motives? Just keep an eye open. If he attacks us in any way, we will respond."

Taichia frowned and handed Satchitta an unopened envelope. "From one of Rakan's men, Gollash," she said. "He gave this to one of our guards to give to you. I wasn't sure whether to open it or not."

Satchitta opened the envelope. Satchitta silently read the letter inside, then put it back in the envelope. "He wants to know the recipe for my favorite soup."

"What?" Taichia said.

"Please write down Shanti's recipe for pea soup and send a messenger to discreetly give it to Gollash," Satchitta instructed. "Whoever he is, he wants to connect with us in a friendly way."

Suddenly the Master grimaced as a sharp pain shot up his spine! Taichia gasped! She jumped up, ran to the table, and poured water into the glass. Then she added a teaspoon of an Ayurvedic compound and stirred the solution. She handed the glass to Satchitta, who drank it all down. Then she adjusted the pillows behind the Master, slipped a blindfold over his eyes, sat on the chair next to him, and silently sat with him until he was asleep.

CHAPTER 30

Bunny put the final touches on her sunflower and iris painting.

She stepped back, gazed at it, then said, "It's hard to believe that Rakan is a sleeping Buddha who thinks he's saving the world. His dream is a sweet one. Who wants to wake up from a sweet dream?"

"Um," Lloyd mused, "what did Dilai Dalai write?"

"Oh," Bunny said. "'If ever there was a time when we needed a man with an ego so crystalized that he believed he could save the world, it's not now.'"

"You and I know that one," Lloyd said.

Bunny frowned. "When we were lieutenants in Genghis Khan's army?"

Lloyd nodded. "We thought we were saving the world, did our fair share of mischief."

"Sure did," Bunny said. "I can understand Rakan's sleepy mind because I've been there during past lives. Seems the world can be divided into two types of people."

"Those who are asleep and those who are awake?" Lloyd asked.

"Yes," Bunny said, "and those who divide the world into two types of people and those who don't."

CHAPTER 31

Mark awoke at dawn the first morning in Bodhi Cave and was surprised to feel Leela cuddled behind him under several yak rugs. Her presence felt utterly delicious to Mark, and he soaked it up like a sponge.

Then something strange happened...

The contrast between the joy Mark felt, and the tension in his physical body from his arduous journey, began to tug at his heart. He felt a trembling in his belly which began to slowly spread throughout his body. Part of him wanted to control the energy, to keep the feelings to himself and not disturb Leela. But the energy continued to flow and to grow in intensity until he felt he was going to burst!

He took several deep breaths and tears began to flow.

Suddenly Leela stirred...

Damn, she's awake!

And that did it: Mark burst into tears, was overwhelmed with shaking and weeping, and cried like he hadn't cried since Floyd's death. Leela put one hand on Mark's heart and the other on his belly. Mark shook, and tears flowed like a monsoon of pent-up emotions. He cried a flood of childhood memories for twenty minutes, let the tears flow until finally he lay still, drained, empty, peaceful, silent...

Mark opened his eyes and looked outside the cave. It was snowing lightly. He took a deep breath, rolled over and faced Leela.

"Who *are* you?" he asked in wonder.

Leela laughed, and with a playful twinkle in her eyes, said, "I don't know. That's why I'm here: to find out."

Then she tickled Mark under his armpits and they both roared with laughter, rolling around in each other's arms for several minutes like children playing.

Suddenly they stopped and lay still, silently gazing into each other's eyes. Slowly, tenderly, Leela brushed Mark's cheek with her right hand and kissed him on the lips. The kiss lingered, and Mark's whole body quickly filled with subtle electricity.

They kissed for a while and the energy turned into fire, into passion, into love, into melting and merging, like sugar melting in a warm tropical ocean, until only the sweet salty taste of oneness remained...

Soon three gulls - two adults: a white one and a brown one, and a small light-brown one - flew into the cave and landed directly in front of Mark and Leela making love. The gulls watched for a while.

Finally, Mark lay still inside Leela.

Leela heard the flapping of wings, opened her eyes, and looked over Mark's head at the birds.

"Gulls?" she said. "This far inland?"

The three gulls squawked, then flew away.

Leela knew that she was pregnant.

CHAPTER 32

An hour later, as Leela and Mark cuddled, Mark said, "I don't understand what's happening."

Leela smiled. "We need to dress and go to Gazabha and meet with the Inner Circle."

"The Inner...?"

"You and I need to talk before we go," Leela said firmly.

"Okay."

"Let's dress, start a fire and talk."

"Okay."

So they did.

It had stopped snowing. After dressing, Mark and Leela sat facing each other around the fire in the morning sun.

Leela said, "I had an intense vision seven days before you came. For five lives I had been with the same person in the vision. Twin brother and sister. Then reversed: twin sister and brother. Then male warriors. Then a prince and princess. Finally, two male disciples of a Baul mystic, a mystic who in this lifetime is my father, Satchitta."

Leela saw that it was too much for Mark to swallow in one gulp, so she paused...

Mark sat with his mouth wide open, stunned. Blinking, Mark asked, "Your *father?* Who?"

Leela took a deep breath. "Satchitta."

"Satchitta? The Enlightened Master?"

Leela knitted her eyebrows. "Why?"

"Lalou was on her way to be with Satchitta!"

"Who's Lalou?"

Mark gasped. "Oh, my God!"

Perplexed, Leela asked, "What?"

"Satchitta!" Mark said.

"What are you talking about?"

Mark shook his head in disbelief. "I came to India to be with Gopal! When I got to Mumbai I found out Gopal had left his body. Then I met a Frenchwoman, Lalou, in a Mumbai restaurant, after escaping from a mob in the marketplace. Lalou—"

"Mob?"

"Later… it's a long story. Anyway, Lalou was on her way to be with Satchitta, in Srinagar!

"Before I met Lalou, I had decided to go to Gopal's commune in Gazabha anyway. Lalou and I were both going north so we traveled together and were lovers.

"We sailed from Mumbai to Karachi, then hiked up the Indus River, parted near Peshawar, she to be with Satchitta and me to visit Gopal's commune, Gazabha, and see Dilai Dalai's scrolls. Part of me wanted to go with her to Satchitta. But in meditation I felt a heart connection with Gopal and promised I'd meet her in Srinagar after I came here. Then I met you."

"You followed your heart," Leela said. She paused then continued: "I mentioned my past lives because the moment I saw you I felt that you are the being from my past lives. Do you want to be with me?"

"My God, *yes!*" Mark beamed. "But this is all… all so..."

"Strange?"

"Yes."

"I understand," Leela said. "It's been strange for me, too, both beautiful and difficult to be the daughter of a Master."

Leela choked on her words. She closed her eyes and her face flushed. The morning sun slipped behind a cloud and a shadow fell on her, accenting the painful feeling in her heart. She hung her head and cried. Mark reached over and hugged Leela as she convulsed and wept. She cried for ten minutes, and her pain triggered Mark's own inner torment. His eyes wandered aimlessly around Dilai Valley outside as he breathed deeply and held her in his arms.

Finally, Leela raised her head and looked at Mark with bloodshot eyes. "Let's go to Gazabha, okay?" she said. "There are twenty-one elders we, ah, I, need to talk with. I'll explain everything after the meeting. You won't understand our dialect, but I'll translate it for you afterwards, okay?"

Mark nodded.

"It's time for me to leave this cave, with you," Leela said. "Are you up for it?"

Mark smiled and held out his hands, palms open and up.

"Okay," Leela said, "you're open. Don't worry about what happens at the meeting. I need to explain to them why I am leaving, and you and I are going to Srinagar."

"We are going? Where?" Mark said.

Leela laughed. "Don't worry. Trust me, we're in for an adventure!"

A half-hour later, Leela and Mark began to hike down the rocky path towards Gazabha. When they came near the edge of the commune, they heard the Zahn bell echo through the valley.

"Everyone will be sitting in silence for ten minutes," Leela said. "It's okay."

Mark nodded.

Five minutes later they entered the center of Gazabha. Leela put both hands on her belly, took a deep breath and gazed into Mark's eyes.

Trust, she thought. *Something bigger than me is running this show...*

She took Mark by the hand, and they walked to the huge circular bungalow with a veranda, Buddha Hall. Leela glanced towards the double front doors. Mark nodded and moved with her to the doors.

Leela opened the right-side door and Mark saw 21 elders sitting in silence. He and Leela entered and sat on two cushions outside the Inner Circle.

One minute later the Zahn bell rang. Everyone in the Inner Circle opened their eyes and took a deep breath. Shanti glanced at Mark and her eyes widened. Then she turned towards Leela and said, "Oh... welcome. Please sit with us."

Mark and Leela moved into the Circle with their cushions. Leela smiled and said in Pukhto, "Thank you. This is Mark."

Everyone in the circle folded their hands in *namaste* and bowed to Mark.

Mark did the same.

Leela began to cry.

She wept for a minute then wiped her tears.

"I can never thank you all enough," she said finally. "It's time for me to be with Satchi again. Why did I leave him in the first place? I thought it was because I was tired of all the jealousy in my friends and others because I was the Master's daughter. Now I know that the others were merely *mirroring* my unconscious jealousy of Satchi."

"Jealousy?" Shanti asked.

"Yes," Leela said, "jealous because I could see that Satchi had something I longed for but lacked. Unknowingly, I left Satchi because somewhere inside I thought I had to find what I lacked on my own. A part of me knew I was spiritually asleep and had to find my own way to wake up. That's what I've been doing since I've been here.

"Living in our beautiful commune for four years and then meditating in Bodhi Cave for the last two years has helped me get in touch with the source of love inside and my connection to

Satchi. It's time to be with him again. You all made it possible through your love. I'm eternally grateful. Thank you."

Leela bowed, touched her forehead to the ground, and sang heartfully:

"Buddhaṃ śaraṇaṃ gacchāmi.
Sanghaṃ śaraṇaṃ gacchāmi.
Dharmaṃ śaraṇaṃ gacchāmi."

The Inner Circle bowed and sang along with her.

Mark bowed with them in silence.

Then everyone sat with closed eyes for a while.

Looking down at the gathering from Cloud Nine, Bunny and Lloyd each sighed deeply, then closed their eyes as well.

Soon everyone in the Inner Circle opened their eyes.

Shanti said, "Let us know what you need for the trip."

Shanti's partner, Rajen, laughed uproariously and his rainbow headband almost fell off his head. He adjusted the headband then said, "It's great you're going! You'll need horses. We'll set you up. And you may have company."

Leela looked puzzled, then her face lit up. "Pathen?"

Shanti took a deep breath and said, "Time to let him go."

"He'll be fine," Leela said. "What about his girlfriend?"

"Punya? That's up to her," Shanti said. "Meanwhile, you must be hungry. There's pea soup and bread and... well, go to my place and I'll meet you there as soon as we finish our meeting here."

Leela and Mark bowed. Then Leela turned to Mark and said, "Everything's okay. Let's eat."

Mark smiled and hugged her. Then they left Buddha Hall and walked to Shanti's bungalow near the center of Gazabha. They went inside and sat on a large hand-knotted oriental rug with a floral design.

Mark asked Leela, "What was that *gacchami* singing about?"

"Sanskrit," she replied. "For me it means…

"I go to the feet of the Awakened One.

"I go to the feet of the commune of the Awakened One.

"I go to the feet of the Ultimate Truth of the Awakened One."

"Oh," Mark said, "and what was the meeting all about?"

Leela brought Mark up to date on what had happened at the meeting, then asked, "Tell me more about Lalou."

Mark shrugged his shoulders. "Lalou? We met by accident in Mumbai. I had decided to go to Gopal's ashram in Gazabha and went to the Mumbai marketplace to find transportation. I'd taken a rickshaw to the marketplace and the driver tried to cheat me after I paid him. He started screaming at me in Hindi, something about *'rupees'*. I gathered by his tone that he was claiming that I had cheated *him!*

"A crowd gathered, and it was obvious that the mob believed the driver's lies. I didn't know Hindi to defend myself. People started harassing and physically threatening me, so I tossed a handful of coins in the air and the crowd dove to pick up the coins and I slipped away and ran into a restaurant around the corner to escape - and that's where I met Lalou."

"And she's with Satchi now?"

"I think so."

"And you and she were lovers, and you were going to be with her in Srinagar after you left here?"

"Yes."

Just then Pathen and Punya walked through the front door. They were dressed in matching fuchsia wool robes and holding hands.

During the two years that Leela had been a Prasad, she had not seen Punya. And now Leela's eyes widened in surprise as she glanced at Punya's full figure, sparking green eyes and lovely angelic face.

Leela took a step back and exclaimed, "Well, look at you! A woman now!"

Punya smiled, curtsied to Leela, and shyly whispered, "Love has its ways."

Leela nodded towards Mark and said, "Pathen, Punya, meet Mark."

Mark stood, walked over to Pathen and Punya and hugged them.

Leela sighed deeply and said, "Mark and I are going to Satchi."

Pathen nodded. Then he turned to Punya, who smiled and nodded.

Pathen took a deep breath, turned to Leela and said, "We're coming with you!"

CHAPTER 33

The weather on Cloud Nine had been stormy with thunder and lightning for several hours. Then it cleared up.

Bunny took a deep breath and said, "Leela's pregnant!"

"The only way to learn about love is to love," Lloyd said. "Like Leela said, she and Mark are in for an adventure."

Bunny shook her head in disbelief. "Mark doesn't know she's pregnant yet! Leela has a longing for the source of love inside; Mark thinks he wants enlightenment; and Satchitta is saying, 'You are already Buddhas. Look inside and wake up!' It's going to be interesting."

"Relationships are interesting," Lloyd agreed.

Just then, Henry, the old male angel on the next cloud, called to Lloyd: "Hey, Lloyd, can we talk for a minute?"

"Sure," Lloyd said, and drifted over to Henry's cloud.

"Mabel is gone now," Henry said. "I heard you and Bunny talking about relating. This wife of mine…. Ah, I've got to talk with someone. I'm miserable with Mabel."

"I don't understand," Lloyd said. "You two look like you're in love, always holding hands."

"That's because if I let go of her hand, she shops. She's shopping now, spends all my money!"

"Oh, that's too bad. How's your sex life?"

"Mabel's a romantic. Last week she insisted we go to the hotel we stayed at on our wedding night. We went to that same hotel and got a waterbed. The sex was so bad that Mabel called the waterbed, 'The Dead Sea'."

"Terrible," Lloyd said. "How long have you been together? Were you ever happy?"

"How long have we been together? Lifetimes, like Mark and Leela. During my last life with Mabel, I turned 99 and the doctor gave me six months to live. After six months I couldn't pay my bill, so the doctor gave me another six months. I lived to be 100. Mabel lived to be 101. Were we happy together? You know why I died before she did?"

"No."

"Because I wanted to," Henry replied mournfully.

"That bad, eh?"

Henry nodded. "My first wife was even worse. I divorced her. Do you know why divorces are so expensive?"

"No."

"Because they're worth it! And Mabel's a sufferer, a real *mahatma*. You know why she doesn't drink?"

"Tell me."

"Because alcohol interferes with her suffering."

"You have a real challenge," Lloyd said. "What are you going to do?"

Henry shook his head in despair. "Do? Old age is when you can do as much as ever but would rather not. I'm done doing. I just needed someone to talk with."

Lloyd shrugged his shoulders. "Seems you're enjoying your misery, Henry. 'Bye." Then he whisked back to Bunny on Cloud Nine.

CHAPTER 34

On a cold sunny day, a week after Mark had met Leela, they sat on a blanket eating lunch in a meadow on a hill overlooking Gazabha.

"I'm pregnant," Leela said, holding her belly.

Mark stared at Leela in shocked disbelief.

Leela looked radiant, Mark stunned.

Mark leaned forward and asked, "How, ah, when, ah...?"

Leela smiled and asked, "Remember when those three gulls flew into the cave the morning after you arrived?"

Mark stared. "Oh... but how do you know... ah...?"

"So soon?"

"Yeah."

"I just know," Leela said. "For a year I had been doing a meditation - watching my breath circle in and out my navel center, near my birth canal."

She patted her belly and continued, "I became very sensitive to this area of my body. After the past lives vision that I told you about, I knew I was to have a baby with this friend from my past lives. You showed up seven days later, when my fertility was at its peak. I just feel it, I just know..."

Mark sat speechless, absorbing the news.

"I, I feel... shocked, scared.... I, ah, don't really know you. This is a... a..."

Leela nodded. "A lifetime commitment? I really don't know you either. I got pregnant consciously. I take full responsibility for raising this child in me. I was born nine months after my parents met. They didn't know each other either before they got pregnant, and we all turned out okay."

Just then the Zahn bell rang, and Mark sat in silent meditation with Leela for ten minutes.

After the meditation, Mark felt centered. He leaned over and hugged Leela. "You sure you're okay?"

Leela smiled, nodded, and said, "I told Rajen and Shanti that I'd stop over to talk about what we needed for the trip. Come to their bungalow with me?"

"Sure," Mark said.

They ambled to the bungalow.

Pathen and Punya greeted them at Rajen and Shanti's door.

Leela took one look at their radiant young faces and asked, "Are you packed yet?"

Pathen and Punya laughed.

CHAPTER 35

A week later, fluffy white snow fell lightly on the frosty ground as Leela, Mark, Pathen and Punya stood in front of Buddha Hall and said tearful good-byes to friends in the Gazabha commune.

Mark was lost in confusion. *Leela, pregnant? Satchitta, a Master? Me, a disciple? What about Lalou?*

His mind was a whirlwind of contradictions.

"Take care, beloved," Shanti said to Leela. "The road to Srinagar can be treacherous this time of year. Pir Pass can have blizzard conditions. Are you sure you want to go now?"

Leela patted her belly. "Now or never," she said. "Something in me needs to move."

Shanti's eyes widened. She looked at Leela's belly, then into her niece's sparkling eyes. Immediately she understood that Leela was pregnant!

"Oh, really!?" Shanti asked, "You really think so?"

"I know so!" Leela said. "If it's a girl I'll name her Shanti."

Shanti shrieked and said, "Oh, Leela, you're amazing!" and silently hugged her for a full minute.

Finally, Shanti let go of beloved Leela and said, "Send word about Satchi's health, okay? Rajen and I may want to be with you all soon."

"Will do," Leela said.

The entire community gathered for a group hug. Then Leela, Mark, Pathen and Punya rode south on their horses along the eastern bank of the Swat River, then east to the Indus River.

They took a harrowing ferry ride with their horses across the raging Indus, then rode like peaceful warriors possessed through

Nature's white fury over snowbound Pir Pass. Once they had crossed the pass, the weather was warmer, and their attitude lightened up.

The worst physical part of the journey was over.

When the four weary travelers finally arrived on a hill overlooking Srinagar, the orange sun was just setting in the west. They paused on their horses to take in the beauty of the area below: the wide winding Jhelum River, snowcapped Shridhara Mountains on the horizon, and the ancient city of Srinagar on either side of the river.

They dismounted and gazed at the full moon beaming a brilliant orange overhead, casting a surreal glow on Dal Lake in the distance.

Leela, Pathen and Punya were exhausted and quickly ate. Then they crawled into yak-rug sleeping bags under an ancient one-hundred-foot Chinar tree.

Mark, however, was on fire. *Leela, pregnant? Satchitta, a Master? Me, a disciple? What about Lalou?*

He didn't know which way was up. Leela had missed her period and was clearly pregnant. He had no clue what it meant to be a disciple of a Master, or even if there was such a state as Enlightenment. He had been lovers with Lalou and had told her he would meet her in the Srinagar ashram. What would he do?

Lost in doubt, Mark meandered through the tall grasses of the meadow towards the moonlit city below. He finally stopped at the edge of the Jhelum River and silently gazed at the full moon reflecting off the glassy surface of the water.

Suddenly… he was in bliss, not knowing what bliss was...

Surprised, he stood for a while bathing in the delicate subtlety of the experience. Then he began to walk along the riverbank, entranced by the luminous life shimmering within the trees and the subtle sparkles in the air.

Soon clouds gathered and covered the moon. He sat at the base of a tree and closed his eyes.

Inside himself he saw a pitch-black sky with streaks of light flickering here and there. He felt a subtle vortex of energy whirling and spiraling deeper and deeper and deeper inside, pulling him like a seductive magnet into a fathomless inner void...

Amazed, in wonder, he let go into the void, into the center of being...

The void continued to spiral on and on, infinitely, forever and ever, pulling him deeper and deeper inside to a centerless center.

Then, suddenly, a beatific vision of a face appeared...

Never having seen Satchitta's face before, Mark knew the face was the Master's! In an instant Satchitta became Mark's Master, his spiritual guide into life's mysteries.

For what seemed like an eternity, Mark continued to sit silently and just be with the experience…

Soon an inner voice, seemingly millions of miles away, faint yet clear, whispered, *"You're going to die."*

Immediately Mark's energy began to contract. He felt a slight trembling and began to come back, back, back, until his eyes opened, and he saw snow falling.

The flakes fell ever so beautifully, like delicate, elegant notes from a flute, a symphony of white magic drifting silently to the ground. Mark sat for a while watching the dancing snowflakes, then took a deep breath, stood up, and hiked back to camp.

He stood above Leela and watched her sleeping peacefully. Then he looked up and saw that it had stopped snowing. Still in bliss, Mark strode to his horse, took his journal out of the backpack, sat down under a tree and began to write:

Tonight, standing, watching
the full moon glimmer on the river,
the back door opened
and the Friend walked in silently.

The pines opened their arms,
hugged me in wonder,
and a star-filled vortex
lifted me down an inner tunnel
with no end.

My eyes opened,
a veil was lifted
from my blind heart,
and the Guest moved in
and kindled the fire
of love eternal.

As I sat under a tree,
waiting, waiting,
for my thirst to be quenched
by heaven's wine,
dawn tiptoed
through a crack
in the garden wall
and revealed the Master's face.

I heard my heart
beating an empty drum,
and, dancing with snowflakes,
bowed in gratefulness
for the kiss on my lips.

An inner sun
illuminated flowers
showering on me
in the valley's empty womb.

Tonight, Satchitta opened the door,
and I stepped into his palace
of love, life, and laughter.

Thank you, beloved Master.

Mark closed the journal, went to his horse, put the journal in the backpack, then slipped under a yak rug next to Leela.

Leela stirred. "Beloved?"

"Seems so," Mark replied.

CHAPTER 36

Bunny took a deep breath, fluffed the cloud she was sitting on, and turned to Lloyd. "Looks like our work is done," she said.

"Mark and Leela are in Satchitta's hands now," Lloyd agreed.

They heard a loud bump in the direction of Cloud Nine.

"I'm looking for Bunny and Lloyd!" a booming voice cried.

"Him again?" Lloyd asked.

"Sounds like it," Bunny said.

God drove his electric golf cart over to Bunny and Lloyd, then got out of the vehicle and looked at the new dent on the right front fender. He peeked over his thick glasses and said, "I have orders here for you two to go back. Your work here is done."

"To Earth?" Bunny said. "Good timing."

"That's my job," God said.

Bunny shrugged her shoulders and remarked, "The thing is though, I don't want to miss the good part."

God seemed confused. He asked, "How do you know there will be a good part?"

"How do I know there won't be one?" Bunny replied.

God scratched his silver mane and said, "Okay, you can stay. But only if you promise to let me know when the good part comes."

"Will do," Bunny said.

CHAPTER 37

Mark rested next to Leela under a yak rug in bliss most of the night, gazing at the glimmering panorama of stars and planets above Srinagar, his heart beating in a subtle rhythm with the pulse of the universe.

Just before dawn's first light, he felt like he would explode if he didn't get up and complete his two-year journey to the feet of a Master. Bliss was beginning to fade, but Mark was bubbling with energy. He slid from under the yak rug and walked about on the hillside, sniffing winter flowers, delighting in the singing of the birds, anxiously awaiting stirrings from his fellow pilgrims.

He didn't have to wait long. A half hour later, just as the golden sun rose over the horizon, he saw Leela awaken and glance at him with amusement, a 'silly boy' smile on her face.

"So," Leela mused, "did the sun rise or did you pull it up?"

Mark laughed, then ran to Leela, took off all his clothes and slipped under the yak rugs with her.

Leela was naked as well, and within minutes the energy in her sex center smoldered. She gently wrapped her right hand around Mark's *lingam* and placed it inside her moist *yoni.*

Slowly, slowly, over the next hour, Mark and Leela played like two conscious children dissolving into oneness…

…sweet…

Their playing excited Punya and Pathen as well, and the teenagers, too, made love.

As the sun rose slowly above the horizon, the lovemaking attracted a flock of mallard ducks which had gathered on a nearby hillock. Sensitive to the mystical dance that was happening below them, the mallards quacked in harmony with the two couples.

Finally, Leela spontaneously sat up and bellowed, “Let’s go!”

Everyone laughed, then quickly dressed.

Within fifteen minutes each lover was on a horse galloping down through the apple orchards to the banks of the Jhelum River, and into Srinagar.

They rode along the banks of the river as the sunlight illuminated hundreds of *doongas*, large houseboats with shingled roofs. The boats floated like lotus flowers on the city’s polluted waters. Numerous mosques and shrines dotted the horizon, their pagoda-like roofs framing the skyline. Merchants emerged from the narrow side-streets, toting bags of raw wool on their shoulders. Craftsmen carried woodcarvings, copperware, tapestries, shawls and carpets. They loaded their wares onto boats and wagons for shipment to other areas of the city and beyond.

The sleeping city quickly woke before the pilgrims’ eyes. Leela led the way as they rode through the wonderland of musky smells, warm colors, and busy sounds of commerce. They passed several old bridges, *kadals*, then crossed over the oldest bridge, the *Fateh Kadal*.

On the other side of the *Fateh Kadal*, they wound through an intricate labyrinth of streets until suddenly they came upon a meadow of golden grass at the edge of the city. A vibrant palette of winter flowers, bushes and trees graced the meadow. A small creek ran through the length of it and cascaded over a sequence of small man-made waterfalls. Thick groves of golden bamboo wove their way along both sides of the creek.

At the far end of the meadow, about twenty laborers appeared to be working on the construction of a large building. A white sign with black lettering in Kashmiri was staked into the ground near the entrance to the building. The English translation of the sign: “Future site of the People’s Bank”.

“This used to be wasteland,” Leela said. “Now it’s a wonderland!”

Leela stopped at the edge of the meadow. Her glance silently pointed out a long row of fir trees lining the other side of the meadow. Behind the trees in the shade was a tall bamboo fence which ran left to right as far as the eye could see. In the middle of the fence hung two wings of a huge copper gate.

Mark looked at Leela’s glowing face.

The Master’s daughter was home...

Tears flowed from Leela’s eyes. She took a deep breath and looked back and forth across the meadow. She dismounted her mare and began to walk with her along a stone path across the grass. The others followed.

They strode along until suddenly, three gulls - a white, a brown, and a smaller light-brown one - swooped down and landed in the middle of a patch of pink and dark-blue flowers in front of them.

Mark and Leela looked at each other in surprise. Each thought, *The same three gulls from Bodhi Cave?*

The gulls waddled about curiously in the grasses then lay down and nestled with each other in the morning sun. Leela arched her eyebrows, then continued to move slowly around the gulls and up to the ashram’s front gate.

Two young male Kashmiri guards and a lovely middle-aged Oriental woman - all dressed in red robes - stood chatting in front of the closed gate. When they saw four pilgrims approaching, they folded their hands and bowed, “*Namaste.*”

This was the common greeting within the ashram, but because of the variety of languages spoken by disciples from other countries, English had been chosen to be the primary language, and Taichia was the primary teacher.

The four pilgrims bowed and tied their horses to a tree.

The Oriental sannyasin squinted her eyes. "Leela?"

Leela smiled and ran to hug her. They danced around in circles until finally they stopped.

"Can we go in, Dahlia?" Leela asked jokingly.

Dahlia laughed. "Not until you introduce your friends," she said joyously.

Leela chuckled. "Oh, this is Mark! Pathen! Punya!"

"Welcome," Dahlia said, then nodded to the other guards, who immediately opened the twelve-foot, ornately decorated copper gate.

As the gate creaked open, gentle gurgling sounds from a series of cascading waterfalls tickled Mark's ears. He stepped inside and saw three small waterfalls at one edge of a large pond which was partially covered with white lotus flowers. Large golden and white carp and elegant white swans cruised the clear azure-green water. A verdant garden area shaded by juniper trees and a variety of giant bamboo graced the rest of the area.

Leela was in heaven; Mark, Pathen and Punya in awe.

Shangri-La!

Once inside the ashram, Mark saw a beehive of men and women of all ages from every part of the world floating about in woolen fuchsia and red robes. He was amazed at their eyes. Not all mind you, but most of the eyes had an unmistakable depth to them, like vast oceans one could joyously drown in.

Pathen and Punya stepped aside as several Indian women ran up to Leela, hugging, giggling and welcoming her in Kashmiri.

Mark looked for someone Western to talk with. Leela had told him that the male disciples were called "Swami," and the women, "Ma", so he asked a tall curly-haired blond Australian Ma, "Do you know a Ma named Lalou?"

"Yes," she smiled. "She's in the kitchen."

Leela tapped on Mark's back. He turned around.

"I asked friends about Satchi," Leela said. "He's taking a bath now. We won't be able to see him till Darshan tonight."

"I'm his disciple now," Mark said.

Leela smiled. "We'll meet him tonight. I'm scared."

"*You're* scared?!"

Just then a familiar face with an unfamiliar slim body came up to Leela.

Leela squinted. "Prema?"

Prema nodded.

Leela admired Prema's new svelte physique.

"You, ah... you are you... aren't you?" she asked.

Prema laughed and hugged Leela.

"Yes," Prema smiled, "but there's less of me now! Great to see you! I heard you were living in Gazabha. Sorry I was such a bitch before you left. Can we be friends again?"

"Sure," Leela said, "I can be a bitch, too. In fact, I enjoy it! How is, ah, Satchi?"

Prema frowned and lowered her head.

"Oh..." Leela said. "That bad, eh?"

Prema raised her head and said, "Well, he's still giving discourses and Darshan but is frail as a rail… and well..."

"Well, what?"

"Um... I'll let him tell you."

"Okay," Leela said. "Prema, this is Mark."

Prema studied Mark's tall, handsome features, turned to Leela and said, "You can pick 'em, honey!"

Then she hugged Mark and said, "Welcome."

Turning once again to Leela, Prema asked, "Who are your other two friends?"

"Oh," Leela said, "Pathen, my cousin, and his girlfriend, Punya. They only understand a little English."

"*Namaste*," Prema said, and hugged Pathen and Punya. Then she turned to Leela and remarked, "I bet you're dying to see Taichia."

"Yes!" Leela said, then moved with Prema and the others through a guarded gate and paused before Satchitta and Taichia's bungalow.

Once there, Prema said, "I'm a midwife now and have a delivery to go to. See you all at Darshan tonight?"

Leela's eyes widened. She touched her belly, and said, "Midwife, eh? Hmm... maybe... um... later..."

Then Leela hugged Prema and said, "Thank you, beloved."

Prema's eyes watered. She took a deep breath, nodded, then walked away.

The moment Taichia looked out her bungalow window and saw Leela, she shrieked and practically flew out the front door with an entourage of five other women, all dressed in flowing fuchsia robes!

Taichia was a tall, elegant brunette with shiny deep blue eyes, a full bosom and a warm smile. She was bubbling over with delight as she rushed up to Leela and hugged her. Then all the other women, too, gathered round and hugged Leela.

Mark, Pathen, and Punya stepped back and enjoyed the show.

Leela was lost amidst the crowd of chattering women for several minutes. Soon the women on the periphery stepped back and Mark could see Leela again.

Leela smiled at Taichia and nodded towards Mark. Taichia walked to Mark and hugged him. "Oh, beloved!" she said. "Welcome, welcome!"

Taichia then turned to Leela and asked, "And oh, Leela, who are your other friends?"

"Shanti's son, Pathen, and his girlfriend, Punya."

Taichia's eyes widened as she gazed into Pathen's eyes. "Oh, Pathen," she said, "you have your uncle's eyes."

"Satchitta's?" Pathen said. "Oh, I..." and he hugged his aunt.

Taichia stepped back, scanned Punya's lovely features, and said, "She's a keeper, Pathen," and hugged Punya.

Pathen blushed and asked, "And Satchitta?"

Taichia frowned and lowered her head. "He's taking a bath now. He's, well, you'll see tonight at Darshan. Now, beloveds, some of Shanti's famous pea soup?"

The four pilgrims nodded, and everyone went inside the bungalow to eat soup and chapattis.

Mark and Leela settled into Leela's old bedroom on the west side of the bungalow. Pathen and Punya stayed in the ghotul. All four were exhausted yet filled with excitement, so they rested in their beds until dinner.

Mark and Leela took a short nap then bathed after waking up. They dried their bodies and were sitting on their bed draped in towels when suddenly they heard a knock on their door.

"Come in," Leela said.

Taichia entered the room smiling, her arms full of food and clothes. "Here," she said, laying everything on the bed, "robes and sandals for Darshan and food for the belly."

Then Taichia's eyes fluttered, and her face turned pale. She took a deep breath and said, "Satchi has been slowly going downhill since he was arrested and poisoned. I don't know how he's lasted this long. He is more and more fragile each day. His back is in constant pain. And his stomach - well, you know how he loves to eat sweets before bedtime."

Leela nodded. "How bad is... is he okay?"

"*Oui* and no," Taichia said emphatically. "Except for his afternoon nap, he won't rest! He is so stubborn! Insists on giving a discourse each morning and receives disciples for *sannyas* initiation each night! Seven days a week! His back! I don't know what to do with him! We've had the best doctors to see him, but..."

Taichia took a deep breath and looked at her radiant daughter. "You," she said reflectively. "You look, ah, ah..."

Leela smiled and held her belly. "Pregnant."

Taichia shrieked and hugged Leela.

"NO! Ah, YES! Ah, wait till he hears!" Taichia exclaimed.

Then she gazed at Mark and asked, "You?"

Mark blushed. "Seems so. I'm amazed."

Taichia laughed and hugged Mark. Then she stepped back, studied Mark carefully, and nodded approvingly.

Leela smiled and said, "Mark feels he is already Satchi's disciple. He wants to be initiated as soon as possible. Pathen and Punya want to meet with Satchi in Darshan before they decide about *sannyas*."

"*Oui!* Of course!" Taichia said. "Tonight. I'll tell Satchi you're here when he wakes up from his nap. Now, beloveds, relax and I'll arrange places for the four of you at Darshan. Oh, what a treat!"

Then Taichia bowed and slipped out the door.

"Your mother is beautiful," Mark said.

"Yes," Leela said, "but Satchi... I'm worried..."

Mark and Leela dressed, then Leela gave Mark the lowdown on the protocol for Darshan, on being in the presence of the Master. Leela and Mark snacked on the food Taichia had brought. Then, with their bellies full and their hearts pounding, they dressed in the robes and sandals Taichia had given them and silently sat with closed eyes in their room and waited...

7 PM. Buddha Hall.

Leela, Mark, Pathen and Punya sat in the front row which formed a half circle around a podium, twelve feet in front of Satchitta's elevated white high-back chair. On Leela and Mark's left, Taichia sat next to Amritam. Dahlia and Lalou sat on Mark and Leela's right, and Pathen and Punya sat on Lalou's right.

320 disciples sat in 16 concentric semicircle rows behind them. Two stenographers sat ready to write down each word Satchitta said. Three musicians played on a tabla, flute, and sitar.

The air was electric!

Mark sat anxiously awaiting Satchitta, his heart racing and his mind a hurricane of thoughts. Suddenly, he glanced outside the large mosquito netting to the right of the podium and saw the full orange moon shining in all its glory. He took a deep breath and sensed a stirring outside.

A moment later, Satchitta entered Buddha Hall.

Physically the Master was a delicate wisp of a man, although his presence emanated an ethereal energy. He walked to the podium with hands folded and his playful, childlike eyes beaming brightly. He glided gracefully onto the podium, stopped in front of his chair, and silently *namaste'd* with folded hands.

Everyone bowed and *namaste'd.*

Mark's heartbeat was almost audible. He felt his face twitching as he returned Satchitta's *namaste*.

The Master had a long white beard and was wearing a violet and green wool robe with a matching knitted cap. He slowly and carefully sat down in the cushioned chair, crossed his legs, and slipped off his sandals.

Dahlia announced, "Deva Leela."

Leela stood, walked to the cushion in front of Satchitta, and sat down.

Satchitta smiled. "So, beloved, you have come. Welcome."

It was a powerful moment. Tears of joy and laughter rolled down Leela's face. Mark and everyone else in the audience who had known Leela had tears in their eyes.

Leela laughed then gulped her tears. "Thank you," she said, then bowed and touched the Master's feet.

Mark's heart almost leaped out of his chest.

The Master grimaced with pain. Still bowed down, Leela didn't see his grimace, and after a few moments she sat back up upon the cushion.

Satchitta adjusted his posture in the chair. Taichia anxiously leaned forward as if the Master was starting to fall, and she was preparing to catch him. Satchitta steadied himself then blissfully gazed into Leela's eyes.

"Very good, beloved," Satchitta said. "You and I can play again and create more mischief!"

A ripple of laughter coursed through the audience.

Leela took Satchitta's words to heart. She took a deep breath as if to swallow the Master's loving words. Then she crossed her hands over her heart, bowed, and once again touched the Master's feet.

Leela remained bowed for a full minute, during which time a pure lake of consciousness filled Buddha Hall with a silence so deep the cuckoos outside fell silent.

Finally, with tears in her eyes, Leela got up and floated over to the cushion next to Mark and sat down.

Dahlia called, "Mark Trimble."

Mark stood, walked to Satchitta and sat on a pillow before him. He bowed, touched the Master's feet, then sat up and gazed into the Master's eyes. Satchitta touched the middle of Mark's forehead with his right thumb for twenty seconds, then draped a sandalwood mala around his neck.

Mark inhaled the fragrance of the sandalwood, arched his head, and gazed passively into the fathomless depths of the Master's eyes.

And that was it... the emptiness in the Master's eyes touched the emptiness in Mark's heart and tears began to flow...

Mark's mind went blank...

The next thing Mark knew, he was sitting on a cushion next to Leela. He had been so lost in the wonder of the Master that he remembered little of what Satchitta had said to him. The next morning though, one of the stenographers gave Mark a hand-written English transcript of Satchitta's words to him at Darshan:

"The tears are good!" Satchitta said. "Anything to say? No? Good, your tears say it all. The heart is opening. This is the only communication possible between a Master and a disciple: a silent opening of the heart.

"Your journey shall be from the head to the heart, and finally to your Center. In fact, there is nowhere to go. You are already who you need to be, here now.

"A Master is needed because you have already journeyed far from yourself, from your heart and Center. You have lived in the mind too long and your heart has become somewhat clouded. But not to worry; it is natural, and I can see that your heart is opening.

"Your new name shall be Swami Anand Chetan, 'Consciousness is bliss' - the bliss of being in your beloved's arms, safe, unconditionally loved. You know this feeling, um? Yes, the same feeling - but now allow this feeling to be with the Whole of Existence.

"You have loved, I can see it in your eyes and your tears. You have felt the pain, the agony, the ecstasy and misery of love. Now love consciously. The love you have known till now was the projection of your dream-mind, a projection of the ideals which society and the priests imposed on you. Love is a flowering of consciousness, nothing else. Love has nothing to do with society's ideals or with another person. Love springs from within, from your very Center, your Being, like a flower spreads its fragrance with no thought of any reward.

"Yes, you can share this love with another person, with a rock even. But the love I am talking about is not dependent on anyone or anything outside you. It is your very nature. Sharing this love is as natural as breathing. You have only to look inside to find the source of love. Love is the periphery, consciousness the Center.

"And when I say consciousness, what do I mean? I simply mean energy, the purest energy. Matter is gross energy. What we call 'energy' is a little purer than matter. And consciousness is the purest energy – 'alive emptiness' if you will - space, zero in scientific terms.

"The difference among the three energies is only that of different frequencies, different wavelengths, that's all.

"Dilai Dalai wrote, 'The mystic $0 = e = mc^2 =$ loving'.

"This mc^2 is only a symbol; it represents material energy in scientific terms. Looked at from the peak of consciousness, all these three energies are one energy.

"But science is knowledge without love. Perhaps that is why Dilai Dalai included the word loving in his equation: to indicate that loving, consciousness, and matter are one. Most scientists are identified with the mind and know little of love; hence scientists criticize Dilai Dalai's statement. Scientists will discover what Dilai Dalai and I are talking about once scientists become meditators and experience Existence as a whole within themselves - form *and* spaciousness! Then their science will be loving, creative. Right now, science is destructive, war-oriented, because most scientists themselves have lived in the head at the expense of the heart. They know only morality or beliefs about spirituality and know little or nothing of love or consciousness.

"So become more and more conscious, Chetan, more and more sensitive though meditation, and your love will grow until you are no more and only love is. Meditation is your path and love is a flowering of meditation.

"Let this be our journey together. Let the earth, sky, people, let everyone and everything be a chance to become more and more conscious. Walking, walk loose and natural, conscious of each step. Eating, eat consciously. Drop from the head to the heart. See, feel, listen, taste, smell from the heart.

"My effort is to bring you to the highest peak of consciousness so you can determine for yourself what is right and wrong. No outside advise will be needed.

"Enjoy and share! Be simple, playful, a nobody. Now go with my blessings."

Tears came to Chetan's eyes as he sat on the veranda of his bungalow reading the Master's words the morning after Darshan. Then he remembered the verse he had written in the middle of the night after his initiation:

Chicken Heart,
Melting Eggs,
"Cluck!"

CHAPTER 38

Chetan and Leela ate breakfast with Taichia on the veranda of their bungalow the morning after Darshan.

After a delicious breakfast of fruits, nuts, fresh cow's milk and tea, Taichia said to Leela, "Satchi wants to see you."

"About?"

"In about an hour," Taichia said. Then she picked up a tray of fruit for Satchitta and walked inside the bungalow.

"I wonder what he wants?" Leela said. "Last night Taichia said Satchi doesn't see anyone till after noon."

"I have to go," Chetan said. "Lalou."

"Oh," Leela said. "What are you going to say to her?"

"I'm sorry but I'm happy? I don't know."

Leela hugged Chetan.

"I know all this is strange for you," Leela said, "but I'm happy too."

They hugged for a minute, then Chetan said, "I've got to go."

He kissed Leela on the lips and left.

Leela had an hour before her meeting with Satchitta. She immediately walked to the administrative office and asked Dahlia if someone could take a message to Shanti and Rajen, telling them that Satchitta's health was failing and that it was time for them to come to Srinagar.

"We're sending clothing to Gazabha in two days," Dahlia said. "We'll send your message then."

"Thank you," Leela said. Then she wrote her message on a piece of paper and gave it to Dahlia.

Her promise to Shanti fulfilled, Leela felt relieved. She walked out of the office and began to play her flute as she strolled along a garden path.

Within a few minutes Leela was dancing along the ashram's side streets like a centaur prancing through the woods. And this was the actual case: the mythical centaur is half-human, half-animal, a metaphor for the conflict between the lower appetites and conscious behavior in humans. Like the centaur, Leela was also split. Here she was, dancing along, frivolous and carefree on the outside, and inside tormented by her grief over Satchitta's tenuous physical condition. Her caring heart was stretched to its emotional limits, and on some level, she knew that Satchitta's approaching death mirrored an anxiety about her own death.

At the sandy edge of the ashram's pond, Leela picked up a stick and wrote in the sand: "Creativity is first receiving then giving love."

First receiving, being open... then giving...

Leela tossed the stick back where she found it, then continued her walk until it was time to meet with Satchitta. As she walked back to the Master's bungalow, she reflected on the Master…

It was clear that Satchitta's body was almost depleted, that he was alive only because of his compassion for his disciples. Taichia had told Leela at breakfast that the Master knew his death was quickly approaching and he had begun to prepare for it.

Now as Leela approached the gate to the bungalow, she became acutely aware of her anxiety, and didn't know what to expect. She managed a slight smile for the guard at the gate, then walked to the bungalow and inside to Satchitta's bedroom.

She knocked on his door.

"Come in," Satchitta said.

Leela opened the door and saw the Master lying in bed propped up with pillows and covered with a white cashmere blanket. She walked to the bed and kissed Satchitta on the right cheek. Then she sat on one of the chairs next to the bed.

Satchitta gazed at Leela with his fathomless eyes. “Beloved,” he said, “it’s almost time for me to go, and I can see by your energy that you are ready. You have the gift.”

Leela looked puzzled. “Ready? Gift?”

“You know that you don’t know who you are,” Satchitta said, “and that love and meditation are one. It shows in your energy. You are almost home. You have a loving heart, rebelliousness, courage, intelligence, creativity and humor.”

The Master paused, smiled, and looked at Leela’s belly. “And you’re ready to share.”

Leela gazed at her father in silence and took a deep breath. “I don’t understand.” Immediately she heard a soft voice inside and asked, “You mean I’m ready to help people, teach something?”

Satchitta nodded.

“What am I... to teach?”

“When the ‘I’ is not, teaching happens,” Satchitta said. “What are you to teach?”

The Master picked up the small brass Tibetan meditation bell from the table beside his bed, held the bell in front of Leela, and rang it, “Ding!” Then he put the bell back on the table and gazed into Leela’s eyes.

Leela chuckled. “Real frogs?”

The Master smiled. “Real frogs.”

Leela laughed, then felt a wellspring of tears bubble up from her belly and cried for a minute. Finally, she gathered herself, wiped her tears, and bowed to the Master.

Satchitta said, “Just be aware of entitled understanding.”

Leela knitted her eyebrows. “Entitled...?”

The Master took a deep breath and explained: “As I said, you know that you don’t know who you are. Neither do others. And you know that you can’t be conscious for anyone else. You know that aloneness is your reality. Bodhi Cave was good for you in that respect. From your centered space of aloneness, love can flow freely now, without attachment or desire for any recognition or reward for sharing your understandings."

Satchitta reached over with his right hand and held Leela's hands. He gazed into her eyes and said, "Soon I will be gone. Simply share by being yourself: empty, open, silent, joyous, sad, playful - howsoever you are! And you have been doing this your whole life! Prema and the others were not only jealous of you because you are the Master's daughter. They were jealous of the natural way you lived: laughing, dancing, creative, loving, ecstatic.

"No, I don't think you'll have a problem with entitled understanding. Only people who are damaged in some way, stuck in their minds, who feel they are unlovable and powerless, try to get power over others by convincing others that *they* have all the right answers, that *they alone* know the right way for others to live. This is entitled understanding.

"These people live in their minds. Without any experiences of meditation or love, they falsely believe they understand what is true and feel entitled to force their ideas on others. These are unconscious people, like Rakan, who try to hide their feelings of inferiority and self-hate by dominating others. They feel they are *entitled* to their self-created role of teacher, pundit, expert, or priest in order to avoid feeling their loneliness, ignorance and self-loathing.

"But you are not one of them. I am only saying this because the mind is tricky, the trickiest thing in the world. We all come into the world helpless children, spiritually asleep, and dreaming that we are damaged in some way, separate from Existence. But the truth is, we are already whole deep inside, and only we can wake ourselves up from this false dream. No one can do it for us.

I feel you understand this and are ready to share your understanding with others."

Leela nodded. "What about Rakan?"

With deep compassion in his eyes, Satchitta said, "Rakan has a keen intellect and the potential to be a buddha. He is not his criminal mind. At his center is consciousness, his Buddhahood. But he is the epitome of entitled understanding, dreaming a sweet dream of world domination. He doesn't want to wake up spiritually. I can tell he is up to something, and it may be time for us to end our experiment here and send sannyasins out into the world.

"Mystery Schools are needed around the world to help people learn to live beautifully, meditatively, and creatively in the marketplace. The marketplace is the real testing ground for meditators."

"Oh," Leela said.

"Yes," Satchitta joked, "you may even have to get a job!"

Leela laughed.

The Master smiled and said, "The source of love, creativity and fulfillment is within. You have already experienced that when one meditates, the sources of joy and creativity spontaneously bubble up and express themselves through one's natural talents and merits, enriching their life."

"You can help others understand this, and that if there is confusion, doubt, it is best to go in: be silent, meditate, and allow the alchemy of awareness to transform problems into challenges. In the light of understanding how to live consciously, problems become opportunities to sharpen one's intelligence and express one's creativity."

Leela patted her belly, and said, "I'm aware of *this* challenge and opportunity!"

Satchitta smiled. "So far so good."

CHAPTER 39

That same morning, Chetan walked into the large ashram kitchen looking for Lalou. The kitchen was a beehive of thirty male and female sannyasins in robes, darting about preparing food and cleaning the area.

Chetan felt a light tap on his right shoulder. He turned around and saw Lalou, whose long blonde curly hair, stately presence, and lovely rosy-cheeked face contrasted sharply with her blood-shot blue eyes.

Lalou wiped her hands on her apron. "I was waiting for you," she said, "but when I saw you and Leela together at Darshan last night, I knew..."

Chetan nodded. "I'm sorry. I never expected Leela to happen, but she did."

"I understand," Lalou said. "It's okay, there is lots of love here. I've been with a few other men since I last saw you."

Chetan took a deep breath. "No hard feelings?"

"I cried a lot," Lalou said, "but basically, my love affair is with Satchitta and the sangha."

"Are you staying for a while?"

"Till my money runs out. You?"

Chetan shrugged his shoulders. "I don't know. I'll see how it goes. Satchitta looks... well, like he's dying."

"I know," Lalou said, and hugged Chetan.

Chetan took a deep breath. "See you later, okay?"

"With the Master, I never know," Lalou said.

Chetan nodded and left the kitchen. He walked out the front gate of the ashram, turned left and walked till he came to a large fountain in the middle of one of the Mughal Gardens.

Suddenly, from behind the marble statue of a tiger by the side of the footpath, a wild-eyed face popped out in front of Chetan.

"Satchitta *is* Lord!" the face declared.

Chetan jumped back.

A tall, curly black-haired, oddly handsome clean-shaven young man in a fuchsia wool robe was staring at him determinedly. The man was wearing a mala and holding a tall wooden staff. Three acupuncture needles were sticking in his right ear.

"Wha-! *What*?" Chetan stammered.

"The Master *is* Lord!"

"Lord of...?"

"Of *everything!*"

"If you say so," Chetan said.

"I need help," the face said.

Chetan could see this was true.

"Listen," the face continued with a heavy New York accent, "I'm Nikhilprem. Niki. I'm broke but I have a plan."

"And you're going to tell me your plan, right?"

"Right. Listen, you've got to help me kidnap the Queen of England!"

Chetan roared with laughter!

"I mean it!" Niki said seriously. "She's in India now. We could get a hundred rupees at least."

"At least," Chetan agreed. "But wait! You've got the wrong guy. I'm not going to kidnap the Queen of England. Not without chaperone."

Niki looked confused. "Chaperone? You won't help? We could *get* a chaperone!"

"No!" Chetan said firmly. He reached into one of the pockets of his fuchsia robe, took out a gold rupee, and handed the coin to Niki.

This proved to be a big mistake. Unknowingly what Chetan had just done was to essentially adopt the Orphan of the Universe for life.

Nikhilprem gave Chetan a hug which practically fractured his ribs. "Thank you!" Niki cried.

The Orphan of the Universe just stood there in tears hugging Chetan. And Chetan's personal reward for all this was knowing that he had just saved the Queen of England from a fate worse than a root canal treatment.

At that moment, an attractive young redheaded woman in an orange robe walked up to Chetan and Niki. Chetan immediately knew the woman had to be related to Nikhilprem in some way. She, too, was wearing a mala, and in addition to the gibbon monkey frantically chattering on her right shoulder, the woman wore only one sandal and was smoking a hand-carved pipe shaped like mermaid. The smoke smelled like pifka.

"Niki," the woman said with an Australian accent, "I've been looking all over for you! Who's this?"

"Chetan," Chetan said.

"I'm Mary. My name means 'Miraculous Goddess of the Titans'."

Chetan felt she was misinformed about that but didn't comment. "Hello, Mary," he said.

"Are you going to help us?" Mary asked.

"No. Excuse me, I've got to go now," Chetan said.

"What's wrong?" Niki asked.

Chetan huffed, "I'm exasperated!"

"Castor oil," Mary suggested.

"What?" Chetan said.

"Castor oil's good for that," Mary said confidently. "It cured my gout."

"I don't have gout," Chetan said.

"You will have if you don't take castor oil," Mary reasoned.

Mary, Chetan would soon learn, was a true sorceress of logic, and for the moment he had to agree with her. "I'll get some," he said, and began to walk away from the eccentric couple.

Niki grabbed Chetan's right arm and asked, "Where ya goin'?"

This was Chetan's second clue that the Orphan of the Universe had bonded with him for life.

"Home," Chetan said.

"Where do ya live?" Niki asked, stepping closer.

Chetan inadvertently inhaled some of Niki's dog-breath and became alert that, *Wait a minute, what have I done?*

In a flash, Chetan saw a picture in his mind's eye of Niki and Mary moving in with he and Leela. Niki would help Chetan make castor oil soup; Mary the Miraculous Goddess of the Titans would help Leela cure the gout she didn't have; and Mary's monkey would pee on the carpet. One big happy family.

In panic Chetan tried to walk away without answering Niki. But Niki persisted: "Where ya goin'?" and followed behind Chetan with apewoman in tow.

"I told you," Chetan insisted, "I'm going home."

"To the ashram? I saw you at Darshan last night. I'm a sannyasin, too. Going to get enlightened."

"Really?" Chetan said, "Good luck." And he tried to walk away again.

"Thank you," Niki replied, keeping up with Chetan.

"Hey, Chetan!" Mary called.

Chetan turned around. "Yes?"

"Do you think the Queen of England is exasperated, too?"

"She will be if you kidnap her."

"Really?" Mary frowned. "Then let's find some other way to make money, Niki. Anyway, we don't have castor oil."

"Right," Niki said. "Maybe we could pinch Saint Faykin's signature from the old registry in that temple in town and sell it. Or we could get one of those ancient religious manuscripts we saw for sale in the bazaar. We could sell them to tourists for thousands!"

"Maybe," Mary agreed, "or give tours of Saint Faykin's grave in Pahalgam. What do you think, Chetan?"

Chetan hesitated. He could see that Mary and Niki were sincere and remembered how self-righteous he could be at times. He didn't want to hurt them, but finally had to say the truth: "Look," he said deliberately, "I'm sorry, but I don't want to sell Saint Faykin's signature or scriptures or give tours. Aren't all scriptures fiction unless the words represent the experience of the reader?"

With surprising reasonableness, Mary scolded Chetan: "Lighten up!" she said. "Have you seen Saint Faykin's tomb in Pahalgam? It's amazing."

"Saint?" Chetan asked. "Listen, selling castor oil seems to be your best bet to raise money."

"Spoiled sport!" Mary scolded again.

"He's okay," Niki said sympathetically.

Just then two rough-and-tumble local teenage punks dressed in dirty brown kaftans interrupted Chetan, Niki and Mary. The two thugs walked up and stood in the middle of the three.

"So, what is this, a cult?" one of the thugs asked in brusque English.

"The penguin cult," Chetan answered matter-of-factly.

The tallest thug looked shocked. "What's this, 'penguin cult'?" he asked.

The two young thugs were standing on Chetan's right. Chetan winked at Niki and Mary out of his left eye and deadpanned: "Usually we wear tuxedos with white shirts and black bow ties and waddle in a straight line following our beloved penguin leader. Sometimes we slide on our bellies across ice."

The two thugs looked at Chetan like he was crazy and began to back away. "Ice?" the tall one said.

Chetan continued, "Tonight is our Sacred Blood Ceremony. What's your blood type? Want to come?"

The two thugs looked at each other in shock. One mumbled something in Kashmiri to the other, then they quickly backed away frowning and mumbling something about "bloody penguins".

Mary's monkey furiously jumped up and down on the Goddess's right shoulder. "Easy boy," she said, and petted the monkey. "Where's the Blood Ceremony?" she asked Chetan.

Chetan laughed. "Only kidding. Look, I'm sorry I was rude. I can be a fool sometimes."

"Me, too," Niki said.

"The Fool is my favorite Tarot card," Mary said.

"Mine, too," Chetan agreed. "See you at the ashram?"

"Sure," Niki and Mary chimed, and they all hugged then parted company.

CHAPTER 40

Four months later, on an overcast spring day, Gollash stood with his hands on his hips and a smile on his face, admiring the new People's Bank building. The large bright yellow circular domed warehouse was an aesthetic marvel, and the project right on schedule. Sakaj day was two weeks away and Gollash had just handed a revealing note for Satchitta to one of the guards at Satchitta's ashram.

Gollash was pleased; Rakan, too. With the success of the People's Bank project and without precedent, Gollash had been elevated to the ranks of the Hassas and had become Rakan's most trusted man.

As he stood admiring his architectural masterpiece, Gollash reflected on his situation. He accepted the fact that his destiny would soon require him to challenge Rakan and he felt ready to suffer the consequences.

This is for me, Gollash thought, *and Asanga...*

Indeed, Rakan's wrathful greed had wrecked Gollash's body but not his spirit. Now the one-eyed, wooden-legged former orphan stood ready to meet his date with fate. He opened his notebook and scribbled some notes outlining the next steps in his plan to foil Rakan.

Suddenly he heard Rakan's voice from behind.

Gollash turned around and saw Rakan about ten feet away, walking towards him with Visiog on his right.

"How are things going?" Rakan asked.

Gollash stashed his notebook in one of the pockets of his kaftan and turned around. "Good," he said nervously. "Good".

"Wonderful," Rakan said. "We're all set for Sakaj Day?"

“The Bank staff needs to complete training,” Gollash said with authority.

“No problem,” Visiog offered. “I’ll take care of it.”

Rakan nodded towards Gollash. “No, let him do it.”

Gollash nodded and bowed.

Visiog frowned. The power had obviously shifted, but Rakan was in Despot Heaven and didn’t notice Visiog’s obvious displeasure with Rakan’s choice.

Rakan addressed Visiog: “Stay here and help with the construction clean up. I need to talk with Gollash privately. AGOK AL-HOOPALOO!”

“Agok al-hoopaloo.” Visiog said half-heartedly.

Rakan and Gollash walked towards the People’s Bank.

Visiog was left standing alone to fume over his demotion. He had been Rakan’s closest confidant, the Hassas who Rakan even trusted to oversee the preparation of his food. The day before though, Rakan had given this responsibility to Gollash. Visiog was furious but determined to reclaim his former seat of power.

I’m entitled to it! he thought.

CHAPTER 41

Later that same afternoon, Satchitta laid in bed in pain. Leela sat on a chair next to the Master.

"It's almost time for our experiment here to end and we have to prepare," Satchitta said. "The escape tunnel is complete and I'm going to advise Amritam to go to Gazabha to start a Mystery School, and you will have to decide where to go."

The Master winced and Leela called, "Taichia!"

Moments later Taichia rushed into the bedroom with two pieces of paper in her hand. She ran to Satchitta and asked, "Are you okay?"

Satchitta adjusted his body in the bed and said, "Water, please."

Leela poured water into a glass and handed it to the Master. Satchitta slowly drank water, then laid the glass on the table.

Satchitta saw the papers in Taichia's hand and asked, "What is that?"

Taichia frowned and said, "A note from Gollash and another from Rakan. They personally came to the main gate at different times this morning and handed these notes to Dahlia. Gollash's note is sealed so I don't know what's in it. Rakan's note is an invitation to the inauguration of the People's Bank next door on Sakaj Day in two weeks. Rakan wants you to be there."

"Oh, this is good," Sachitta said. "I will be there."

Leela and Taichia were shocked!

"WHAT?!" Taichia shouted. "NO! ABSOLUTELY NO! No, do you hear?"

"Please, may I have the notes?" Satchitta asked.

Taichia huffed, put her left hand over her heart, and handed the notes to Satchitta. The Master opened Gollash's note and read it. Then he read Rakan's invitation.

"Send Rakan a note saying that I will be at the celebration," Satchitta said softly. "Make arrangements. Accept his invitation. May I have some chai? And please ask Amritam, Shanti, Rajen, and Dahlia to join the three of us here for a meeting so I can explain."

CHAPTER 42

Shortly after dawn the next morning, Chetan shook Leela's right shoulder as they both lay in bed. "Leela! Leela!" he cried.

Leela quickly sat up in bed drenched in sweat. She turned to her left and saw Chetan staring wide-eyed at her.

"What's the matter?" Chetan asked.

Leela eyes fluttered. She took a deep breath and looked vacantly around the room. "The matter? A dream."

Chetan leaned back and studied Leela. "You were screaming in your sleep. Are you okay?"

"I... we... were on a ship," Leela said. "At night. Pitch black. Everyone running around screaming, crying. The ship had hit something, was floundering, tilting at a steep slope, bow upwards, going to sink any minute. I was a man, you, my wife. You held our infant boy. We had overcoats on, pajamas and nightgowns underneath. I was putting you and our baby in a lifeboat. The captain was shouting, 'Women and children only!' You and our baby were crying as your boat was being lowered into the icy sea below. 'Don't worry!' I shouted, 'I'll be on another boat. See you in New York! Love you!'"

"That was it?" Chetan asked.

"That was the last I saw of you and our child," Leela continued. "Your lifeboat disappeared into the night. My whole life flashed before my eyes: banks, wealth, power, huge estate, servants, manipulating people to gain wealth. 'The masses are sheep. They need me to lead them.' The entitled understanding Satchi was talking to me about yesterday! My life had been all about wealth and power. I'd spent little time with you and the baby.

"The ship shifted, lurched suddenly, was almost vertical. I hung on to one of the masts and saw what looked like an iceberg in the water below. I knew I was going down with the ship into the icy water, and for ten minutes I saw the futility of my life, how I had wasted it in the vain pursuit of power, wealth and manipulating others. For what?

"Then the ship and I were swallowed by the ocean in one gulp, and I... I heard you call my name just now."

"Just a dream," Chetan said soothingly.

"No," Leela said, "more than a dream! *Felt real!"*

"Past life?"

Leela nodded. "Um, but I don't understand."

"Let's get ready for discourse," Chetan said.

There was a knock on the door and Leela said, "Come in."

Taichia opened the door and walked in, her eyes red with tears. "He's in terrible pain now. I sent for the doctor. No discourse again today."

Leela motioned for Taichia to sit next to her. They sat silently with each other for a few moments. Then Leela excused herself, dressed quickly, and walked next door to Amritam's bungalow. She knocked on the front door and waited.

A minute later, Amritam opened the door and stood with weary brown eyes in his bathrobe. His long white beard hung to the middle of his chest, and the copper-colored skin on his face looked more wrinkled than Leela had ever seen it.

"Namaste," Leela said.

"Namaste," Amritam replied.

"Excuse me," Leela said. "No discourse this morning."

Amritam nodded. "I was up with him all night."

"Oh," Leela said. "Do you have a minute? I need to talk with you."

"Come in," Amritam said, and Leela entered the bungalow with him. Amritam pointed to a couch. They both sat down and Leela explained her dream to Amritam in detail.

Finally, Leela concluded, "And that's what I saw: my whole life wasted with wealth and power. I'm worried about a lingering belief I have from the experience."

"What belief?"

"That I have to die for my beloved and child to live."

At that moment, Amritam's beloved, Premdip, brought a tray of chai into the room and graciously laid the tray on a table in front of Amritam and Leela.

"Thank you!" Amritam and Leela chimed.

Premdip left the room as Amritam poured chai into two cups. Then he turned to Leela and said, "Do you know of any other past lives?"

"Quite a few. But this one was intense! And that belief..."

"Well," Amritam said, "the only way to know whether it was a past life or just imagination, is to do *jati smaran*."

"I've heard Satchi mention that. What is it?"

"Someone you trust guides you back through a deep relaxation process into the realms of your unconscious mind. If upon taking you back, the same experience is repeated, only then can you be sure it was a past life and not imagination."

"It felt so real!" Leela insisted.

Amritam studied Leela closely. "You're still trembling. Just learn from the experience and move on. Remember, you're not the mind. Whatever you experience, you're not that. You're the *watcher* of the experience, whether a dream or a past life."

Leela closed her eyes and took a deep breath. "I felt guilty after the dream, stupid really. Saw how I'd wasted my whole life on wealth and power. Took my wife and son for granted, hardly spent any time with them. There was no love in my life. In the end I died miserable, heartbroken."

Amritam smiled. "Good! Now you don't have to repeat the same mistakes *in this life!* You don't have to die for anyone else to live."

Leela sighed and said, "But I feel I did something horribly wrong in that life, manipulated people and need to be punished."

"NO! Absolutely not!" Amritam said emphatically. "That's the beauty of consciousness, the compassion of Existence. Until we become conscious of the secrets of our unconscious mind, we repeat the same mistakes over and over, life after life, are caught in a vicious circle of good-bad, reward-punishment. There's no need to be punished in this life for something we did in a past life. Our past lives were essentially just a dream. *This* life is a just dream! Wake up here now!"

Leela took a deep breath. "Satchi's so sick," she said, "going to die soon. He said I was ready to share my understanding of love and meditation with others. But what do I know? During one life I'm a tyrant, financial manipulator, political power-monger, a beggar really, because my behavior is determined by those I attempt to control. In the next life I'm the manipulated, the powerless victim of the political, economic and social hell I myself created in my past life as a tyrant! And in still another life I'm a rescuer - priest, nun or social worker - helping the types of people I destroyed in my past life as a tyrant. On and on. How stupid!"

"THE GOOSE IS OUT!" Amritam shouted.

Leela was startled. She fell back on the couch, then laughed. "Damn! There I go again!"

Amritam laughed. "More chai?"

"Yes, thank you."

Amritam poured chai and said, "You're too hard on yourself. These are intense times. Rakan is up to his mischief again. Like Satchitta told us recently: it's almost time to drop the experiment here. You heard him: he asked me to start a Mystery School in

Gazabha. Premdip, Taichia, Shanti, Rajen, and whoever else wants to go with us can go. I've had the same doubts as you about sharing my understandings. But let me tell you two fables Satchitta shared with us in discourse before you came back...

"It's been said that Chinese Medicine, and specifically acupuncture, originated when one man decided to kill another man whom he perceived to be his enemy. The man shot the enemy with an arrow but only wounded him in the leg. The wounded man had had painful migraine headaches for years before being wounded, but after his leg healed, he no longer had the headaches. He attributed the disappearance of the migraines to the infliction of the leg wound. *This* realization was the beginning of his discovery of *other* acupuncture points and meridians, and eventually the discovery of acupuncture, a science which has benefited mankind for centuries.

"Then Satchitta told another fable about a criminal in a certain city who was brought into a hospital on the verge of death from wounds inflicted during a drunken brawl which the criminal himself had started in a pub. The attending physician didn't know this patient was a criminal. He treated the patient and saved the man's life. The day the criminal was released from the hospital he went back to the same pub where he had been beaten up in the brawl, and he murdered eight innocent people.

"In the first story a man had the negative intention to kill another man, and the end result was a positive benefit for mankind - acupuncture. In the second story the surgeon had the positive intention of saving his patient's life, but the result was a negative one: the slaughter of eight innocent people.

"The point that Satchi was making rang true for me, Leela. Through meditation I've had insights into my past lives. I've lived as a tyrant, a rescuer, a victim, and countless permutations of these archetypes. The mind's nature is duality, so that *overall*, any action which my *mind* tells me to take is going to have *both* positive and negative consequences!

"Life is vast! We don't know all the ramifications of our actions. Personally, I've experienced the futility of trying to save the world or help others in any way that my mind says, because *my mind* has only created an endless circle of misery for myself.

"Satchitta said that the *only* way out of this cycle is by meditating and experientially understanding that the mind itself is the *root cause* of misery and that consciousness is a stronger energy than thought. In the light of consciousness, the darkness of mind and misery simply disappear. The more I'm conscious, the more my actions will help others. The key is to relax, live as consciously, spontaneously, and joyously as possible, and trust that Existence will guide me moment to moment. As Dilai Dalai wrote, 'Ultimately the only way I can help others is to be conscious myself.'"

Leela nodded, took a deep breath, and closed her eyes. She sat with Amritam in silence for several minutes, then opened her eyes and said, "Thank you. I feel better."

Just then they heard a knock on the door. Amritam stood, walked to the door, opened it, and stood facing Shanti and Rajen.

"You heard about the horses?" Amritam asked.

"Yes," Shanti said. "Do you know the owner well?"

Amritam nodded. "He has a huge ranch not far from here, 350 horses, more than our population. He has bought food from our farm for years and is completely trustworthy. He'll make good use of this property."

"Come in," Amritam said. "Leela's here. She needs to know about all this, too." Shanti and Rajen entered the room and nodded to Leela.

Amritam walked over to a dresser, opened the top drawer, and removed a piece of faded yellow parchment paper. He handed the paper to Shanti and said, “Here’s the deed to our property, and this is what we need to do...”

CHAPTER 43

During one of Lloyd's past lives in China, he invented golf. He was Duffer Ching, a mystic who taught that the "no-goal" of golf is to strike a round stone with a wooden staff over a long distance into an empty hole with as few strokes as possible.

"The no-goal," Duffer taught, "is emptiness."

Now, a thousand years later, Lloyd was playing golf again at the Cloud Nine Country Club.

One morning he returned from playing golf and laid his bag of clubs next to Bunny.

"How was your game?" Bunny asked.

"So-so," Lloyd said. "The holes looked smaller."

"Perception is everything," Bunny said.

"Seems so," Lloyd agreed.

Just then an old man in a flowing white gown floated by. He stopped and squinted towards Bunny and Lloyd. "Where's my glasses?" the old man asked.

God had lost his glasses again.

"I don't know," Lloyd said.

Bunny saw that God was about to crash into a storm cloud and cried, "Hey, watch where you're going! You'll get hurt!"

The old man maneuvered around the storm cloud and floated away.

"He's really getting old," Bunny said, "losing it. Still imagines that he's some God Almighty. He's harmless enough though. Maybe it's best to keep humoring him."

Lloyd shook his head and said, “No, we’ve humored him too much. He’s delusional and harmful to himself and other folks who believe his nonsense. I need to talk with him.”

Then he flew off to chat with God.

CHAPTER 44

The evening sky was pitch black and the merciful monsoon rain poured down like a river, cleansing the parched land in and around Srinagar.

Chetan felt that the intensity of the rains amplified the collective feeling of anguish among disciples in the ashram. Satchitta was clearly dying, and all his disciples felt it on some level or other.

The air was heavy with moisture and grief.

Inspired by Satchitta's statement that meditation was his path, Chetan had spent as much time as possible in meditation during the four months he had been in the ashram. Usually, his heart was full of gratitude being in the Master's presence during the morning discourses and evening Darshans. But on this evening his mind and heart were in turmoil. He felt the need to take a walk to release his anxiety. He hugged Leela good-bye in their bungalow and walked with an umbrella through the Mogul Gardens in the pouring rain.

Suddenly Niki jumped from behind a bush and hollered, "We're coming with you!"

Startled, Chetan jumped back!

Next to Niki, Mary stood with a wide-eyed grin on her face. The gibbon monkey on her right shoulder was dressed in a band leader's outfit and nibbling on Mary's lotus flower earrings.

"Oh?" Chetan said.

"Yeah," Niki said. "We heard you're going to America. I'm from New York. I'll show you around. My cousin Louie is a bag man for the Garbanzo Family. I have connections. In New York it's all about connections."

Chetan didn't recall signing Niki's adoption papers, or Mary's either. But the Orphan of the Universe and his soulmate must have thought that they had signed the papers for him.

"Who told you that?" Chetan asked.

"Who needs to know anything?" Mary offered.

"Look," Chetan said, "forget New York for now! Can we get out of the rain?"

"Over there," Niki said, pointing to a nearby pavilion. The three walked underneath the dry open-air pavilion.

Chetan pulled a leather pouch of pifka from his right pants pocket and said, "Here." He untied the strings of the pouch, pulled out a pipe, and filled the pipe with dried green leaves. "Lalou and I smoked on the way from Mumbai," he said.

"We've smoked with her, too," Niki said.

"I like it," Chetan said, and he lit the leaves.

They took turns smoking.

After about ten minutes, Niki said, "Good stuff."

Mary said, "Rainbow trout."

Chetan, Mary and Niki stood silently smoking for several minutes. Then Chetan said, "I heard that we could rent boats. Want to go with me?"

"We can't," Mary said. "We've got to get back to work."

"Oh," Chetan said, "in the ashram?"

"Yeah," Niki said, "but thanks."

They all hugged, and Niki and Mary walked away.

Chetan was soaring. He hustled into town and rented a small rowboat. The Jhelum River was swollen and raging from the heavy rains, but Chetan was excited! He had loved white-water rafting with Jeff and Wayne in Missouri.

He climbed into the boat and rowed madly across the widest part of the river. In the middle of the river, a large board on the bottom of the boat suddenly popped out! The boat quickly filled with water and began to spin in circles and sink!

Chetan couldn't see either shore in the pitch-black night and pouring rain. Instinctively he jumped out of the boat and began to swim across the raging current.

Tossed and turned by the current, it took all his strength to swim ashore, but he finally made it and grabbed onto a thick tree root at the river's edge. Exhausted and ravaged by the strong current, Chetan clung to the tree root and gasped for breath for several minutes.

Suddenly he felt a painful knot in his navel center. He retched and vomited again and again. He instinctively felt as if the pain had been locked away and stored in his belly by Floyd's suicide. Then in his mind's eye he saw a vision of Floyd. He saw Bridget and Hank and how he had blamed them for Floyd's suicide. The blame was the pain Chetan felt inside now.

Retching and vomiting, he let go of the blame: "I'm sorry!" he cried to the apparitions of Bridget and Hank. "You're not to blame! I'm sorry!"

For several minutes Chetan cried and retched and let go of his guilt and blame in the raging current.

Finally, he pulled himself on shore and lay on his back. He noticed that it had stopped raining and a full moon was shining above. He gazed at the glimmering moon above, and Satchitta's face appeared within the moon.

Chetan burst into tears, a torrent, a monsoon of tears. He cried for the longest time until finally, when the tears had cleansed his heart, with his eyes closed, a past life flashed before his mind's eye...

Chetan was a four-year-old boy standing in front of his father, who Chetan intuitively knew was Satchitta in this life. He had loved his father dearly but, in his vision, he saw his father leaving home, and as a little boy he really didn't know why.

It was revealed to him now in his vision that the reason his father had to leave was because a living enlightened Master had recently come into his father's life. As a young adult in that life Satchitta had been a meditator for ten years without a Master. But from the moment Satchitta's Master came into his life, the truth of Satchitta's relationship with his own wife surfaced and revealed that what Satchitta and his wife believed was love wasn't love; it was unconscious possessiveness – and Satchitta's wife felt the lie more than he did. For several months she had a secret affair with another man, then asked Satchitta to leave.

It broke Satchita's heart in that life to leave his beloved son. But Satchitta's heart needed mending by a Master, and in that life little Chetan needed to grow up experiencing love and guidance from primarily only one parent: his mother.

Chetan laid on the shore on his back. He closed his eyes and felt his heart. Due to his new understanding that there was no one to blame for what happened during his past life with Satchitta, Chetan felt a space open up for Satchitta... and for Hank, Bridget, Floyd, Camille, and for himself.

Compassion happened.

Chetan took several deep breaths and saw Satchitta's face inside himself. The Master related this story:

"A cunning businessman is walking along a ridge above a vertical cliff when he slips and falls. As he plummets towards the jagged boulders far below, he grabs onto a branch and breaks his fall.

"The man quickly realizes how hopeless his situation is. His grip on the branch is loosening and there is no way he can climb up the cliff. He realizes that he certainly will be killed if he falls.

"Only God can help me now, he thinks. *I never believed in God, but what have I to lose now?*

"He calls out, 'God, if you exist, please save me. I never believed in you, but if you save me, I'll believe in you.'

"There is no response, so he calls out again, 'God, I really mean it! If you save me, I'll believe in you!'

"Suddenly a voice booms out from above, 'Oh no, you won't!'

"The voice startles the man so much that he almost loses his grip!

"'Yes, I will!' the businessman insists. 'If you save me, I'll believe in you!'

"God calls out again, 'No, you won't! That's what they all say.'

"The man argues with God and finally God relents. 'Okay,' God says, 'I'll save you. Let go of the branch.'

"'Let go of the branch?' the man says. 'Do you think I'm crazy?'"

In an instant Chetan got it: pifka was a branch he was clinging to because he didn't trust that whatever he was feeling in any moment was okay.

I don't like what I'm feeling? Change it! Smoke pifka!

He realized he was wasting a precious opportunity to be naturally conscious each time he smoked pifka. He realized that the next river he had to cross was one that only being conscious each moment could help him cross - *without* the branch of pifka!

It was his choice moment-to-moment: to be or not to be.

The future remained unknowable, but in that moment, Chetan sat up and gazed at the full moon reflecting on the river. He stood, walked to the river's edge, reached into his pocket, took out the pouch with the pifka and pipe, and dropped the pouch into the swift current.

He looked up to the moon and said, "Thank you, Beloved Master."

Then he walked back to the bungalow and into his bedroom. Leela gasped when she saw Chetan soaked to the bone. “Look at you!” she said. “What happened?”

Chetan lowered his eyes. “Understanding, and gratitude for Satchitta.”

Leela nodded. “Want some chai?”

CHAPTER 45

In the middle of one of Srinagar's Moghul Gardens, Archdoppe Dildoh and Holy Gooft Doedoh studied each other suspiciously, each prelate determined not to give an inch in their negotiations to secure a truce between them.

Dildoh had fifteen soldiers with him, armed with Stealtz Rifles. Doedoh also had fifteen armed soldiers with Stealtz Rifles.

"Enough bloodshed!" Dildoh began, holding out a handful of *Kashmir Beacon* news clippings to Doedoh. "It's been a year now, and you've killed over twelve hundred of my people since Rakan started his Saint Faykin's tomb campaign in *The Beacon.* I don't know why we didn't see this earlier! But thanks to Gollash, now it's clear that Rakan has been baiting us against each other all this time."

"I know! I know!" Doedoh sneered. "And you've killed over eleven hundred of my people. How can we settle this? Fairly!"

Dildoh's suspicion deepened. "I don't trust you," he said. "You welched on our last agreement."

"That wasn't my fault," Doedoh protested. "The... listen, we're in this together. If we combine our forces--"

"First the money!" Dildoh interrupted, holding out his hand.

Doedoh motioned for four of his soldiers to remove the huge chest of gold rupees from his bullock cart. The soldiers lifted the heavy chest and put it onto Dildoh's cart. Dildoh opened the chest and smiled.

Doedoh said, "You'd better follow through with your part of the bargain."

"Don't worry," Dildoh said, "You can have Rakan's ore mines, weapons factories, and other businesses. And you can make the People's Bank into an orphanage if you want. This chest is enough for me. This time there will be no mistakes."

Doedoh firmly shook Dildoh's limp right hand, and said, "We have a deal!"

CHAPTER 46

Early evening, two days before Sakaj Day, Taichia, Leela, Amritam, Shanti, Rajen, and Dahlia sat on wooden chairs around Satchitta's bed at the Master's request. Satchitta was dressed in a full-length white robe and white knit cap and lying propped up by pillows surrounded by flowers. Leela was almost five months pregnant and showing.

"Beloveds," Satchitta began, "we were fortunate that Gollash gave us advance notice of Rakan's plan to destroy the ashram. Now we can plan our course of action. As I said two weeks ago, I visited Gollash on the spiritual plane and have seen the purity of his heart. I accepted Rakan's invitation to join him on Sakaj Day because Gollash suggested that it would be best for me to accept the invitation and not arouse Rakan's suspicion that we know what he is up to. I could always cancel at the last moment.

"Gollash made it clear that Rakan will not stop until the ashram is destroyed. It's been essential that we don't evacuate the ashram prematurely or Rakan's spies in the provinces will detect and kill us on the road. It's also essential that we follow Gollash's instructions or Rakan will launch a full-out invasion of the ashram."

The Master reached over, picked up several sheets of paper from the table next to his bed, and said, "Here are Gollash's notes. So far everything is going according to plan. Any questions?"

Taichia insisted, "It's too dangerous! We don't want you to go to the People's Bank on Sakaj Day!"

Satchitta nodded, closed his eyes for several moments, opened them, and said, "True, it is dangerous! Rakan's spies and guards from the province will all be gathered there for the celebration.

But that is why the evening of Sakaj Day is optimum for our departure. Rakan and his gang will all be at the celebration.

"Second thing: in his note Gollash insisted that I be there on Sakaj Day in order for him to destroy Rakan from within. He didn't say how he plans to do this.

The Master took a deep breath and softly, lovingly said, "So that is why this is all about trust, beloveds..."

Satchitta waited until he saw that everyone's heart was open and deep in trust, then concluded, "But please, don't worry about me. I shall leave the body within the hour."

Utter shock rocked the room!

Everyone jumped up!

Taichia burst into tears and collapsed upon the Master's feet. Shanti, too, was crying, but managed to put her arms around Taichia and hold her. Leela burst into tears, laid her head on the Master's chest, and wailed the loudest.

Satchitta knew this was natural and allowed ample time for his devotees to grieve. For over fifteen minutes everyone wept. Then slowly, slowly they began to calm down. Finally, the Master said, "Please sit."

Taichia sat up and held the Master's feet. Everyone else sat on chairs around him. Some crying and whimpering continued as all six of Satchitta's closest devotees sat entranced.

When there was utter silence, Satchitta said, "I felt I would be safe if I followed Gollash's plans. But now it's not possible. Existence has other plans for me, and I have total trust in Existence. Someone will have to go in my place... or not. Decide among yourselves what to do.

"Rakan may succeed in destroying our ashram but not our love. You have me in your hearts. No one can destroy your love. My only prayer is for you and our beloveds to dancingly disappear into your beings. With great laughter, disappear! With songs on your lips, disappear!

"I have not told you everything until this moment because I myself know only the moment. Life changes, and it's almost time for you to leave on the wind and spread our love. Amritam and Taichia will transfer the deed to our property to our friend who owns the horses, and those who wish to go with them to Gazabha, shall go. Leela, what about you?"

"America," Leela said.

Then she jumped up, wrapped her arms around the Master's chest and wailed. Satchitta let Leela cry for several minutes then gazed at Taichia. In the Master's eyes was more compassion than Taichia could handle and again she collapsed at his feet. Shanti stood and put her arms around Leela.

Everyone had tears in their eyes.

When Leela and Taichia settled down a bit, Rajen guided Leela back to her chair. Taichia remained on the bed holding Satchitta's feet.

Finally, Satchitta said, "Whenever you are with yourself inside, you are with me. It's time to stop clinging to my body and commune with me in silence. Everything I've spoken has just been to prepare you to be with me in silence. Truth happens only in silence. When you are conscious, silent, I will be with you even when my body is gone.

"Going back to Gazabha would be easy for you, Leela, and I know you love challenges. It is good. We grow in intelligence by going into the unknown. But be aware: there are Rakans everywhere. Everywhere, more or less, there is a conspiracy between so-called religions and vested interests, the self-appointed 'protectors' of the stagnant *status quo*. Organized religions destroy people's intelligence by giving them unverifiable beliefs which kill their ability to question and experientially explore the truth of their inner nature. And the power-mongers in government and business exploit these unintelligent people by telling them that *they themselves* are the servants of the people and the people should do what they tell them to do. For the most part, they are all unconscious and the results have been disastrous world-wide."

The Master closed his eyes for several moments, then he continued: "But remember the *total situation*: people have power over you only if you give them your power. Most of the so-called common people in the world never grow up; like the power-mongers, they are unconscious and remain childish. They are always ready to give away their power. The economic law of demand and supply applies. That is, by giving away their power, these childish people are in effect demanding that someone come along and supply them with what they demand. They don't want to consciously mature and take responsibility for their own life. They unconsciously demand that someone else take the responsibility and dominate them. They *create* the power-mongers by giving away their personal power and responsibility for their life. They give away their power to those who think they are entitled to dominate them.

"Once an individual takes back the responsibility for their life, they free themselves from the power-mongers. With freedom comes responsibility. One must evolve through meditation and develop the ability to respond moment to moment with awareness if one is to remain free. It's an eternal journey.

"The dominated and the dominating are all sleeping buddhas, dreaming the dream of the ego, of a false belief that they are separate from Existence. Someday, some life, each one will understand the futility and misery of the ego and will awaken through meditation. But one must go In. It takes understanding and guts.

"I know from my own experience that the Dream has no beginning, but it does have an end. Spiritual awakening is the end of the Dream. Meditation is the flower and compassion the fragrance. Understanding the whole situation through meditation, you will be able to help all types of people just by being yourself. No effort will be needed.

"Don't be concerned with the priests and politicians. Respond creatively moment to moment to the situations that life presents to you. Trust Existence. Just be aware of the priest and politician within your own mind and have a good laugh at yourself! Be ordinary, natural, Leela. Do you understand?"

Leela nodded and took a deep breath. "How can I thank you enough?"

Satchitta grimaced with pain and said, "By being conscious, aware, *sammasati*. Go In."

Forty minutes later, Buddha Hall was filled with 324 of Satchitta's disciples. The Master was lying propped up on pillows in his bed on the podium. Three disciples played on a sitar, tabla and flute on one side of the podium. Taichia and Leela sat on chairs on either side of the bed at the feet of the Master. Chetan sat in the seventh of twenty-one semicircular rows of sannyasins surrounding Satchitta.

Sweet music filled the air.

Satchitta motioned with his hand and Taichia handed the Master a small bowl of sweets. Satchitta slowly put a sweet in his mouth, closed his eyes, and savored the sweet for several minutes.

Then he took a deep breath.

A moment later Satchitta opened his eyes, scanned the audience, and said, "Remember that you are a Buddha. *Sammasati*." Then he closed his eyes.

Everyone closed their eyes...

A silent synchronicity filled the hall...

The musicians brought their music to a whisper...

The symphony of birds that had been singing outside the hall suddenly became silent...

A lone bird serenaded...

The musicians stopped playing altogether...
The lone bird, too, stopped singing...
Silence pulsated with light...
All was still for fifteen minutes...

Suddenly everyone felt the mood change...

Chetan opened his eyes. With tears of gratitude, he gazed at Satchitta's body lying on the bed. Then he looked at Leela. Leela turned, gazed at Chetan with teary eyes and smiled.

Chetan smiled.

Gradually there was movement in the hall. The birds begin to sing again in a chorus of joy and delight.

The atmosphere changed into celebration!

The musicians began to play softly. Disciples stood with tears in their eyes and began to sway. Many sannyasins began to dance and several hugged silently.

Taichia laid a rose on the Master's chest and kissed his forehead. Leela stood and laid her head next to the rose. The musicians began to play celebration music, and everyone danced around the podium in a whirlwind of tearful ecstasy, spinning and grinning like children around a maypole!

Fifteen minutes later the music reached a crescendo. Six swamis placed Satchitta's body on a wooden pallet garlanded with flowers. They hoisted the pallet and carried it outside the hall with everyone following behind them singing chorus after chorus of "Om, Shanti, Shanti, Shanti".

The caravan stopped at the side of a four-foot-high wood pyre in the middle of the ashram. The pallet with the Master's body was placed on the pyre.

Everyone gathered around as Taichia torched the pyre and flames quickly engulfed Satchitta's body. Leela and Chetan sang and danced around the flames, whirling in ecstasy.

The celebration went on into the middle of the night, until only glowing embers remained of the pyre and Leela fell asleep in Chetan's arms.

CHAPTER 47

At dawn the next morning, fifty Hassas stood at attention in the Tomb Room in Rufus Temple as Rakan burst through the door with Asanga and Gollash.

"Sit, idiots!" Rakan roared. "What's this I hear about Satchitta?"

All the Hassas sat down. Visiog hung his head and said, "Those flames that were seen in his ashram yesterday..."

"Yes, yes, go on!" Rakan said impatiently.

Visiog said no more, for he knew that Rakan had heard the rumor.

Rakan pounded the table and screamed, "NO! DAMN HIM! They will worship him as a saint now and the ashram will be as strong as ever! What now, eh, Visiog? This was your great idea!"

Visiog turned to Asanga and said, "Your turn."

"For what?" Asanga asked.

"To prove yourself!" Visiog sneered.

"How *dare you!"* Rakan shouted.

"Everyone here has been tested to a greater degree than Asanga," Visiog said emphatically. "You know my loyalty, master. What if Asanga were to do away with Leela, his old lover, now that she's back? She is Satchitta's only offspring. That will cripple the ashram!"

Rakan's eyes lit up. The High Honchah turned to Asanga and said, "Yes, Plan B, good idea! Isn't it, *son?* Leela!"

Asanga feigned surprise, then said confidently, "Sure, I'll do it!"

Visiog glared at Asanga suspiciously.

Rakan liked what he had heard. It was his life's fulfillment to have his son take over responsibility for his empire. *But Asanga must prove himself first!*

"Yes," Rakan said to Asanga, "The goose will be cooked! Now I want you to personally go to the ashram gate with ten guards and invite Leela to The People's Bank inauguration tomorrow."

Asanga nodded, stood up, left for the ashram with ten Hassas, and later gave Rakan Leela's note accepting his invitation.

CHAPTER 48

Sakaj Day began like any other monsoon day.

It rained.

Leela and Chetan stood on the veranda of their bungalow, and each took a deep breath. The Master's daughter pulled the hood of her beige cashmere cape over her head, took Chetan by the hand, and asked, "Are you ready for this?"

"What do you think?" Chetan said.

Leela studied him. "Okay, let's go."

They walked from their bungalow through the ashram and out the front gate. They took a right along the main path of the People's Park and walked to the bright yellow People's Bank building.

Leela stood before the bank holding Chetan's hand.

The area was crowded and noisy. Everyone, including Rakan, was wearing Sakaj Day faux donkey ears, a tail, and horse blinders aside their eyes.

Rakan stood at the entrance to the People's Bank with Gollash, Asanga, and Visiog at his side.

Rakan shouted in English, "Quiet, everyone! QUIET!" Immediately there was silence.

"We have special guests today," Rakan announced, and waved his right hand towards Leela and Chetan. "Won't our guests join us inside?"

The crowd applauded loudly.

Leela glanced at Chetan and whispered, "Here we go. I hope the soup's good."

The couple walked into the People's Bank with Rakan, Gollash, Asanga and Visiog. A large portion of the crowd followed them inside.

Rakan stopped in front of a large buffet table arrayed with every kind of seasonal fruit and vegetable available in Kashmir. Everyone gathered around Rakan.

Leela looked behind her and saw that the double front doors were being locked by one of the Hassas. A veil of terror fell over her face.

What if...

Rakan swept his hand over the table and proudly proclaimed, "Here is the fruit of our labors! Now a toast to our neighbors!"

Asanga picked up a clear glass of fruit juice from the table and nodded to Leela and Chetan. They each randomly picked a glass of juice.

Rakan, Gollash, Visiog and several other Hassas picked up glasses of juice, and Rakan toasted Leela and Chetan:

"Here's to our neighbors, here's to our friends, here's to a friendship which never ends!"

Chetan and Leela drank to the toast.

"AGOK AL-HOOPALOO! Hee-Haw!" Rakan shouted.

"AGOK AL-HOOPALOO! Hee-Haw!" the crowd roared.

Leela was shaken by the shouting and took a deep breath.

Suddenly she felt trapped by the crowd, by Rakan, by the Hassas, by the locked building!

This is no game! she thought.

"Must be some chant," Chetan said nervously.

"Must be," Leela agreed. "Maybe it's time to go."

"Now everyone, go!" Rakan shouted. "There's not enough room here for everyone to celebrate!"

Leela was relieved. She started to back away when Rakan added, "But our special guests must stay and have some of Leela's favorite pea soup!"

The crowd laughed and cheered and began to file out of the building, leaving Leela and Chetan alone with Rakan and fifty Hassas.

"Of course," Leela said, "I'd love some soup."

"You would?" Chetan whisped. "I thought you wanted to go."

Leela turned to Asanga and said, "Funny meeting you here."

"Yes," Asanga said with a sparkle in his eyes, "friends are friends."

Rakan smiled. "Come, Leela, and your friend, ah, ah..."

"Chetan," Chetan said, as he put out his right hand to shake Rakan's hand. But Rakan ignored the gesture and left Chetan's hand dangling in the air.

"Yes, Chetan," Rakan said, turning away, "join us for some of Leela's favorite pea soup."

"Delighted," Chetan said.

Rakan furtively called over Snakji and whispered, "Quick! You know what to do with the maegin. Make handwritten placements with the names of Leela, Chetan and Gollash and place them on one side of the dining room table. Make placements for Visiog, Asanga and myself on the other side of the table."

Snakji rushed into the foyer and added a deadly portion of tasteless water-soluble maegin to a bowl of soup. He quickly scribbled the names of each guest on paper from his notebook and placed a name on the table in front of each chair as instructed.

Rakan allowed ample time for Snakji to complete his task by bragging about how beautiful the People's Bank building was and how the poor of Srinagar will be benefitted by his generous donation to the community.

When the handwritten placements had been laid on the dining table, Snakji opened the door to the foyer and waved to Rakan.

Rakan rubbed his huge belly and declared, "Now let us enjoy Leela's favorite pea soup!"

Snakji stood at the entrance to the foyer as Rakan, Asanga, Visiog, Gollash, Leela, and Chetan passed by him into the large high-ceiling room. Then Snakji entered the foyer and closed the door behind him.

In the middle of the spacious room were two rectangular tables. On one small brown wooden table was a big pot of steaming soup and six large ceramic bowls filled with hot soup.

The other larger dinner table was covered with a white silk tablecloth. The centerpiece vase contained an assortment of colorful flowers. Three chairs faced three other chairs on the either side of the table, and handwritten placements with the name of each guest lay next to a wooden spoon wrapped in a white silk napkin.

"Ah, the soup looks hot and ready to eat!" Rakan said proudly. "Asanga, won't you do the honor?"

Asanga walked to the small table and put the first three bowls of soup on a rectangular tray.

He began to walk over to the placements for Leela, Chetan, and Gollash, when suddenly he appeared to stumble and spilled a little soup on Rakan's right foot!

Everyone looked down in horror at Rakan's foot.

Meanwhile, Asanga turned the rectangular tray with the three bowls around 180 degrees and put the tray on the dinner table.

"How careless of me!" Asanga apologized. He pulled a handkerchief from his pocket and wiped Rakan's foot.

Red with anger, Rakan quickly composed himself. "That's okay," he said, "accidents happen."

Asanga wiped the three bowls dry with a napkin, walked over to the side of the table where Leela, Chetan, and Gollash were to sit, and placed a bowl of hot pea soup in front of each handwritten name.

Gollash took a deep breath and sighed. He knew that the soup in the bowl previously intended for Leela was now in front of him.

The soup in Gollash's bowl had been spiked with maegin by Snakji.

Asanga turned to Leela, and said, "Careful, it's hot!"

Leela looked into Asanga's deep brown eyes and saw love!

My God! Leela thought. *He knows!* She took a deep breath and immediately her tension vanished. Leela felt she was safe.

"Everyone, eat up!" Rakan said. "Let's not waste another drop, eh, Leela?"

Leela studied Rakan. "No," Leela said, "we wouldn't want to do that."

Asanga put the last three bowls of soup on a tray and laid each bowl on the table in front of handwritten placements for Rakan, Visiog and himself. Then everyone sat down to eat.

Rakan could hardly contain himself as he watched Leela happily eating soup. He finished his bowl long before anyone else and started blabbering: "This animosity between us has gone on too long. We're neighbors now. This is a new beginning, a new dawn. The People's Bank shall be a symbol of our eternal friendship...."

On and on Rakan blabbered...

Leela kept nodding as Rakan ranted on. When she finished her soup, she said, "Best soup I've ever had! How can I ever thank you enough?"

"You already have," Rakan said. "You already have." He wiped his thin lips with a napkin and said, "I hate to see you go, but please come again soon, will you? You haven't lived till you've tried our homemade chocolate cake!"

"I look forward to that," Leela said. "Bye."

"*Namaste*," Chetan said.

Leela and Chetan walked hand in hand out of the People's Bank and back to the ashram.

CHAPTER 49

In the evening of Sakaj Day, Rakan sat alone on a couch in the foyer of Rufus Temple gloating over the latest issue of *The Kashmir Beacon.*

Gollash hurriedly limped on a crutch into the foyer and shouted, "Dildoh and Doedoh! Someone has to put out the fire!"

Rakan glanced over the newspaper and asked, "What fire?"

"That fire!" Gollash insisted. "You know, those killings. Dildoh and Doedoh are at it again! In Pahalgam! Someone must go and put out the fire or the people of Kashmir will turn against us for instigating the war between them. But who? Who? This is crucial! Who shall we send?"

Rakan beamed with pride. His son, Asanga, had just proven himself with Leela. He was the man!

"Asanga!" Rakan said. "Gollash, send him in here. And get me some more of that pea soup, will you? Tasty stuff! Give everyone the rest of the day off and tell the guards to go to sleep. I don't want to be disturbed. Understand?"

"Yes," Gollash bowed, and began to walk away.

"Gollash," Rakan asked tenderly, "are you feeling well? You look pale."

Gollash swallowed hard. He had just vomited four times and was trying not to die before he could do what he had to do.

"I'm fine," Gollash said. "It's been an exciting day. I need rest."

"You deserve it," Rakan said.

No, you deserve it! Gollash thought.

Five minutes later, Asanga walked into the foyer. Rakan looked up from his newspaper and said, "Asanga! Son! I need you to go to Pahalgam and cool off Dildoh and Doedoh. They're at it again. More bloodshed."

"Now?" Asanga asked.

"Is there any other time?" Rakan asked.

Asanga was stunned at the profundity of his father's words. *Yes, now is the only time,* he thought. *And this will be the last time I'll see you.*

Strangely enough, Asanga felt gratitude swell up in his chest. Tears fell from his eyes and rolled down his cheek. He bowed to his father and said, "I'll leave immediately."

Then as Asanga was about to walk out the door, he turned around, looked into his father's eyes and said, "I love you."

Upon hearing those three precious words that no one had ever said to him before, Rakan stared in amazement. He silently watched Asanga walk out the door, then quickly shook off the uncomfortable feeling of sentimentality. He gathered himself, and roared, "Gollash! Where is that soup? I'm famished!"

Seconds later, Gollash arrived back in the foyer with a hot bowl of Shanti's pea soup on a tray.

"Here it is, master," Gollash said, holding back his tears and struggling to stay alive. *We both must die for others to live.*

CHAPTER 50

Soon after sunrise the next morning, Visiog stood with absolute authority at the head of the long table in the Tomb Room in Rufus Temple. Forty-nine Hassas sat before him.

In command at last! Visiog thought. Then he bellowed, "Brothers, beholders of truth, AGOK AL-HOOPALOO!"

The Hassas raised their right fists and cheered!

"AGOK AL-HOOPALOO!"

"We shall overcome our adversity!" Visiog roared. "We shall destroy the enemies who have taken the lives of our beloved master and Gollash! All hail, Rakan, our master forever!"

The Hassas all cheered! "AGOK AL-HOOPALOO!"

"Where is Asanga?" Snakji asked.

Visiog replied, "He left for Pahalgam. He told me that Rakan ordered him to deal with Dildoh and Doedoh. They're fighting again."

Then Visiog turned to the Hassas and shouted, "Brothers, let's storm the ashram, find the culprits, destroy their axis of evil! Justice will prevail! AGOK AL-HOOPALOO!"

"AGOK AL-HOOPALOO!" the Hassas roared.

"Bare your swords and ready your guns, men!" Visiog roared. "We're going to war!"

The Hassas cheered and Visiog led the terrifying brigade of vengeful vigilante priests on horseback out of Rufus Temple and through the streets of Srinagar towards Satchitta's ashram.

Shop owners and their patrons screamed and jumped away as the onslaught of screaming horseman raced through the city. The black-caped horde quickly reached Satchitta's ashram and screeched to a halt in front of the two tall front gates.

"Break open the gates!" Visiog shouted from atop his black stallion. Twelve Hassas jumped off their horses and quickly broke open the front gate with hammers and metal bars, only to find...

...the ashram empty...

...not a soul around...

...no one...

It was obvious to all the Hassas that the ashram was vacant.

As riled up and bloodthirsty as they were, the horde of cutthroats hesitated to storm the ashram. There was no one to fight.

No one, only utter silence...

Visiog spurred his horse into the ashram and manically rode around inside, screaming, "Come out! Come out! We know you're here! Come out, cowards!"

The other Hassas, too, rode around the ashram on their horses looking for someone, anyone, to kill.

But no one was there.

After a futile attempt to locate one person in the ashram, Visiog ordered the Hassas to tie up their horses and leave their guns and swords outside Buddha Hall. Then the new commander-in-chief gathered his forty-nine storm troopers inside Buddha Hall.

Visiog attempted to give a long-winded, inspiring speech to his deflated troops, but soon gave up. After twenty minutes of blabbering, Visiog concluded his speech by holding up his right fist in the air and proclaiming, "The ashram has been destroyed! Our first victory together!"

"Victory!" the Hassas responded half-heartedly.

Just then a lone armed soldier appeared at the entrance to the Hall.

Then another...

...and another...

...and another...

Within seconds, dozens, then hundreds, then two thousand professional soldiers could be seen through the wall of mosquito netting around the hall, all armed with the new Stealtz Rifles that Rakan had sold Dildoh and Doedoh.

Visiog stood in the middle of Buddha Hall and looked through the mosquito netting in astonishment. He saw the hoard of soldiers around the hall and was prepared to fight to the death.

Dildoh and Doedoh stood with their generals outside the main gate of the ashram, prepared to fulfill Visiog's death wish.

CHAPTER 51

Midafternoon on a sunny day, Leela, Chetan, Punya, Mary and her monkey, Lalou, Prema, and twenty other sannyasins stood anxiously waiting on one of the wharfs in Mumbai.

Look!" Punya cried, pointing to Asanga, Pathen and Niki running up to them panting heavily. Niki held out a large leather sack and said, "We sold all the horses, got a fantastic price!"

Chetan lowered his backpack from his shoulder and said, "Here, put it all in here with the rest of the gold from my bank."

Asanga stuffed the sack of gold on top of the gold that Chetan had withdrawn from his bank.

"Great," Chetan said. "No luck so far finding a ship. Let's try others."

Chetan led his friends down along the pier and asked three more Captains if any of them were sailing to America soon.

No luck.

"Only one more left," Chetan said, looking further down the pier. "Maybe...WAIT! Couldn't be!" He pointed to a beautiful white clipper ship lowering anchor a hundred yards away.

"THE QUEEN!" he roared and ran towards the ship.

"CHETAN!" Leela shouted. *"Wait for us!"*

"Come on!" Chetan shouted back. He ran down the pier until he came to the last ship in the harbor. His friends ran behind him. Mary's monkey fell off her shoulder, landed niftily, and scurried to catch up with her.

As Chetan got to within fifty feet of *The Emerald Queen,* a familiar voice with an Irish accent shouted "Mark!" from the deck.

Chetan looked up and saw Ethan decked out in white Captain's regalia! "It can't be you!" Ethan shouted. "But it is you! How the hell are you, mate?"

Ethan ran down the gangplank and onto the pier to hug his friend. By this time, the other sannyasins had caught up with Chetan and stood in awe watching the two men hug.

"You look great, Ethan!" Chetan exclaimed. "I'm Chetan now."

Ethan looked bewildered. "Chay-who?"

"Chetan. Hey, look, this is my friend, Leela."

Ethan was stunned by Leela's beauty. He stood wide-eyed and watched her gracefully walk up to him.

"Chetan told me a lot about you," Leela said.

"Oh, no!" Ethan said. "I didn't do any of it."

"Yes, you did," Leela said, "and we're going have fun doing more!"

"We?" Ethan said. "Who, ah, *we?* Are you going with me? To 'Frisco?"

"If you want us," Chetan said. "And I have a few other friends."

Chetan turned and nodded towards the other sannyasins.

"Bloody hell!" Ethan said. "These are *all* your friends? What's with the red getup everyone's wearing?"

"What's a 'getup'?" Leela asked.

"Clothes," Chetan said. "We're sannyasins," he explained to Ethan.

"I knew you'd make it!" a familiar voice shouted from the gangplank.

Chetan turned and saw Vedant striding off the gangplank towards him carrying a backpack on his shoulders.

"Vedant!" Chetan cried and hugged him. "How are you?"

"Packed and ready to go home finally!" the old salt said. "Made enough these last four years to buy a farm, start a family."

"At your age?" Chetan kidded.

"Never too old to love," Vedant said, and wiggled his head.

"Sannyasins? What the hell's going on?" Ethan demanded.

"The truth is," Chetan said, "Leela is five months pregnant with our child. Her other lover, Asanga, is standing there after having escaped from a murderous father and two prisons of sorts. Niki is a New Yorker who defies description and has a pure heart like his beloved, Mary, the Miraculous Goddess of the Titans, with the monkey on her shoulder there. Lalou is the blonde, waving with Prema. Pathen and Punya are the teenage sannyasins holding hands. And the other sannyasins are friends who want to go to America with us. We're willing to work. Here's some money."

Chetan handed Ethan the large backpack of gold rupees. "I got my savings from the bank this morning and we got a good price for our horses."

Ethan felt the hefty bag and was stunned.

"MARK!"

Chetan swiveled to look up on deck. "REV? *SAUL?*"

A strikingly handsome man with a tanned face, full black beard, and wire rimmed glasses waved at Chetan.

"Mark!" the man shouted again.

"No, it can't be!" Chetan exclaimed, "Saul!"

Saul ran down the gangplank and hugged Chetan.

"You look great!" Saul said. "And who is this?"

"Leela," Leela replied. "What's this, a family reunion?"

Tears of joy rolled down Chetan's face. He put his hands squarely on Saul's shoulders and studied him in amazement. Then he turned to Leela and said, "You won't believe how much this man has changed."

Leela smiled. "Try me."

Chetan turned back to Saul and said, "What... my God, what happened? Last time I saw you, you..."

"I was almost dead," Saul agreed. "Well, you're to blame, rascal! I worked at O'Doul's for a while before I hooked up with this rogue and his crew. Would you believe it, Mark? Ethan tried to steal my girlfriend at O'Doul's, right in front of my eyes! Said to her, 'Leave him for me.' The nerve!"

Ethan laughed. "But did she go with me, Mark, ah, Chetan? No, this man's a lady-killer if ever there was one!"

Leela was shocked. "You kill ladies?"

"No, believe me," Saul replied, "they kill me!"

Everyone who understood English laughed.

Leela studied Ethan and smiled seductively. "Chetan tells me you're the ladies' man."

Ethan blushed, then slapped Chetan on the shoulder: "Oh, she's trouble, mate, with a capital T."

"Don't I know it," Chetan said.

"I thought you came to India to meditate, to find a live Master." Saul joked.

The remark changed the energy.

Chetan tapped his heart. "I'm with a Master."

Everyone fell silent for a moment.

"Oh," Ethan said, "Gopal?"

"His son, Satchitta," Chetan said. "Her father."

Ethan, Saul and Vedant stared wide-eyed at Leela.

"Her *father?*" Ethan said. "You're joking." He looked into Leela's deep brown eyes and said, "Damn! No, you're not. She looks like the real deal."

Chetan tapped Ethan on the chest and asked, "And how about you? Where's your dad? How did you get to be Captain?"

Ethan blushed and laughed. "Almost had me throat cut on one of me binges. Singapore. Meditation helped a lot, but I still wanted a drink once in a while. Anyway, I woke up in a pile of rubbish, alive somehow - and that was it. I just grabbed my balls - excuse me, ma'am - and said to myself, 'Ethan, if you want to hold on to your family jewels, you'd best go cold turkey - *or else!* Six months later my dad saw I was sincere and put in a good word for me at the office. Mr. Cornwall gave me my own ship. My dad retired in Donegal."

"Ireland?"

"The same," Ethan said. Then he waved his arms towards the stately *Emerald Queen*, and exclaimed, "Blimey, she's a beauty, eh?"

Chetan patted Ethan on the shoulder and said, "You deserve it."

"Well come along then! We could use a good mate! Or three! Oh, hell, I don't care! All of you can come! I need all the help I can get."

Leela's eyes lit up. "You *mean...*?" she asked excitedly.

"Sure!" Ethan said. "Welcome aboard! Even the monkey!"

Leela shrieked! She threw her arms around Ethan's neck and hugged him with tears in her eyes. *"Really?"* she asked.

"My God!" Ethan exclaimed, with Leela still hugging him. "She's a fireball!

Mary flung her arms around Chetan's neck as her monkey held on for dear life. Within seconds everyone began to hug one another and celebrate.

Mary screamed and jumped up and down: "I can't believe it! We're going! We're going!"

"I can't believe it either!" Niki shouted. "Is this our ship?"

"She is, mate," Ethan said to Niki. "And who's your, ah, lovely girlfriend?"

"Mary," Mary said. She fluttered her eyes at Ethan, nodded towards the monkey on her shoulder, and said, "And this is Willie."

"Monkey business if I ever saw it!" Ethan quipped. Then he turned to Niki and asked, "How long have you known Mark, er, Chetan?"

“As long as I can remember,” Niki said sincerely. “What day is it?”

Ethan laughed and gripped Niki’s forearm firmly. “A madman if I ever saw one! Just the kind of bloke I want on my crew!”

Ethan threw his arms around Mary and Lalou’s shoulders and said, “I promise I’ll be a gentleman, ladies.”

Mary cuddled up to Ethan and crooned seductively, “I promise you’ll break your promise.”

“Oh, Lordy!” Ethan cried, lifting the backpack full of gold aloft with one arm and hugging Mary with the other. “I deserve this! Now get your gear on board, mates, ladies. We’ll introduce ourselves later. But be ready to work your bloody arses off! This is no free ride, no picnic. I’ll count this loot later. It feels like it’s way too much. You’ll need some of this when we get to ‘Frisco. Don’t know where you all will sleep, or what you’ll eat, but that’s your problem! We sail in the morning!”

Ethan put his Captain’s hat on Niki, and jokingly declared, “Captain he is! Good to have you aboard, mate!”

CHAPTER 52

One forenoon a week later, most of *The Emerald Queen* crew lounged on deck. Chetan played Ethan's new guitar and sang "Rise Above the Storm" as Asanga plucked his *aektara* and tapped a rhythm on his kettle drum. Leela whirled around the deck, dancing to their celebration music. All the sannyasins and most of Ethan's crew joined in the dancing as well, letting go of the tension that had built up during previous day's horrendous storm.

The celebration continued until everyone was exhausted and it was time for lunch. Then one by one, the dancers began to wind down and go to the galley to eat. Chetan and a few others remained on deck.

Chetan laid the guitar down, picked up his journal and stood at the bow of The Queen, gazing in awe at the vastness of the ocean. He took a deep breath of salty air, then heard a sweet voice call from behind: "Don't throw it."

Chetan turned around and watched Leela stroll up to him, hand in hand with Asanga.

"How did you know?" Chetan asked.

Leela kissed Chetan's cheek and glanced at the journal.

"I just know," she said. "To you the journal's just a dream, and maybe no one else will ever read it or understand why you would leave the security of your home and risk your life in search of a live Master. So what? Don't throw it overboard. Keep it... or give it to me. I'll keep it for myself and our baby here."

Chetan shrugged his shoulders and nodded.

Leela smiled and said, "Writing was your way of loving yourself, explaining yourself to yourself."

She turned, gazed upon the vast expanse of ocean, looked back down at the journal, and added, "It's love, Chetan, share it. Whether others choose to receive it or not, doesn't matter."

Chetan licked his lips and took a whiff of the salty air. Laughing, he said, "Maybe you're right," and tucked the journal under his arm.

"Asanga and I are going below for lunch," Leela said, "Wanna come?"

"Soon," Chetan said. "I want to write about the storm while it's fresh in my mind. You two go ahead."

Leela nodded, and she and Asanga strolled away.

Chetan turned, laid the journal on the bow and began to write:

•

Seems like eons ago since I last wrote...

I'm looking out now from the bow of *The Emerald Queen* at the calm ocean. It's the day after the storm. Hard to believe that it's the same ocean as yesterday, a gentle warm wind blowing now from the southeast, the brilliance of the dazzling sun overhead making my eyes squint...

The contrast between yesterday and today is remarkable. Yesterday's storm almost sank the ship! Waves towered above us like angry mountains roaring in the ferocious winds. I almost went overboard myself - would have gone overboard if it hadn't been for Niki!

The whole scene seems like a dream now, *is* a dream! It was amazing: when death felt certain, there was no fear, only the intensity of the moment as I rode out nature's fury. Not even an old salt like Ethan suspected that the storm would hit.

I was up in the crow's nest. We had been sailing due east, parallel to the storm south of us. Suddenly the storm turned ninety degrees north and headed straight towards us like a banshee hellbent on destruction! The winds became intense within a half hour! Ethan called for me to come down and help lower the masts, so I made my way down to the deck.

Towering waves started crashing onto the deck, and Ethan barked orders for everyone to help tie up the sails. Then Ethan ordered me to help Niki.

Niki and I were starboard tying up a sail with rope when we both looked up and saw a monstrous wave looming above us like a gigantic claw of death. Don't ask me how, but Niki just grabbed the rope, wrapped it around both of us, and hitched it to a hook on the mast - just as the huge wave came crashing down on us! Almost knocked me out, and I damn well know I would have gone overboard and drowned if it hadn't been for Niki. But the rope saved us.

Tears of gratitude as I write now.

Thank you, beloved Niki!

At the storm's peak, as *The Queen* was being hurtled around by the angry waves like a matchstick, Ethan was at the helm barking orders to the crew, and I felt that I had done all that was humanly possible to do in the moment. In fact, there was too much help. Fifteen sannyasins were on deck tripping over each other, desperately trying to follow Ethan's orders and help the rest of the crew. I felt it was futile to do anything more than just ride out the storm, so I ignored Ethan's orders and went below to make sure Leela was okay. On the way down I passed by Mary, who was helping to batten down one of the hatches. Mary was calmly singing the children's song Leela had taught her, "What's One More Raindrop?"

I ran to Ethan's cabin, opened the door, and saw Leela strapped safely to a sturdy wooden chair. The chair in turn was tied with a rope to a brace on the wall. Leela was rocking her body back and forth in an easy rhythm, singing the same lullaby as Mary:

"What's one more raindrop?
Soon the tears will surely stop.
What's one more raindrop
to an open heart?"

Funny how things happen... the moment I saw pregnant Leela gently swaying back and forth in the chair during the horrendous chaos outside, my heart opened. I felt so much love that… well, the gratitude I felt was overwhelming.

The storm began to calm down the moment I felt the gratitude, as if the weather outside was in synchronicity with the peace I felt inside.

I closed the cabin door and went back on deck.

Within an hour the winds were relatively calm and steady.

A miracle...

•

Chetan put his journal down on the bow of the deck just as Leela came behind him.

"I wasn't very hungry. Can I see?" she asked.

Chetan handed the journal to Leela, kissed her lips, and went to the galley to eat lunch.

Leela read what Chetan had just written and tears came to her eyes. She felt so grateful to be alive. She turned around and saw Niki playing with Willie in a lifeboat, and Ethan enchanting Mary with tall tales of his adventures sailing around the world.

Asanga came up to Leela and hugged her. Then he turned around and silently gazed out upon the deep blue sea.

Three gulls - two adults, a white one and a brown one - and a small light-brown one - swooped down and landed on the deck.

They look familiar, Leela thought.

Leela reached into her robe, took out a few morsels of bread left over from lunch, and tossed them to the gulls. The gulls gobbled up the crumbs, then flew high into the azure sky. Higher and higher they flew into the infinite space beyond the beyond, until finally they disappeared.

Leela sighed.

The Master's daughter then opened Chetan's journal and began to write:

•

The sun, sea, and salty air are all singing with my heart:
Alive! Alive! Alive!
This moment and this moment and this moment,
so small, yet all is contained in this vertical moment.
This moment is all...
the sound of my heart…
the touch of the wind...
the smell of the sea...
the blue of the sky...
the taste of my tears.
This moment is all.

•

CHAPTER 53

Bunny and Lloyd laid their poker hands face down on the cloud they were sitting on.

"Well, what do you say now?" Lloyd asked.

"Life goes on," Bunny replied. "Some adventure with Leela, Chetan and the others, eh? But you know, this disembodied game isn't for me anymore. Let's go back."

"Wait a minute!" Lloyd said. "When you were Dilai Dalai, you--"

"You mean Hueng Tsiang," Bunny corrected. "Like Rajaba was for you that lifetime. Dilai Dalai was somebody else's name for me."

"Okay," Lloyd said, "but why the change? Why go back, with all the misery and pain of living in a body?"

"Because a body provides something substantial - time and space, pain and pleasure, flesh and blood - for our witnessing nature to disidentify from. Right now, we don't feel. So let's play with feeling again! Until we dissolve into our witnessing nature.

"You saw Leela's and Chetan's egos dissolving during the time we've been with them. What transformation has happened with us during the same time?"

"I see what you mean," Lloyd said. "It's risky."

"It sure is," Bunny said. "You with me?"

"Do we have to go now?" Lloyd said, turning over his cards. "I finally have a good hand. Full house, kings high."

Bunny smiled and turned over her cards.

"My God!" Lloyd gasped. "All hearts. A royal flush! You win! Again! Time to look for a new womb."

Bunny chuckled, gathered the cards, shuffled them, spread them face down on the cloud, and said, “The fetus in Leela’s womb is available for a soul to enter. Let’s each pick a card. Lowest card will be born to the Master’s daughter.”

THE DILAI DALAI SUTRAS

If, according to physicists and mystics, all matter in the universe can be reduced to the size of a matchbox,
why diet?

•

Two hearts beating as one may need medical treatment.

•

Love is a rose with thorns,
consciousness the fragrance.

•

A mystic knows he knows nothing,
and his beloved gladly agrees.

•

How can energy and matter exist if not for space to exist in?
The mystic $0 = e = mc^2 =$ loving

•

Every human is doing the best they can to be conscious,
to spiritually wake up here now, including me.

•

Silence is Beauty's language,
Laughter her tears.

•

We are mirrors of each other.
Turning the mirror inside, I am you.

•

Transcendence:
Everyone thinks I'm nuts, and I agree.

•

All "isms" are prisons.

•

Where did life begin if not in the bathroom?

•

Love is a game where losers are winners
and winners are losers who love themselves anyway.

•

If children ran the world, priests and politicians would have
an excuse for behaving like children.

•

No man likes a sarcastic woman, unless her bikini's too tight.
No woman likes a sarcastic man, period.

•

Death is life's shy lover.

•

To see everything in black and white
is to have a zebra's intelligence.

•

If God made the world,
who made the space for God to be in
before God made the world?

•

Bankruptcy just means
you had more fun
than you thought you would.

•

There's no such thing as a free lunch,
although "I forgot my wallet" works sometimes.

•

Whenever you have had too much fun,
go to church.

•

Ultimately the only way I can help others
is to be conscious myself.

"In God We Trust"?
It's more like, "In the Mystery We Doubt".

•

If ever there was a time when we needed someone
with an ego so crystalized
that they believed they could save the world,
it's not now.

•

Ancient Persian Proverb:
Kiss a camel and you will know love.

•

Ancient Egyptian Proverb:
Kiss a moralist and you will move to Persia.

•

If an empty mind is the devil's workshop,
what's that smile doing on Buddha's face?

•

Reincarnation:
men were women,
women were men,
sheep were priests and nuns.

•

I've said too much already.
Communion happens in silence.

•

If I had two cents for every time that I forgot something,
I wouldn't remember where I put the money.

•

A friend in need was your enemy
before you won the lottery.

•

Donald spent thousands of dollars on speech therapy
before he removed the clothespin from his tongue.

•

No one was the wiser, certainly not Emperor Wen Ching,
when he signed the Imperial Order
making one plus one equal three.

•

TV is a good way to kill time,
and intelligence.

•

If cleanliness is next to godliness,
why do priests have dirty minds?

Life is serious.
Take avocadoes for instance.

•

If you have a choice between true love and a free lunch,
why choose?

•

Isness is the unity of opposites.

•

Love is all around
until you lose your wallet.

•

I could solve the problem
if there was one in the first place.

•

Gravity is the outer bliss of consciousness
disappearing into an inner void.

•

Seriousness is hilarious.

•

All my ego's personalities
could populate the Cleveland Zoo.

•

The world will be filled with laughter
as long as priests and politicians make promises
they never intend to keep.

•

Truth cannot be said.
Eyes never lie.
Two wrongs make a right
if you have a cunning lawyer.

•

If nobody knows who I am better than me,
maybe I am nobody.

•

The concept of work began when priests convinced folks
they had to be someone other than who they already are.

•

What do you get when you cross a nun
with a Watusi warrior?
A smiling nun.

•

I don't need a job.
I need a spiritual lobotomy.

•

To joke about everything is neurosis.
To enjoy the neurosis is meditation.

•

The heart gets a toothache
from the candy of cleverness.

•

Banana peels were made for wedding aisles.
What does law have to do with love?

•

Home is where the heart is, and drooling Uncle Gus.

•

Love is overwhelming if it's love,
over-the-hill if it's business.

•

A child is in wonder.
An adult wonders why.

•

Which came first, love or chocolate?

•

The sweet smell of success
can easily turn to dog breath.

•

Truth is ice cream,
feelings the cone,
silence the taste.

•

Some things just aren't funny
unless they happen to someone else.

•

It's easy to read a man whose heart is an open book:
the pages are blank.

•

As a centerfold ages,
her center folds.

•

Divine guidance can be heard by the pure of heart,
and crackpots.

There's no sense just wandering around in a daze,
get elected and be paid for it.

•

"Holy" wars are proof
that someone's getting the wool
pulled over their eyes.

•

Don't give up until you realize
you weren't doing anything important anyway.

•

Sometimes don't you just want to scream?
My place or yours?

•

For years I thought "euthanasia"
was a Boys Club in Hong Kong.

•

Religious education made a lasting impression on me.
Only ten more years of therapy
and I'll be able to laugh without crying.

•

Don't let personal problems get you down.
Let the news do that for you.

•

The real tragedy of a broken home
is that you can never get a plumber
when you need one.

•

This is the dawning of the Age of Hilarious.

•

It's hard to say which smells worse,
dogma or cat litter.

•

I'll never forget what's-his-name for saving my life.

•

Priests sold me my neurotic mind.
Can I return it and get a refund?

•

Weathering life's storms builds integrity,
and soaks the carpet if you leave the window open.

•

A true artist becomes one with his work,
which in time may require ego surgery.

•

Peace of mind comes like a gentle breeze,
and goes with the neighbor's loud music.

•

My life had a purpose, a goal, a dream to fulfill,
then I found my glasses.

•

Osho

•

A moralist rejoices in the pleasure of indignation.

•

A vulnerable man is attractive to women,
but not in the Lady's Room.

•

A sign of intelligence was detected today on Capitol Hill,
but no one there was intelligent enough to read the sign.

•

Temporary Insanity:
a woman shopping, saying, "I can't afford it."

•

What does a saint have that a sinner doesn't?
A good press agent.

•

Some people are unique imitations,
others imitate uniqueness.

•

A disciple goes where love grows:
from a seed to a tree,
a tree to a flower,
a flower to a fragrance,
to the Master inside.

•

A young man mistakes lust for love,
an old man skin cream for toothpaste.

•

Where does life come from and where does it go?
And is there indoor plumbing there?

•

"The Dark Night of the Soul" is any cold night
you have to get up to pee.

•

The more a person talks about their relationship,
the less the possibility they have one.

•

There is a logical reason for everything,
except Brussels sprouts.

•

He who laughs last
will usually not wash the dishes.

•

Discipline will make a man out of you,
unless your name is "Fluffy".

•

Self-improvement is pulling yourself up
by your bootstraps when you're barefoot.

•

The ego loves challenges,
like who to be next.

In the eyes of trust,
falling snow looks
like silence sounds.

•

Is who I am who I am not?

•

The deeper I feel I am not,
the more I am misunderstood.

•

All I do is writing on water.
The space I am is the water.

•

Let-go is creative.
Silence is creative.

•

Thank you for you.

May your fragrance spread beyond the wind
and your love have roots in the earth.

Osho is an enlightened Master who left his physical body in 1990. His vision encompasses the spiritual wisdom of the East and the highest potential of Western science and technology. His unique meditation techniques are designed to allow the release of accumulated stress in the body, mind, and heart to make it easier to experience the thought-free state of meditation.

Osho's books, audios, and videos are sourced from spontaneous discourses before live audiences and can be downloaded free at www.oshoworld.com.

Anyone who has a sincere longing to experience the truth of being human can be a disciple of Osho. Shunyo Mahom is a devotee of Osho. www.shunyo.org.

There are many Osho sannyasins and meditation centers throughout the world. An authentic seeker will find devotees of Osho with whom they can explore Osho's insights into love, meditation, creativity, and celebration.

www.oshowiki.com and www.oshotapoban.com are resources for Osho Meditation Centers and Osho sannyasins around the world.

Thank You, Madhuri, for help editing.

www.ingramcontent.com/pod-product-compliance
Lightning Source LLC
Chambersburg PA
CBHW070638310726
48982CB00001B/328

* 9 7 8 0 5 7 8 3 3 1 4 5 4 *